WILD GOOSE CHASE
GREEN VALLEY HEROES BOOK #8

KILBY BLADES

www.smartypantsromance.com

Dedication

To my grandfather and all the other surrogate dads

Content Warning

This book is a work of romantic comedy. However, grief and PTSD are present as motifs. It begins four years after the main characters suffer a mutual loss and are finding their own way back to life. Though you should be aware of these elements, you should also be aware that Wild Goose Chase is heavy on humor, ends happily, and doesn't dwell on the trauma of the past.

PART I

Chapter One
CHASE

"Chase! You're going to miss the beginning!"

Violet's insistent voice traveled from her living room to her kitchen. I stood at her counter, cutting garnishes for a tray full of drinks. It was fall in Tennessee, but her counter looked like Barbados in endless summer.

"I'll be right there!" I hollered back appeasingly. I'd already hooked tiny umbrellas over the rims of five peach passion fruit daiquiris. Now, I was sliding in striped paper straws. In a few seconds, I'd pour virgin daiquiris from a separate blender into twin Paw Patrol cups—slushies for my godchildren, Bri and Trey.

Using a pair of kitchen shears, I snipped the ends of the last two straws, right-sizing them for their smaller cups, then balanced a toothpick speared with strawberries on the rim of Bri's. After pouring the kids' drinks, I dried my hands on a kitchen towel, threw it over my shoulder, and picked up the tray.

"What'd I miss?" I played a dangerous game, walking with the drinks while stealing glimpses at the screen. *Man Enough* was our Thursday night obsession—a reality show in which eighteen strapping singletons vied for one woman's love. *Entertainment Monthly* called it the most egregious display of toxic masculinity ever to appear on network TV. I called it a fascinating study in gender psychology.

As the only man invited to girls' night in, I took the predicted amount of shit about the shortcomings of my brethren. I'd also learned a few things. Watching an elimination-style dating show with Violet and her friends had been eye-opening. Thursdays were a highlight of my week.

"Adam is sulking over last week's date." Jules rushed into a blunt summary. "Eric's in the gym. And Marcus is in the confessional going on about his feelings. Again."

"Marcus is the best man in this whole competition," I defended.

"Marcus won't last another week." Jules rolled her eyes.

"The others ought to take a leaf out of *his* book," I preached.

"Which leaf is that?" Jules side-eyed me.

"Be nice," Violet teased. "Last I checked, Chase was your ride home."

"Yes, Jules, be nice," I parroted.

I shot Jules a triumphant smirk as I handed over her daiquiri. Jules was perennially grumpy. She was also Violet's oldest friend, though the two of them couldn't have been more different. While Vi was sugar and spice and everything nice, Jules was just…sour. Her features were as sharp as her tongue—severe blue eyes and a diamond jaw defined her pale, slim face. She wore a permanent scowl, not unlike Clint Eastwood's. The two of us caring about Violet so much was the only reason we put up with each other.

"This looks amazing, Chase," the far more gracious Tatum offered when I handed her a drink. Tatum had what I thought of as a pageant smile—wide and toothy and bright-eyed; she was polished in a way that matched her coiffed blond hair. Tatum always looked like she'd just won something. Nikki—lipstick-free and perpetually in yoga pants—was far more understated. She threw me a smile as she took hers, then shifted her attention back to the screen.

"Here you go, bud. Drink it slow this time." I waited for Trey to take his cup with two hands. When it came to not spilling, he wasn't great. He also wasn't great at avoiding brain freezes. Such was the enthusiasm of being four.

Seven-year-old Bri looked up at me with heart-tugging sweetness. "Did you remember the strawberries, Uncle Chase?"

I threw her a wink, then handed over her smoothie, complete with strawberries from my farm. I'd planted three rows of bushes just for her. This kid loved strawberry everything—strawberry milkshakes, strawberries in her oatmeal, strawberry preserves—tubes of strawberry lip balm were stowed in every bag she owned.

Setting the tray on the ottoman, I plucked up the final two drinks, handing Violet hers and settling next to her on the love seat. But I held off on watching the show. Violet's raw appreciation of my mixology skills was the reason why I made drinks.

Her eyes fell shut upon her first, indulgent sip. It gave me time to look at her, unabashed. Violet LaRue's beauty was rare. Her full lips were lush, with a natural pout. An expansive crown of ginger curls framed her face. Her skin was the tawny brown at the center of a perfect peach, with nutmeg freckles dropped across her nose. Her dark eyes—still so lovely in spite of the fatigue that came with parenting—sparkled with intelligence and wit.

"You know I love passion fruit," she said in a contented sigh.

"I do know that," I returned.

"I needed this today." Her lips melted into the smile that got me out of bed in the morning. She reached to the table next to her and handed me a pork empanada. Finally at ease, I settled in my seat to enjoy *Man Enough*.

Today's challenge was to cook a feast for Chelsea, the bachelorette. The suitors had all day to prepare a meal. At sunset on the beach, they would present their tables. Chelsea would go down the line, sitting with each suitor and tasting the meals speed dating-style. One suitor would be eliminated at the end of the night.

"That Eric guy is so smarmy." Tatum spoke of the man currently on-screen who sat crouched in the jungle, hiding inside a bush. He'd used mud from a river to camouflage himself, held a knife in his teeth, and had a wild look in his eyes.

"What's he hunting?" I asked Violet, still catching up.

"He thinks he's gonna catch a wild boar."

I reveled in the way her voice lowered when she spoke only to me.

"Chelsea doesn't eat pork," I pointed out.

"You'd be surprised how few men actually pay attention," Tatum said sourly.

"Reminds me of my ex," Nikki groused. "Brought me home roses every Valentine's Day. Would've been sweet if I hadn't told him ten times I was allergic."

"Have you noticed that he never has a shirt on?" Violet chimed in. "And he's always doing push-ups. Like, everywhere…in the kitchen, by the pool."

"He's shinier than decent people." Tatum's Georgia accent was thick.

"He's clearly in it for the publicity," Nikki opined.

"I don't know why Chelsea can't see through him," Tatum grumbled.

A kind of sadness hit me in my gut. "People see what they want to see." I said it almost to myself. I ought to know, considering I was an expert in being second choice. All my life, I'd found myself in the friendzone. It turned out women went for alpha men.

I definitely wasn't that—not big and boastful, not large and in charge. Instead, I was reliable and steady. You'd think that'd be worth something, I was living evidence it's not. I was the guy who didn't get the girl.

"What she should've seen was him hitting on all those women that one night at the club," Jules came back.

For once, Jules and I agreed. Eric was a piece of shit.

"It's not okay to hit people," Trey informed the room after taking a loud slurp of virgin daiquiri.

Trey was smart for four years old, and he looked the part owing to his green, plastic-framed glasses.

"Hitting on someone isn't the same as hitting someone." Bri spoke to her little brother with the authority of a kid twice her age. "Being hit on is like playing tag, except for grown-ups, and they use compliments instead of hands. When you want to date someone, you say nice things."

"I thought Eric liked Chelsea." Trey seemed confused.

"Eric likes a lot of women," Jules explained.

"I think Eric likes himself best," Trey concluded.

Bri nodded, seeming to accept the explanation. Violet and I exchanged a look. How the hell did they figure out this shit?

"Uncle Chase, can I sit in your lap?" Trey asked.

"C'mere, bud." It was way past his bedtime, but Violet let him stay up each week for girls' night in. I took a long sip of my drink before lifting him up. Five minutes later, he was fading, his eyes drooping and his glorious mess of deep brown curls brushing my chin as his cheek lay on my chest.

"Momma, can Uncle Chase read us stories?" Bri whispered, perhaps sensing that Violet would send both of them to bed.

"Uncle Chase is watching the show, honey," Violet answered at the same time as I said, "Only if we can read *The Lorax* again."

"You don't have to," Violet whispered as Bri gave a little squeal.

"I know I don't have to." I put my hand on Violet's shoulder to keep her in her seat. She seemed a second away from getting up. The look she gave me struck up one of our silent conversations.

Chase, you do too much.

I have a promise to keep, Vi.

You spoil my kids rotten.

Kids deserve to be spoiled.

You know I can never repay you for this.

Good. You're not supposed to.

I ended our silent argument by turning back to Bri. "Go on and brush your teeth, shortcake. And get your book ready. I'll be up there in five."

"Night, Momma! Night, everyone!" Bri scurried away before Violet could protest.

I rose with a sleeping Trey on my shoulder and walked him up the stairs. His was a Star Wars-themed room I'd fixed up myself. Above pale wainscoting, the walls were painted dark blue and dotted with stick-on gems that looked like stars. Bright-glowing light saber fixtures flanked his bed. Lamps that looked like storm troopers sat atop his desk and a Chewbacca beanbag chair sat in the corner.

It was easy to deposit him on his bed. Easy for me, at least. He was getting too big for the petite Violet to carry.

"Night, buddy." I knew he wouldn't hear me, but said it anyway as I placed his Baby Yoda stuffie in his arms. Carefully, I removed his glasses and placed them on the nightstand. A minute later, I was on Bri's floor with my back against her bed.

The Lorax was her favorite everything—her favorite book and favorite movie. She was such a good reader we took turns, me reading the odd pages and her reading the evens. The book was propped up on my knees, and she lay crosswise behind me, reading over my shoulder.

I could tell she was getting tired when she tapered off in the middle of a page. I looked back to find her breathing even and her eyes shut. Bri was unmistakably Violet's, right down to the freckles on their nose. Her curls were looser, her skin was a lighter brown, and her hair was more dark auburn than dark ginger—other than that, they were twins.

After closing the book, I rose from the floor, walking lightly, so as not to make noise.

"G'night, shortcake," I whispered only once I'd gotten to the door. She had bionic hearing. Any louder and I'd wake her up.

"G'night, tallcake," she whispered, half asleep.

This little girl killed me. I looked down at her sweet, pudgy face for another long moment before backing out of the room, closing her door and leaving it open a crack. Sometimes, I loved Bri and Trey so much it hurt.

"Uncle Chase?" her small, sleepy voice called to me as I made my first step down the hall. I backtracked and opened the door.

"Yes, darlin'?"

"We forgot something," she said sweetly.

"You need to use the bathroom?" I asked.

From the faint glow of her purple night-light, I saw her shake her head. "We forgot to say night-night to Daddy."

Something tightened in my chest again, but it was a different kind of something. Not love this time, but guilt. Todd may have died in the line of duty, but he would always be their dad.

"We did forget."

I strode back into Bri's room, my voice light, even as I was gutted. On the far side of her bed, a framed picture of a very small baby Bri being held by a beaming Todd was on the table.

"Night, Daddy," she said in a voice that broke my heart, not because it was sad —because it was earnest. Todd was as real to Bri as he was to me and Violet.

"Night, brother," I said next.

I would do well to remember that. That Todd had been my best friend and that I'd made a promise to take care of his family. That I needed to find a way to do that without wishing I had his life. I would do anything to bring him back, and to not be in love with Violet. Easier said than done.

Chapter Two
CHASE

"You're looking good, brother," I said to Forrest Winters as he greeted me with a fierce hug. It was true. He carried a sort of glow. He stood a little taller, which was saying a lot for a man who already stood at 6'3". His beard had an extra shine. And everything about him seemed content.

"Domestic life suits me." His smile was smug.

"Sierra's still putting up with your shit?"

Forrest gave a low chuckle. "She still wants me, believe it or not. She's loving life on the lake."

"When are y'all gonna have me over? I wouldn't mind some of those bacon bites she makes." I waved him inside. When Forrest suggested we catch up, I'd invited him up to the farm. I'd been bored since the peach harvest, so hosting was a win-win. I liked to cook and he liked to eat.

"We'll have you over once the remodel's done. I'm on my sixth week without a kitchen."

"I didn't know you were having work done, man."

"We were only supposed to replace a few appliances. Now, we're close to a whole new kitchen. But what Sierra wants, Sierra gets."

I couldn't help but laugh. "She's got you wrapped around her finger."

"The only thing I wrapped around her finger is a ring."

"Holy shit. You proposed?"

"Last week." Forrest looked even more smug now. "Matter of fact, I was hoping you would host our engagement party. Return to the scene of the crime, and all."

The Noble Pig was a supper club I ran in spring and summer—an open-air farm-to-table restaurant with a menu I cooked myself. The meal was served on china—more country chic than formal—on a long table on the most idyllic of my orchard roads.

The intimate experience was a favorite for dates—it was where Forrest and Sierra had their first. The Noble Pig had been written about in magazines. I'd started it after months of obsessively cooking weekly dinner parties for my baffled friends. Turning my dinner parties into a supper club that could serve as an outlet for my manic culinary phase had been all Violet's idea.

"Hell yeah I'll host your engagement party," I agreed.

"We're working on dates with Sierra's folks. Might be around Thanksgiving. They're coming in from California."

Forrest came farther into the house he hadn't seen the inside of since my remodel.

"Place looks great." He took an approving look around.

"Yeah, well, nervous breakdowns are underrated." I scratched the back of my neck. "Turns out when you quit your job and move in with your parents, then start big projects to get your mind off of things, you can get a lot of shit done."

"How are Laurel and Pete these days?" Forrest had known my folks for years.

"*Where* are they is more like it. Down some river in Vietnam."

"How long have they been away this time?"

"Going on four months now. I'll send you a link to my momma's blog."

They were deep in their retirement travel and, God bless them, they had earned it. They'd run the peach farm for a solid thirty years. After that, they'd delayed a series of vacations on account of my troubles. All of that had ended in a drastic measure born out of self-preservation and tough love: they'd handed me the deed to the farm.

I'd spent the first week after they left glaring resentfully at the deed—my inheritance mocking me from the kitchen table, the legacy they'd always known I didn't want staring me in the face. The sixty-acre farm was mine to sell or rent, or to let go to seed. But I couldn't disrespect their life's work. So I'd brushed myself off, gotten over my own bullshit, bucked up, and taken to the fields.

"You hire a designer or something? I know *you* don't have this much taste."

Forrest took an appreciative look around, admiring a living room he hadn't seen in quite some time. The worn rug had been removed and the floors beneath refinished—they were now stained a modern brownish gray. The cherrywood doorframes and finishes had been painted over in white. Drab wallpaper had been ripped out from floor to ceiling. Chair rail molding now bisected light and dark shades of blue gray on top and bottom. But the decor really finished it—pops of color amid a palette of grays that matched the stone platform that housed my wood burning stove; a corner with stands for my guitars and banjos; a comfy couch long enough to lounge on, even with my tall frame.

"The kitchen's not the only place I know what I'm doing," I boasted. "All this woodwork was me."

I'd spent the past two winters restoring the farmhouse to its original beauty. I'd used contractors for the foundation work and basement refinishing, but I'd done the cosmetic work myself. I'd taken craftsmanship classes—invested in sanders and belt saws and lathes. I'd restored the detailing to its former glory, from the ornate mantelpiece in the dining room to custom railings on the stairs.

"But who taught you how to do the rest? You been watching those property brothers on HGTV?"

I put my hands on my hips and took in with satisfaction all the elements that made my house a home. "Naw, man. I didn't pick out any of the furniture or the colors. This is all Violet's touch."

Forrest gave a long whistle, looking even more approving than before. "She really fixed up this place. No offense to your momma's taste, of course."

"More like my grandmama's taste," I commiserated. "The way it looked when I grew up here was pretty much the same as it looked when my momma did."

"Where's Jameson?"

Forrest eyed the empty dog bed in the corner. Jameson was the other thing that had come with my deed. The first time I'd met him, his face-licking had awakened me out of a drunken sleep. I'd opened my eyes to find my mother standing over me, where I'd passed out on the couch. In her hand was the empty bottle of whiskey I'd polished off the night before. That was when she told me I needed to stop drinking until I got myself together—that the only Jameson allowed in the house for a while was my dog.

"He spends most days in Violet's barn. You know, I raised him from a puppy. I'm the one who feeds him and takes him to the vet. You think that boy'd be loyal. But I'm telling you—he likes her better than me."

I led Forrest through the living room, then the dining room, then the kitchen, which I'd knocked down a wall in order to double in size.

"This is really nice," Forrest said with the kind of appreciation that could only be shared by a man in the middle of a remodel of his own. "I know I've been to the Pig a few times, but it's been a while since I came inside the main house. I don't think I've been here since right after you quit."

To call what I did "quitting" was putting it lightly. I'd spiraled into an incapacitating depression that had served as an abrupt end to my firefighting career. The last fire I'd fought, three men from Tennessee hadn't come home. One of those men had been Todd.

"Grab some plates," I instructed as we passed through. The lunch I'd made was on the porch, a wraparound affair with a nice view of the orchards from the back. I'd put our spread under a mesh food tent in order to keep out the flies.

"You ought to start a sandwich shop," Forrest complimented two minutes later around a mouthful of turkey club. "What the hell did you put on this?"

"I make a special mayonnaise. Smoked paprika. Umami salt. That kind of thing."

Forrest took another indulgent bite, which made me chuckle. Forrest Winters had never met a sandwich he didn't like.

"Asking you to host my engagement party is only the first reason why I'm here," he said after polishing off two-quarters. His expression sobered. "We need you back."

His "we" had to be the National Forestry Service. And then "needing me back" had to refer to becoming a firefighter again.

"I'm happy where I am." I repeated the same line I'd said to others who'd come knocking. Hell, I'd already refused Forrest twice.

"You must have time," he went on. "The Noble Pig is closed for the season."

"I've still got a farm to run."

"I know you do. But this is more than just me on my annual pilgrimage. Those other times, I just wanted my friend beside me again. This time, I need you. You're a damn good firefighter, Chase."

"Past tense," I was quick to say.

"I'm not asking you to come back as a duty firefighter." He went on like I hadn't spoken. "I need you on my Council on Wildfire Prevention. This is some real-deal shit. Federally funded. Not some rinky-dink local subcommittee. Our charter is to set the national standard for how we fight wildfires."

"I told you. I'm not a firefighter anymore."

"I don't care what the hell you call yourself. The simple fact is, only three ranked command leaders were there."

He looked as haunted as I felt. And he didn't need to say where *there* was: in the thick of the deadliest field of the deadliest wildfire on record.

"So call Thompson," I suggested.

"Thompson's in hospice, with cancer."

Shit.

"I didn't know."

When he spoke again, Forrest's look was apologetic. "That leaves me and you."

I put down what was left of my sandwich. I wasn't hungry anymore.

"You don't know what you're asking."

He fell silent for a long minute. Just when I'd convinced myself he planned to drop it, he spoke again.

"Look, man. I know you were in a real dark place. I know you've worked hard to rebuild your life—"

"You're damn right I did."

"But I also know you blame yourself for Todd's death."

I shut my mouth.

"I'm offering something a thousand guys in your position will never get: a chance to find out what really happened that day. A chance to make it right."

I didn't realize how hard I was clenching my jaw until my teeth gnashed together.

"Nothing can make it right," I managed to grind out.

"No," Forrest protested. "Nothing can bring him back. But making it right? Now, that's something different. Making it right means doing everything in your power to see it never happens again."

I had questions that I didn't dare to voice—to do so would make Forrest think that I was actually considering this.

"The project's sponsored by the Secretary of the Interior," he went on. "She's giving us investigator status, and unfettered case file access to the three deadliest wildfires in the history of the US. Our job is to find mistakes and failure points, then to rewrite the manual for how firefighters are trained. And we don't just hand off our findings to some department that says they'll execute—they want us to teach the training ourselves."

I remained quiet, my protests dampened by the merit of his offer. His reasons for why I ought to do it weren't wrong. But my reasons weren't wrong either. Taking the job would force me to relive the trauma, even if I never picked up a hose again. For four years, I'd worked hard to not feel so broken—to look forward and leave the past behind. I wasn't ready to look back.

"I've got other people who depend on me now. I can't just walk away."

"I'm not asking you to walk away. I'm asking you to split your attention. You know as well as I do, these fires are becoming more extreme. If amateurs keep trying to train these guys to fight the kind of fires they've never seen, a lot more guys like Todd will never come home to their families."

Chapter Three
CHASE

I woke up from a restless sleep to find gratitude in Saturday. Saturday was my busiest day of the week. I fed the animals in the early morning, worked the farmer's market 'til noon, then headed to Green Valley to keep an eye on Violet's kids while she went to class.

It was off-season now, but Saturday nights in summer were supper night at The Noble Pig. On those days, Violet dropped her kids off at the farm. A stool for Bri and a stepladder for Trey were permanent fixtures in my kitchen. Saturdays never felt like work—they felt like how things were supposed to be. Saturdays reminded me I'd built a life.

A life you can't just walk away from, a voice inside me said to the part of me that wanted to accept what Forrest proposed. Working on the protocol that could have saved Todd sounded more than a little tempting. But I couldn't forget how broken I had been. Losing Todd the way I did had made me catatonic. I'd suffered what the doctors had called a mental break, diagnosed as such given my inability to function.

I'd kept myself together long enough to attend his funeral. Then, I'd gone home and gotten in bed. I didn't get up for days. When I'd stopped answering my phone, my firefighter brothers had paid me a visit—the kind where I didn't answer my door, so they'd had to knock it down. They say I didn't talk for two full weeks. I don't remember most of it. What I do remember is people hovering over me, telling me all I needed was time. What I'd needed was serious help from trained professionals who knew about grief and trauma. And not just from that day—the accumulated trauma that came from working that kind of job.

"Woman trouble?" my well-meaning, if oversexed, employee inquired. Cody had been helping me at the farmer's market for two years. He had all the cockiness of your average twenty-two-year-old, but he was a good worker, and I liked the guy.

"You think every damn thing boils down to woman troubles."

"That's 'cause every damn thing does."

The look I gave him told him he was full of shit.

"Is the farm in trouble?" he quizzed.

"It does all right."

"Someone piss in your corn flakes this morning?"

I rolled my eyes in lieu of supplying an answer. He smirked back at me, unperturbed.

"Do you have any health or legal problems?" he prodded. "Were you abducted by aliens who performed depraved experiments on your weak human body? 'Cause if it ain't none of that shit, it's got to be a woman."

"Did you ever think that maybe I just had a long night?"

It had been a sleepless one. Drifting off had taken hours. Thirty minutes after I did, I'd awakened in a cold sweat. I hadn't nodded off again until the sun rose.

"Fine. Be mysterious." Cody threw me a haughty look.

Since proving him wrong would force me to explain my dilemma, I let it lie.

And I couldn't think of it as a dilemma if I didn't have a choice. Even if I wanted to go back to the forestry service, my biggest responsibility was Violet. I'd promised Todd that I would take care of her if anything ever happened. It would only, always, ever come down to that.

* * *

Four hours later, I stood in Violet's kitchen pinching the crust shut on a chicken pot pie. I'd handmade the dough myself; my freezer-chilled butter and ice-cold water technique would ensure it came out flaky. Across from me, Trey was face deep in the mixing bowl which, only seconds ago, had contained the dough for no-bake peanut butter bars.

Bri stood at the counter, staring absently at uncut bars that had already been smoothed into the pan. I'd tried to cheer her up by putting on the frilly apron she'd given me when she was four. It was pink and it said "Uncle Chase." It was usually good for a laugh but she hadn't cracked a smile. She'd been down in the dumps since we got home.

"What's up, buttercup? You don't want to lick the spoon?" I jutted my chin at the one she held in her hand.

"When will Mommy be home?" Bri pouted.

"Her class ended a little while ago." I kept my voice light. "I'm sure it won't be long."

"But I want to show her the vid-e-o." She stretched out the word to three times its normal length. She was a championship whiner when she turned it on.

"Your momma's got to go to school, just like you," I pointed out.

"Mommy's too old for school," Trey supplied.

"You're never too old for school," I protested. "Your momma does a lot for you. Now, it's your turn to support something that's important to her. It's important to her to get her degree. She's doing it to better herself."

"But Mommy's already good the way she is." Bri was still put out. "She doesn't need to be better."

"Bettering yourself just means achieving your own goal," I explained.

"She'll miss all my soccer matches." Bri was scowling now.

"I caught the whole game on video. She won't have to miss a minute," I appeased.

"Did you go to college, Uncle Chase?"

"No." I shook my head. "I went straight to the fire academy, just like your dad. Then I was a firefighter for a long time. After that, I went to culinary school."

Trey took a break from his bowl-licking. "And that's where they taught you how to cook."

"I was already good at cooking before that. They just taught me to cook better."

"That's just like Mommy," Trey concluded. "She's already good at making our house pretty. Now she wants to help other people's houses."

"I don't want Mommy to get another job." Bri was still fixated on Violet. "If she has two jobs, she won't have any time for us."

Violet chose that moment to walk through from the garage into the kitchen.

"Mommy!" Trey jumped down from his stool and ran to Violet, planting a sugary kiss on her lips. It gave me time to lower my voice and speak to Bri.

"Don't be too hard on her, shortcake. Your momma's doing her best. Now, here's my phone. Go on and show her a video of your game."

For the next twenty minutes, I busied myself cleaning up the kitchen as Violet caught up on the day with her kids. Trey sat on Violet's lap as Bri leaned on her shoulder and showed her the video. I could see that Violet was tired, but she gave what she had left to her kids.

"What smells so good?" she wanted to know when she finally found me at the sink and greeted me with a hug.

"Chicken pot pie and peanut butter bars." I'd just put the latter in the fridge to chill.

"Next week, can we make fruity krispies?" Trey asked.

"Sure we can, bud." Fruity krispies were Trey's favorite dessert, not that he had ever met a dessert he didn't like. They were like Rice Krispie treats, except you made them with Fruity Pebbles. They were cloyingly sweet, so I cut in some plain Krispies to take off a bit of the edge.

"Maybe not next week, Chase." Violet lowered her voice to speak only to me. "I mean, I don't think I'll need you to come."

"Is class canceled next week?" My mind was already racing to alternatives. "Maybe we could all go to the haunted hayride. It's opening weekend. Tickets just went on sale."

I expected Violet's face to light up with the suggestion, but she looked uncomfortable.

"Actually, Jules is coming over to watch the kids." She said it in a way that made me suspicious. Doubly so when she wrang her hands. "I figured, every once in a while, you could use a break."

"A break from you and my godkids?" My voice lowered along with hers.

She shifted her gaze to Bri. "Kids, why don't y'all go have your screen time in the other room?"

Chair legs scraped across the floor as both kids fled the kitchen at a running break. I might've smiled if I hadn't gotten such a funny feeling. Violet had a right to ask anyone she wanted to watch her children. But what the hell was going on? I'd watched these kids every single Saturday since Violet's first semester in school.

"Is Jules coming next Saturday or every Saturday?" I tried to keep the hurt out of my voice.

"Just next Saturday. Some Saturdays." Violet looked like she wanted to cry. "I don't know."

"Vi…what the hell is going on?"

"Next week, I need someone…not just for the afternoon. I need someone to stay late."

I softened somewhat. "You know you could've asked me. I know you're hung up on being a burden, but spending time with Bri and Trey is no burden to me."

But my words did not appease her. If anything, she seemed more fraught. Whatever it was that made her want Jules instead of me, she was having a hard time getting it out.

"I have a date," she finally said. Her voice was no louder than a whisper. "I didn't want to ask you to be here while I go out with another man. I know he's been gone four years, and it's time for me to move on, but you being here to witness it doesn't feel right. I mean, you were Todd's best friend."

"You're dating again?" My mouth reacted before my mind could tell it no. I could hear the incredulity in my voice. "Since when?"

Her thin voice told me she was nervous. "Since I got asked out."

Years spent in the fire service had taught me to keep a neutral face. People hadn't always been in great shape whenever I'd arrived on a scene. But I'd seen third-degree burns that hurt me less than this.

"Look," she continued. "I'm not even sure I like the guy, but I know I'm overdue. It's time I get back on the horse."

I took my time before speaking, knowing I had to choose my words. My reaction now had the potential to break something in our friendship. It was clear she thought she had to hide all of this from me. But I couldn't abide her doing that.

"I think it's great that you're dating again," I lied through my teeth, then chased it with an absolute truth. "He wouldn't want you to be alone."

"Yeah. I know." She looked miserable. "It's just… A big step."

Once again, I compartmentalized my feelings.

"You don't have to hide anything from me, Vi. I've always been your friend too."

It was my second lie in a minute, because I'd never been her friend—had never not wanted more than she could give.

Chapter Four
VIOLET

Well, that went well.

I barely managed to keep my thoughts to myself as I watched Chase's truck disappear. He hadn't even wanted to stay for pot pie. It confirmed the worst possible outcome: I'd gone and made things weird.

Not the very worst outcome, I consoled myself.

At least he hadn't overtly disapproved. But he'd done the next-worse thing. He'd given me the look I couldn't read. I'd known this man for going on nine years, and too many parts of him were still a mystery to me.

I still knew what I needed to. Chase Greenleaf had been my savior. The man was a saint. He'd been broken himself when he'd damn near saved my life. He'd given his time, his money, and every shred of normalcy a thirty-year-old bachelor could ever hope for. And I'd taken, taken, taken. It was time I found a way to strike out on my own and give him back his life.

Jules picked up the call I placed on the second ring. My phone sat on my shoulder as I opened the oven and removed the pie. "You don't have to worry about watching the kids next Saturday," I told her after a brief greeting.

"Violet. If you keep canceling dates, your chances of ever having sex again reduce to nil."

"First of all, I feel called out. Second, I won't apologize for all the times I chose Netflix over chill. Third, I didn't even cancel this time. I'm calling to tell you I told Chase about the date. He's fine with it. He said he'd watch the kids."

Silence from Jules was rare. The woman thought a mile a minute and her mouth was never far behind her thoughts. Especially when it came to Chase, she always had an opinion.

"I like it," she finally decided. "No sheltering. No mollycoddling. Just rip that Band-Aid right off."

I smarted at the imagery and redirected. No time for regrets. What was done was done.

"What the hell am I going to wear?"

Jules heaved a dispassionate sigh. "We've been over this."

"No… You've made a preposterous suggestion to which I have never once agreed."

"That blue dress'll get you rode hard and put away wet." Jules was matter-of-fact.

"That dress will get me arrested for indecent exposure."

"Fine. Have it your way," she huffed. "I'll check my closet for a turtleneck and some mom jeans you can borrow."

"I just want to feel comfortable," I protested, wanting her to take pity. "The rest of me will be awkward enough, going on the first date I've been on in over eight years. And, by 'comfortable,' I mean 'age-appropriate.' I can't run around in the kinds of things I used to. I'm not twenty anymore."

"You're not a hundred either," Jules mumbled under her breath.

I didn't expect her to understand. Jules still had the same tight ass she'd had when we were eighteen. She did questionable things like eat clean and run triathlons. I, on the other hand, carried the residual weight of two pregnancies. Since high school, my fondness for carbs had only grown.

"Baby steps," I chided. The idea of going out with a man thrilled and terrified me in equal measure. I was certain the kissing part would make me feel like I was cheating on Todd. But Jules was right about my dry spell. The naked truth was, it had outgrown that designation some years earlier. It had now progressed to a D-4 drought. I pressed mute on my phone before shouting into the living room for the kids to wash their hands. No need to blow out Jules's sensitive ears. She had a short fuse for loud noises or ruckus of any kind. That made it just as well that Chase was still game to watch Bri and Trey. Jules loved my kids by extension of being my oldest friend, but Chase just plain loved my kids. Those were two very different things.

"I've gotta hop off. Time for dinner," I told Jules once I heard the shuffle of small feet.

"Hey—have they scheduled the trial dates yet?"

"Yeah. They're not for another ten weeks."

The unresolved nature of my lawsuit was yet another heavy burden on my heart. Just thinking about it made me bitter. The original suit had been filed six months after Todd's death and taken nearly two years to get a verdict. Now, it had been more than a full year since we'd lost the case.

We—as in me and the widows of two other Tennessee firefighters who had died in the same fire as Todd—we'd all filed the same suit. Most survivors of fallen firefighters received decent benefits from the state firefighter's fund. But all three of us and our children had been denied on a technicality: our partners had been killed out-of-state.

It was a circumstance the policies hadn't been written to address. The state insurance coverage had been underwritten as just that. Payouts were entitled to survivors of Tennessee firefighters killed in Tennessee. But jurisdiction was becoming more complex. As catastrophic wildfire incidents grew nationally, an increasing number of relief crews fought wildfires across state lines.

No survivor benefits were why I'd had to take so much charity these past few years. They were why—in the darkest hours of my own grief—I'd had to pick myself up and find a job. They were why I lived in fear that, when they'd needed me most, I'd been stretched too thin to be there for my kids.

"I'll be there with you," Jules vowed. "Not just the days you have to testify— every day they hold open court. I want that judge to know who I am."

"The last judge who knew who you were nearly placed you in contempt," I reminded her.

"Then I guess I'm lucky they assigned a new judge."

Everything about her comment reminded me why I loved Jules. Everyone needed a ride-or-die friend.

* * *

I KIND OF LOVED MY office, a converted storage barn that had once housed tractors and farm supplies. Years after the last bag of fertilizer had been opened, the air still held a whiff of the scent. The ground floor had been converted into a showroom space for the events business I ran. Six smallish tables were appointed with different settings—everything from blue gingham on white with mason jars and simple plates for barbecue, to fine bone china and antique crystals. It gave clients more than a sense of variety in terms of our offerings—it gave a taste of the quality their guests could expect.

The second-floor loft was the space that housed my desk and all my files. Chase's Irish setter, Jameson, had his own cushy setup in a comfy corner and stayed with me most days. The enormous center window had once been a shuttered cutout used to load bales of hay. Now, it was framed up with colonial panes that overlooked the orchards to the west, the lake due north, and the forest just beyond. There wasn't an inch of this place that had a bad vista, but for my personal tastes, my office had the best view of the farm.

"Good morning. Noble Farms." I spoke in my phone voice, which was twice as chipper as my everyday tone. Not that I made it a practice of sounding unfriendly—brides-to-be telegraphed vocal excitement. Sounding half as excited as they were was just part of my job.

"Oh, yes—hello! I'm looking to speak with the person who handles events. I'd like to book a date for a wedding."

"I'm Violet, the events director. I'd be happy to help. Have you taken a tour of our event spaces?"

I already knew she hadn't. If she had, she would remember me. Apart from my part-time events coordinator, who served as my boots on the ground who came on-site for each event, the events department at Noble Farms was a one-woman show.

"Oh, no, I haven't toured," the woman gushed. "But I'm sure we want to book you for our wedding. Our dinner at The Noble Pig was unforgettable. The way it felt? That's how I want our wedding guests to feel."

"Our chef is amazing, isn't he?"

"Girl, everything was amazing. How far out are you booked? I'm hoping you've got my date."

Two minutes later, I hung up the phone and wrote out the appointment in my calendar. The happy couple would be by on Friday at 10. Our touring hours were inconvenient for working people, but Noble Farms was in demand.

"Ready for our weekly staff meeting?"

A familiar tingle crept down my spine. Chase had entered the barn, along with his deep, rumbling voice and his sexy farmer vibe—a worn T-shirt that made his muscles pop and jeans that sat low on his hips and fit just right. Chase Noble Greenleaf was a tall drink of water, with deep auburn hair and a beard to match, and sun-kissed skin from his time spent outdoors.

Mention of our weekly meeting always made him poke fun. As he climbed the stairs to my office, he peered at me playfully with soft green eyes from beneath the brim of a worn baseball cap.

Focus, Violet. Today's an important day.

"Right on time, as usual." I managed a bright smile. Rising from my seat, I plucked the folder containing the report I'd painstakingly prepared off of my desk and headed to the conference table.

"How's your day so far?" He pulled me into a friendly hug. Our customary greeting never failed to remind me how good he smelled, which never made any sense given how much he worked outdoors. He should have been all dirt and dust and sweat, but, by some strange magic, his skin held sunshine, and peaches, and forest trees.

"We booked two more weddings—December and June."

He fixed me with a smile. "Does your boss ever tell you, you're doing a great job?"

"My boss has an overblown sense of praise for my contributions."

"Maybe my employee doesn't like taking credit where credit is due."

This was why I had to do what I was about to do. Even if the idea of doing it terrified me.

When the life insurance debacle had threatened to leave me broke, Chase had created a job for me on the farm, a job that centered around the only thing I'd ever done well. I'd been building my own interior design business when I met Todd, but after we got married, he hadn't wanted me to work.

After I made it out of the worst of my grief, I tried for two straight months to find work with an established design firm. I didn't get a single offer that paid a living wage, let alone one that would let me take care of my kids. That was when Chase had swooped in—told me people had been approaching him about renting the farm as a venue. He'd made it sound like becoming his events manager would be doing him a favor.

That turned out to be a bald-faced lie, which became abundantly clear a week after I'd accepted and received my first paycheck in an amount that was approximately two and a half times more than what the job was worth. After that, the perks just kept on coming. Flexible hours. Unlimited vacation. Full benefits for me and my kids. A 401k plan, to which Noble Farms made a substantial monthly contribution.

Chase had built me this loft office with his own two hands, complete with a full modern kitchen and an enormous day bed in the far corner that was perfect for naps. Not my naps, of course. When he'd given me this job, Trey had been an infant and Bri had been two. Chase had built an office where I could bring my kids. I'd made it my mission to pay him back.

"Let's get down to business." I slipped on the pair of glasses I didn't strictly need. More than I cared about my mild astigmatism, I cared about looking official for my meetings. Chase giving me a fake job had made me hell-bent on earning real profits. I was determined to make all he'd done for me worth his while.

"If you'll join me on page two…" I jumped right in. "I just closed the books on the second quarter. Net income was up seventy-six percent from Q1 and fifty-one percent year-over-year. The change was driven by expanding the schedule to accommodate more bookings but mainly by ancillary service sales."

"I've been getting compliments on the wedding planner," Chase commented without looking up, overplaying his straight face now. Man, he was laying it on thick today.

"The wedding business is doing well…" There was no point in not admitting it. "But not strictly because of planning. The affiliate program for preferred vendors is bringing in a nice passive income."

Chase nodded as his eyes scanned, his brow furrowed in concentration as he read the numbers I'd put on the page. Not only was this good news—I was proud of the report.

"All of this adds up to something exciting." My heart began to race. There was no going back now. "We can afford to hire another person. We can hire someone at a fair wage and still grow your profit margin by twenty-five percent. If your investment pays off like I hope, it'll add up to more event business. Pending your approval, of course."

Chase's gaze continued to skim over the paper. He seemed genuinely impressed, but I was making a big ask. Hiring me as a charity case was one thing. Now, I was asking him to grow his business for real. I was offering greater profitability, but I didn't know whether he'd ever really wanted to commit to this. I waited in suspense as he took his sweet-ass time.

"This is missing something."

My alarmed gaze flew to my report. "What?" I had to know. I never did my monthly reporting without checking it twice.

"Your projections for next year don't account for your own increase in salary. Anyone who can create profit growth like this deserves a raise."

I sighed. "Chase, we've been over this. You already overpay me. By a lot."

"You're right. We have been over this. Violet, you are not overpaid. You're underpaid based on the value that you add."

I gave him a look that told him I was not having this conversation again.

"Do you approve my new employee or not?"

Then I did the thing I rarely did—I stared him down. Stood my ground was more like it. Sometimes, I had to with him. If I didn't set boundaries, Chase would give me even more than he did.

"Yes, you can hire your new employee," he relented.

"Thank you." I dampened the fierceness I'd just displayed, letting gratitude color my tone. "I know you're a busy man, but I'd like you to be part of the interview process."

"What Violet wants, Violet gets," he quipped in a way that riddled me with guilt.

I wanted him to participate because it was his business and his money, because he was the owner of the farm. I needed him to participate because it was imperative he get along with the next person. Unbeknownst to him, the new employee would be much more than the second member of the event management team. They would be my replacement. Chase didn't know it yet, but I was planning to leave.

Chapter Five
CHASE

It was Thursday night. Girls' night in. *Man Enough* was on the TV. The clock on Violet's date was ticking faster. It was supposed to happen in two short days and I was not okay. I'd spent all week working a laughable plan designed to remind her of the beauty of her singlehood.

Monday, I'd given her a raise to reinforce her sense of financial independence. Tuesday, I'd made sure she overheard a conversation between me and Cody about the high rate of psychopathic murderers women met on dating apps. Wednesday, I'd left the paper open to an article about the benefits of friendship over romance. Despite my best efforts to make her think twice, I hadn't heard a word about her canceling. Violet was still going out on her date.

"So, tell us about this guy!" Tatum whisper-hissed. I caught the question as I came down Violet's steps. I'd just put her kids down to sleep. Instead of continuing down the stairs and entering the conversation, I lingered. I told myself I wasn't a creeper—that I was just a guy in search of information—that just for a minute, I would eavesdrop out of sight.

"His name is Rodney," Violet began.

Already, I hated this guy. What the hell did people call him? Rod?

"I met him at a wedding—I mean, one of the weddings I helped coordinate for the farm. We've run into each other a few times now, but he only just asked me out. He owns one of the companies we use for stage rentals, but he also plays in a bluegrass band."

"What's he look like?" Tatum pressed on.

"I don't know." Violet continued. "He's average height. Good-looking with bright blue eyes. Divorced. Likes hunting and fishing."

Who cared about bright blue eyes? Green eyes like mine were rare. But why was I even comparing myself? It wasn't like Violet and I could get together. She was the only woman on earth who was uniquely forbidden to me.

"Where's he taking you?" Nikki wanted to know.

"I don't know." A hint of annoyance came into Violet's voice. "If I did, it wouldn't be a date."

"If you don't know where you're going, how do you know what to wear?"

"I'm guessing he'll tell me if I needed to wear something out of the ordinary. And I don't need to plan every minute of everything. I'd like to be surprised."

I made a mental note of that, then scolded myself to throw said note away. I had no use for knowing what Violet considered her ideal date.

"So what do you like about him?" Tatum sure did have a lot of questions. I might have burst into the room to save Violet from the interrogation if I hadn't wanted so many answers myself. However much it pained me, I hung on every word.

"Honestly, I don't know." Violet sighed. "My only requirement at this point is that he's not some psycho killer."

Her comment should have gratified me to the extent it vindicated my scheming. But it only made me sad.

"Apart from that," she went on. "I think I just want all the basic things that a woman in my situation would appreciate. I want an honest-to-goodness man, someone who makes me feel like a woman."

I frowned, not knowing what that meant in this day and age.

"And he's gotta love my kids. That part's a deal breaker," she continued with determination.

"Who's watching Bri and Trey?" Nikki asked.

"Chase." Jules finally spoke, the first time she had since I'd reached the bottom floor.

My ears perked up to hear whether anyone would say more on the topic, but the room went abruptly silent.

"And all of y'all can quit grilling her about it," Jules finally said. "She'll tell you all about it when it's through."

The topic switched right then and I hung back for another solid minute. Once enough time had passed, I plodded heavily with my steps when I finally walked back into the room.

"Kids are down," I reported.

"Thanks, Chase." Violet was always sincere. She plucked my fuzzy navel off the coffee table and held it out to me as I sat down. I'd made it with blood orange juice and a schnapps I'd distilled myself from my homegrown peaches. I threw her an innocent "you're welcome" smile, feeling sorry-not-sorry for the eavesdropping I'd done.

"I think he's really showing up this week," Nikki was saying.

"Who is really showing up?" I asked, trying to shift my focus to the show. I had to keep my feelings off my face.

"Eric," Nikki and Jules said at the same time.

Eric. My least favorite suitor. The one who, for the life of me, I couldn't understand why Chelsea still kept him in the game.

"Y'all gotta explain this one to me," I told them plainly. "How the hell did he not get voted off? He keeps crashing her dates with other guys. Like, *bro*, wait your turn."

"Those aren't his finest moments," Tatum agreed diplomatically. "But he did save her from that spider. And he did fix that creak in her bedroom door. And he really handled those guys who tried to get fresh with her in the bar."

Titterings of agreement sounded throughout the room. But I remained incredulous.

"So, wait. A guy buys a can of WD-40 and fends off a harmless insect, and all else is forgotten?"

"Those guys at the bar might not have been harmless," Violet pointed out.

"Trust me, Chase." Nikki turned to me and preached. "There's no such thing as a perfect man. There's only things you love about them and bad habits you can break. She can train him not to interrupt, but doing something when something needs to be done? Women everywhere are looking for that."

"Marcus wouldn't have stepped to those guys at the bar." That, of course, was Jules.

"Are you serious?" I looked at Jules like she had lost her senses. "Eric's brilliant plan nearly started a bar fight. You can't protect your woman if bottles are flying everywhere."

Violet shrugged. "I see it. I see Eric's appeal."

"Fascinating." I didn't even say it sarcastically. Some of the things I heard in this room had me floored.

"You taking notes, Chase?" Jules ribbed.

I cast her a sly glance. "Maybe I am."

"Chase doesn't need to take notes." Tatum looked over at me with a playful smile. Her voice held humor, but when I threw her a dismissive eye roll, she blushed.

"She's not wrong," Nikki concurred. "Chase is tall, dark, and handsome; proprietor of a successful farm; and an award-winning chef, and firefighter."

"I'm not a firefighter anymore." My response was reflexive and there was an edge to my voice. Being called that in the present tense made me prickly.

"Chase served his country faithfully. *Any* woman would want a man who did," Violet said appeasingly. She knew how being called a firefighter bent me out of shape. "But that's not why Chase is a great catch. He's steady, kind, and reliable. Chase is a catch because he's such a nice guy."

She couldn't have known how a comment like that would affect me. Especially coming from her. I knew she'd only been trying to help.

"I appreciate your conscious rejection of male objectification," I said jokingly to Violet before swinging my gaze back to Nikki and pretending to look hurt. "I'm a former firefighter. Not a piece of meat."

The punchline got me the laugh that I had hoped for. Regular conversation ensued. I acted as natural as always. But, that night, I didn't find it easy to get to sleep, not because of what had been said—because of all the memories it brought up. Of a much younger me and a much younger Violet and the something I'd hoped had been growing between us. And how that thing that was growing had wilted and died the second Todd had come along.

* * *

YOU GIVEN IT ANY THOUGHT?

Forrest's text came through just as I hopped into my utility truck, which was more like a super-slim ATV. It drove on the road like a normal truck, albeit a diminutive one. It was narrow enough—and rugged enough—to drive through the orchards in the rows between the trees. Perfect for the repairs I was doing to some of my irrigation systems.

I thought about it the day you asked me, I tapped out as the engine idled. *I appreciate the invitation, but no thanks.*

Forrest's next text came in quickly. *I'll be there in half an hour.*

I heaved a heavy sigh and shook my head. I knew what he was trying to do. I also had a farm to tend to. I was also grumpy from lack of sleep. I didn't have time for this.

I've got a lot of work in the orchards today, I returned honestly.

And I've got a lot of time on my hands, he shot back right away. *Don't worry. I'll let myself in.*

Two hours later, as I made my way back up to my house, I wasn't surprised to see Forrest's truck parked outside. I was doubly unsurprised to find him on my couch. When he stood to greet me, he had a beer in his hand and a sucked-clean plate of small chicken bones in front of him.

"I see you found the wings in my fridge."

"Man, I could drink that buffalo sauce," he commented with reverence.

"Old family recipe," I said.

"Remind me to thank your momma." He greeted me with a hug.

"Not that it ain't nice to see you, man, but I can tell you—you're wasting your time with all of this investigation talk."

"Tell me that after you see this," he challenged, bending to pick up a leather messenger bag. He opened the top flap and pulled out a file.

He pinned me with a serious gaze. "I could get in trouble for showing you this. It's real-deal government classified."

"You don't have to show me anything," I returned in an even voice. "I'm sorry, but I can't join you on the investigation. I've got too many responsibilities here."

"I'm *showing* you…" he said pointedly. "Because you, of all people, deserve to know."

Interesting choice of words.

"Deserve to know what?"

He handed me a heavy file, one far too thick to read in my living room at four o'clock when I was sweaty from the fields.

"That the public story and the classified story about that day are different."

We both knew what *that day* was. There was only one day the two of us had ever talked about like that—the day Todd and two other men had died on that mountain. Correction: the day I had let him die. The day I had been the one in charge, and they had died on my watch. The day I had ruined his family's lives.

I had never been named in the incident as a person of interest or a person at fault. My name had never been raised in open forums and I was under no public scrutiny. But some people in firefighter circles—myself included—blamed me for sending them into that fight. It was a fight which, in the clear light of aftermath, everyone agreed they had been bound to lose. The question was, why hadn't I seen it at the time?

"Give me the Cliff's Notes version," I implored.

"The Secretary of the Interior thinks the fire was suspicious."

"Suspicious?" I repeated. "Suspicious in what way?"

"Read the file, and you'll find out."

"Do you mean you want me to read the file so you can suck me in?"

"Todd was our best friend. And if I didn't try to put the best person on the case, I wouldn't be a friend to him at all."

His comment made me properly chagrined.

"I'll read the file," I acquiesced.

"Read it soon," Forrest said. "Like I said, it's classified. I can't leave it here with you for long."

Chapter Six
VIOLET

Chase seemed not-okay when I got home from my class on Saturday. I saw on him a look that I often resembled myself. He wore a smile on his face, performing a little as he played Monopoly Junior with Bri and Trey. But his eyes told me something was wrong.

It wasn't the kind of thing I could ask him about in front of the kids. I would wait until they went upstairs. Chase had thought to take them to the movies so they wouldn't be home when my date arrived. It was thoughtful and it made me think that Chase really was fine with me dating. I couldn't dwell on why I was disappointed.

"Mommy!" Trey exclaimed the second he noticed me standing in the door. As usual, he ran and launched himself toward me, practically jumping into my arms for a hug. "What did they teach you in class today?"

I started in on a brief overview of lighting design while I issued a hug to Trey, a hair stroke to Bri, and a shoulder squeeze to Chase. They were playing on the living room floor, so I lowered myself to watch them finish the game. Once it was over, I shooed Bri and Trey upstairs to get ready for the movie while I helped Chase clean up the set.

"What time is he picking you up?" Chase casually asked as he put deed cards in color order. I didn't like that he was still keeping up his façade.

"Hey," I said gently. "What's going on with you?"

The troubled sigh he heaved confirmed that something really was wrong. "Am I that easy to read?"

I shrugged. "I wouldn't quite call you *Captain* Obvious. Maybe *Lieutenant* Obvious or Driver Engineer."

It was a good joke, but he barely smiled.

"Chase, what is it?" Now I was alarmed. "Do you need me to stay home?"

The instantaneous suggestion proved how readily I was willing to give up this date—that I didn't really wanna go and was maybe looking for an out.

"What? No. I'm sorry. Really, Vi—I'm fine. And the kids will be fine, too. I don't want you worrying about me. Worry about having a good time on your date."

He looked miserable as he said it—so miserable I rolled my eyes.

"I won't have fun on my date if I'm out there worried about you."

His eyes darted toward the stairs, as if to make certain the kids weren't coming.

"I got a visit from Forrest. He wants me to come back."

I trod carefully. "He's wanted you to come back since the day you left."

Chase leaned back against the couch. "This time, he's serious about it. He's been over twice in the past week. You know how he gets when he really wants something."

"Yeah, I do know how," I murmured, even as my heart began to race. Now it was me who was pretending to be okay when I was not. I had already lost my husband to the Green Valley Fire Department. Had been on tenterhooks every time he went out on a big call. I'd lived in a constant state of legitimate anxiety. If Chase went back to the fire service, I'd be right back in that mental space again. I honestly didn't think I could take it.

"So now you know what's bugging me," Chase rejoined. "Which means you can stop worrying about me. Now, go get all gussied up for Rod."

That last part was delivered with playful sarcasm, but I managed a small smile.

"I never should've told you his name."

From there, Chase stood up and extended his arm downward, lifting me to standing. He was still built like a firefighter was, his muscles rock hard beneath his shirt. He pulled me up like I weighed nothing, then both of us were up. He was tall enough and I was short enough that he towered over me, then fixed me with that soft, green gaze.

"Thanks for caring enough to worry about me." He gave me a small smile.

"Thanks for telling me what was wrong." I gave my own small smile and hoped he couldn't see me blush. He pulled me in for one of his hugs and—I couldn't help it—I melted in.

Chase's hugs were epic, born of a time when both of us had been deep within our grief—a time when I would break down from the overwhelm and cry on his shoulder for what felt like hours. In the early days after Todd's death, there were moments when we had literally clung to each other, offering comfort that was intimate and raw.

We'd moved past a lot of it, but the hugs? They had stuck. They were steady. And warm. And safe. Somewhere along the line, I'd realized Chase was so much more to me than a shoulder to cry on. And that I liked his comfort a little too much.

He kissed the top of my head. I didn't want to let go, which was a sure sign that I should. When we pulled back, he pinned me with a reassuring look.

"Now go get ready, and don't worry about me. I promise. I'll be fine."

* * *

It turned out I was not fine. Thoughts of Chase returning to the fire service had me rattled. So did going out with a man who wasn't Todd. It was triply unsettling that I couldn't remember how I was supposed to act on a date. It had been so long since I'd even been on one.

Todd and I hadn't strictly dated, not in the traditional sense. He used to say he'd fallen in love with me at first sight. It had certainly felt that way. We'd met each other simply—one night out to dinner with mutual friends. After that, he was everywhere.

It didn't take long for him to decide that I was his, and he was mine, and that the two of us needed to be together. That was how he had been—bold and confident, bossy and charismatic—but so lovable, you couldn't help but follow his lead.

Not long after we met, he went away to training school. We were long distance for a while. On one of his weekends home, I got pregnant with Bri. From there, it was doctor visits and shopping for a house, and eloping in Las Vegas. It was a few brief months of domestic bliss. Then, Bri came and we really were a family. We were so happy, I never looked back, never regretted it, never thought twice most days. But I hated the days he went on calls.

"Violet." Rodney smiled brightly when I opened the door. His teeth were so white, they gleamed—a contrast to his weathered, suntanned skin. "You sure do look nice."

"You, too," I complimented, though he looked the same as he did every time we'd met. That wasn't to say he was underdressed for our date, but rather that he overdressed for the kinds of simple tasks he'd been there for when I'd seen him on the farm.

He had on expensive jeans and a crisp, button-down shirt that had its top two buttons undone; his face looked like it was chiseled out of stone; his longish hair was wavy and framed his face like a lion's mane. As usual, he looked like he'd spent more time on his appearance than I had—not that there was anything wrong with a man who took pride—and he wore a lot of cologne.

"You all ready?" He looked over my shoulder in a way that told me he was curious about my space. He knew that I had kids. I prided myself on the fact that my house didn't look like a Gymboree. It was old and smallish, so I'd run with shabby chic. The pieces I'd accumulated from garage sales and thrift stores were tastefully assembled—a mishmash of light, weathered wooden furniture and reclaimed chandeliers. I'd made smart choices in my neutral paint colors and had splurged mostly on resilient rugs and seating with uphol- stery I could clean. It wasn't my dream house, but it was home and I was proud of what I'd done.

"Let me just grab my purse." I backtracked a few steps to pluck my bag off of the front table, then joined him on my front stoop. My purse wasn't large, but it had all my important things. Lip gloss, which I always wore; a Taser my friend Loretta had taught me how to use; and my emergency fifty. It didn't have much real function in the age of Apple Pay, but my dad had taught me to carry one.

Out on my driveway, I found a huge surprise—huge in the literal sense. The largest Hummer I'd ever seen took up the space of two cars. It was bright yellow and all suped up, with grills and racks and the kinds of lights up top I couldn't even name. The thing was so large, it looked like it could comfortably seat eight.

Rodney opened the passenger door. Even with the chrome step that dropped down for me to set foot on, getting up into that thing felt like mounting a horse. After shutting me inside, he jogged around and got in. He started the engine, but didn't move the car. I swung my gaze over to him, to find him staring in the rearview. He couldn't have been scanning for nonexistent traffic —we were sitting in my driveway. He was looking in the mirror. At himself.

"We going off roading in this thing?" I made my question sound light. This was a lot more car than I usually saw in Green Valley, which was saying something for a place where men compared the size of their trucks.

My voice jarred him out of whatever he was doing and he finally engaged the gear shift. "No, but we're headed somewhere remote."

His attention shifting to the road meant that he hadn't seen my frown. It was a creepy thing to say to a woman on a date. "Not too remote, I hope."

"I figured we'd head to Sky Lake, do a little fishing. When I can, I like to catch my food. You ever been to the western campground? It's got a nice place to see the stars and build a fire. What I catch there is some of the best lake trout you'll ever eat."

It did sound mildly romantic. Showed that he was down-to-earth. It might even save me from my own self-consciousness. I was dreading what folks would say when they saw me out with another man. Green Valley was a small town. Wondering what to say if I ran into one of Todd's friends was giving me legitimate anxiety.

"Oh, okay. Fishing sounds nice." I turned back toward my recently vacated driveway. "But maybe I ought to go back and change my clothes."

"Don't worry, darlin'." He winked a blue eye. "You won't have to lift a finger."

Rodney made good on his word. Just over half an hour later, he settled me into a reclining chair on the lake to let me sit back and watch him fish.

He'd built up a fire in the pit behind us and set out a steel campfire grill. He'd brought along a well-stocked cooler—beer for him and hard cider for me. Our backdrop was beautiful—the sunset and the lake. I appreciated the effort and the nature energy, and would have liked the company a whole lot more if Rodney hadn't spent the whole time talking about himself.

Technically, I had asked him questions in a small talk kind of way. That was what people on first dates did. I just hadn't expected his answers to be so lengthy. Simple questions, like where he was from and what had gotten him interested in the party rental business yielded answers that were thorough to the extreme.

Rodney didn't just give the long version of the story—he meandered. By the time the fish was cooked, I was starting to feel like I had in my class that morning—like I was in a lecture and I ought to be taking notes. But there were silver linings to his interest in himself. He was attentive to me, but not *too* attentive. As in, he didn't seem too interested in physicality or sex. Not feeling cornered into confronting expectations I wasn't ready to meet felt like relief.

"How long you been working for Chase?" He finally let me get a word in edgewise after he fixed me a plate.

"A few years now," I replied. "But I'm in school for interior design; double major in business administration."

"Impressive." Rodney's bright-eyed nod and approving look seemed sincere. "I like a woman with a mind for business. What are you gonna do with your degree?"

I took a deliberate breath, not sure I had ever said this out loud. "I've put away some money. I'm hoping to come into a little more. Once I've saved up enough, I'm going to buy a building."

"A building?"

I nodded. "That old horse and tack store downtown? The one that's been vacant for more than a year? The one that nobody wants because it's so dilapidated?"

Rodney frowned in thought. "The one on the corner of Valley and Main? On the block behind Eager Beaver's?"

I nodded. "I can't afford it yet, but I've got my eye on that place. I want to open a studio of my own."

Rodney gave a low whistle. "Buying a building is no joke. I own a few myself. Do you know Dick?" Rodney was really looking at me now.

"Dick who?"

"Dick Wiener, the commercial real estate agent. He's your go-to guy for commercial property. If you don't know him yet, I'll introduce the two of you."

From there, Rodney resumed another long stint of talking about himself. To his credit, some of the horn-tooting he did this time was on my behalf. Telling him my plans for my business had yielded a rundown of all the people he knew who might be able to help.

He noticed at least a half hour too late that the night was getting cold. It wasn't until I asked for a blanket that he suggested we pack up.

"You want to head into town for a nightcap?" he asked once the camp was cleaned up.

"Another time?" I asked sincerely. It was only ten o'clock but I was tired. I was always tired as the mother of young children; but the night air and him droning on hadn't done the situation any help. I was also fairly certain that two weeks' worth of emotional buildup had finally come crashing down now that the moment I'd anticipated had finally arrived.

He drove me back to my place in more balanced conversation, a fact that I was thankful for. The porch light was on when we approached the house. The Hummer was loud and I hoped that it wouldn't wake up my neighbors. But that thought rested in the back of my mind when I remembered what might happen next.

I couldn't rightly say that I felt much chemistry with Rodney. But I was on a date and the man was about to walk me to my door. I'd had years to think about the moment that was about to happen. I should have been prepared. Should have had a plan to set boundaries. Should have had a frank conversation with myself about what I was ready to do. But I had no idea what I would do if he came in for a kiss.

"I had a real nice time, Violet." He said it as he helped me dismount from the car—kept hold of my hand as he walked me to the door. It was the first time he'd touched me all night. I was grateful for the fact that he really had been a perfect gentleman. But I couldn't get a read on how much he liked me. And I couldn't tell what he might do next.

"I'm headed out of town on Tuesday. A little expedition in the bush. But I'd like to see you again. Maybe the week I come back. Can I give you a call?"

I nodded stiffly. I would have agreed to anything right then. Could he tell that I was trembling or was that something I could only feel on the inside?

"Great." He stopped walking and peered down at my face. We'd stepped up on to my stoop—it was as far as we could go without walking through my door. He rounded on me and took my other hand.

"Rodney." I heard the panic in my own voice, but was lost for what to say. He hadn't actually kissed me yet. Could I proactively say no to something he hadn't tried?

He took a step closer. That was when I heard a ruckus coming from behind the house. I frowned, stepping back instinctively. If there was a prowler or a rogue animal on my property, I needed to check it out. The closer I listened, the better I was able to identify what I was hearing. The rumbling sound was getting louder, but where was it coming from? I took another step away from Rodney and craned my neck to look past my front hedges. That was when I saw a tall male figure emerge from behind the garage. It wasn't a prowler. It was Chase.

Chapter Seven
CHASE

It hadn't been a good idea to take the kids to a movie, an animated Disney princess sort of thing. Being an involved godfather, I'd seen my share. The heroine was strong and self-determined, noble and wise, overflowing with dreams and potential. Then she met some 'roided-up prince and everything went to shit.

Walking out of that theater, I tried to marshal my thoughts, but they couldn't stay off of Violet. Worries about losing her to one of the many undeserving yahoos who lived in these parts infiltrated my mind. I kept myself together long enough to cook, feed and read stories to the kids. But after they were down, I had too much time to get to thinking about the many ways in which encouraging her to date could go wrong.

First, I turned on the porch light, then obsessed over every outdoor noise, thinking any little thing might signal her return. When that put me at the edge of my wits, I briefly regretted having agreed to babysit through an event I clearly couldn't handle. Somewhere between eating my feelings with the help of the homemade strawberry ice cream I'd whipped up with the kids that morning, I poured myself a glass of bourbon, and made a concerted effort to think healthier thoughts.

Maybe you can't be with Violet, but she's still a treasured friend.

Friends look out for friends, especially when it comes to new people.

It's natural for anyone who feels protective of her to want to lay eyes on this guy.

The least I can do for Violet is slap her date with "don't fuck with her" vibes.

No sooner had I cooked up a solid plan to insert myself into the situation than the sound from a very large engine cut through the quiet of the night. I'd concluded the moment Violet arrived home was the right moment to bring her trash out to the curb. I was suddenly pleased with myself to have been slow to fix the recycling bin with the wonky wheel. I could roll it silently across the lawn, but where would the fun be in that? Only the noisiest one would do.

This is it.

I hurried through the kitchen and opened the garage door, swiftly grabbing the bin and beginning to make my way down the drive. The heavy plastic wheels trudged crudely over the pavement. I kept my gaze forward, pretending not to notice the ruckus I was making or the enormous yellow Hummer parked in front of the door.

His choice of transportation was a virtual guarantee that he was compensating for something. Not to mention, driving a gas guzzler like that made him a climate change–denying asshat. I could make it all the way to the street and get away with not looking at them directly. It would be a different story once I turned back toward the house.

"Chase?" Violet said it loudly enough for me to hear her voice over all the noise. I hazarded a glance, steeling myself for whatever backlash I might be facing. I looked up, pretending to be startled, then I gave a little wave. I made a fuss of situating the bin in a precise position next to her mailbox, then doubled back to greet them at the front door.

Yards away from reaching this guy, I was already sizing him up. I recognized him from the farm. Like Violet said, he was one of our wedding vendors. The gimlet eye he fixed me with as I made my approach told me interfering was the right decision. I had to send a message to this guy.

Without hearing him speak a word, I knew two things: he had an alpha complex; and he saw me as a threat. I didn't know what Violet had told him about me, but it didn't matter right then. I was about to tell him everything he needed to know.

"Chase Greenleaf." I extended my hand in introduction; for Violet's benefit, I smiled. It only behooved me to seem friendly. She wouldn't know that I'd given him a nice, firm shake. She also wouldn't know that the enormous Breitling on his shaking hand was a flex meant to be seen by other men. Its face was so large, it looked more like a dive computer than a timepiece.

"Right," he replied. "Chase. You're Violet's boss."

"Actually, I play many roles in Violet's life." My voice was saccharine sweet. "Violet helps me with my business, but she's the one in charge. But we go farther back than that. Me and Violet are family. And I'm the godfather to her kids."

"Oh, that's right." Rodney feigned sudden recollection. "You were here babysitting. It's nice that you did so I could take her out—show her a good time."

Unlike *some* men, I wasn't under the mistaken impression that caring for children diminished me. I arched my eyebrow in a way that let him know his comment had left me unfazed. Caring for children was a joy.

"It's not babysitting when you love them like your own. Violet's raising two amazing kids." Before he could respond, I dove back in. "And—sorry—I didn't catch your name."

Something in his blue eyes hardened. "It's Rodney. Rodney O'Toole."

It was only by the grace of God that I didn't lose my shit right there. This guy had a first name and a last name that were both euphemisms for penis. And by all accounts, he seemed like a total dick.

"I understand you're one of our wedding vendors." I said it with a straight face.

He weaved his head back and forth, ambivalently. "That, and a few other things."

I swung my gaze back to Violet, who was watching the exchange like it was set point at a tennis match. A look of clear unease displayed on her face.

For that brief moment, I did regret crashing the party. It wasn't her who I wanted to make uncomfortable—it was him. Now that I'd done what I'd gone there to do, it was time for me to leave.

"Well, it was nice to meet you, Rod. Glad you got her home safely. Maybe I'll see you around the farm."

With that, I raised my left hand to my face, like all I was doing was stroking my beard. But I wanted Rodney to see my naked left hand. He needed to know that I wasn't some glorified babysitter. I was Violet's unmarried, straight, male best friend, father figure to her kids, and someone who could clearly take him in a fight.

"Vi, I'll see you inside." My voice softened when I spoke to her. I walked between them, into the unlocked front door. Instead of closing it, I left it open as I disappeared into the house, out of sight but never out of mind.

* * *

"So...how was your date?"

I let Violet find me unloading the dishwasher when she wandered inside.

"Why don't you tell me?" She crossed her arms in front of herself and called me out with a single eyebrow quirk. "You ought to know. You were there."

I knew better than to dare deny I'd done what I'd done. So I did the only thing left that made a lick of sense. I crossed my own arms in front of myself and confessed.

"I just wanted him to know you've got people—folks who'll smack him down if he steps out of line. I'm thinking he got the message."

"I guess now that he knows the score, you won't *ever* be pulling anything like that again."

She gave me the same look she gave the kids sometimes—the one that said, "you can't beat me, so don't even try."

I grunted noncommittally, then set the rocks glass I'd just plucked out of the dishwasher in front of her. Then, I walked backward toward the freezer, where I'd hidden a carafe out of reach on the top shelf.

She didn't know about it. It wouldn't have been ready to drink until now. But bourbon punch was her favorite. It had lemonade and pineapple juice; it was steeped in orange slices and bing cherries; I'd put in fresh cane juice from my farm and enough bourbon that it would never freeze.

Without asking whether she wanted some, I shook the clear container and watched her eyes light up as it dawned on her what I'd made. Once all the ice crystals were shaken loose, I poured both of us a glass.

"So. How was your date?" My question was less sardonic this time.

I hoped and prayed she wasn't about to tell me she liked Rod.

"It was okay." Something in her voice was tentative.

I couldn't decide whether to be worried that something bad had happened or elated at her ambivalence.

"He seems like an okay guy," she went on.

"Where'd he take you?" I did my best to ask with the curiosity of a friend.

For now, I would compartmentalize my feelings. I could do it long enough to see how Violet really felt about how things had gone. It didn't escape me, how going on your first date after your husband passed away would be a big step for anybody. The part of me that didn't want to sabotage any man who even looked at her the way I saw her wanted her to be happy one day.

"He took me fishing. On Sky Lake."

My incredulity couldn't be helped. "You went fishing in *that*?"

I was secretly pleased that the outfit she wore hadn't been too sexy. Don't get me wrong—Violet would look delicious in a burlap sack, and the sweater dress she wore flattered her. But it was a far cry from anything you'd think of for catching fish.

"He went fishing. I watched."

I blinked. "Let me get this straight. His idea of showing a woman a good time was making you watch him catch your dinner?" I tried not to let my triumph show on my face, but it was hard. Dates were all about connection. Even I knew that—and I hadn't been on a date in years. That fact alone told me this guy had zero game.

"It was…nice," she defended, her voice unenthused.

I did a mental fist pump as I hummed in understanding, using my listening voice. "Mmm-hmm…"

"He built us a fire, set me up with a chair, made sure I was comfortable while he caught our dinner."

I didn't like the idea of her going with a stranger to a remote, wooded location. Shit. I watched true crime.

"How was the fish?" I resisted the urge to ask her for a detailed description of the full menu. You could tell a lot about a man based on what he served for dinner.

"It was good. Simple. Very fresh but just seasoned with salt and pepper."

I tried to tamp it down, but suspected I looked a bit triumphant. All of this new information had me pleased. This guy was an obvious amateur. Judging from how quickly she'd followed me inside, there had been no goodnight kiss. And on the off chance that there had been, I would bet my whole, entire farm that said kiss hadn't been any good.

"How were the kids?" she finally asked, and I rolled with the change of subject.

"The kids were fine." I didn't mention that I'd covered for her when the ever-perceptive Bri had asked which friend Mommy was going out with. "We made fruity krispies when we got back to the house. Neither one tried to draw out bedtime. Trey got right to sleep."

"I mean it, Chase. Thanks for watching them." Her face was lovely and her gaze was sincere. A few simple words from her—one glance—was never too little to remind me how I felt.

"Like I said. It's not babysitting when it's family."

Chapter Eight
VIOLET

By Monday morning at work, my date was practically forgotten. I'd received the predicted Sunday morning calls from the girls. They'd asked different questions than Chase. Did he seem like a solid guy who had his shit together? Did he do anything that was a deal breaker? Was he a good kisser? Did Rodney have a big rod?

"Yes," "no," "I don't know," and "it's way too early to think about that" had been my answers. Knowing Rodney had gone out of town was a relief. It meant I wouldn't have to navigate whatever came next—no worrying about what further contact meant, and when and whether he would really call.

All the better for me to focus, I thought as I put down my bag and sat at my desk chair. I'd posted a job description for a special events manager. I didn't want to hire an "events assistant" or an "events associate." I wanted the title to signal that this role was high level. As I'd written in the job description, I wanted a unicorn—someone who would take to the role like I had and really fly.

I settled in with my coffee, closing all extraneous windows on my computer, wanting to dig into my task. Then, I silenced the phone on my desk. Taking calls was part of the job, but I didn't want to be distracted. The person I brought in to take over after I left the farm had to be right.

I wasn't halfway through reading my first résumé when my cell phone rang. I always kept it on in case something was happening with my kids. I thought to send it to voicemail if it turned out to be anyone other than the day care or the elementary school, but I picked up when I read the caller ID.

"Hey, Katrina," I greeted my attorney with more cheer than I felt. Talking to her always put me on edge, not because she was intimidating—because every phone call from her held the potential to give me hope, or to destroy it, or to take me back to a time when the pain was fresh.

"I'm getting ready for the court date." My brightness took effort to manufacture. "We're still on for that, right?"

I pushed away my coffee, suddenly too jumpy for more caffeine.

"That's why I'm calling. The retrial doesn't have to happen if you don't want it to. DCH just made an offer. Half a million dollars to settle the suit."

Half a million dollars. I repeated the number to myself.

"As in, US dollars?" I said out loud.

"Yes. They want to give you a lump sum."

But I didn't understand. "That's 100,000 dollars over what the policy was supposed to pay out."

"They're offering extra for pain and suffering, and to offset legal fees." Katrina's voice was always sober. I'd concluded that aspect of her manner was part of what made her a great attorney. Her lack of emotion didn't make her seem cold—it made her seem like a straight shooter. She gave off the vibe of a person who simply told the truth.

As the news began to set in, confused tears sprang to my eyes.

"After all they put me through…" The first words I was able to speak came out in a whisper. "After four years, dragging me through the mud and fighting me tooth and nail, they suddenly decide to make me an offer? Why?"

A slight creaking sound in the background told me Katrina was reclining in her desk chair. It was a habit I'd noticed when meeting with her at her office.

"The lead attorney on the case says the insurance company has a new general counsel. Given how many lawsuits insurance companies are party to, the general counsel is nearly as important as the CEO. They're saying they want to settle because the new GC likes to deal with cases like yours in a different way."

"So the insurance company had a change of heart?"

"Insurance companies don't have hearts," she came back bluntly. "They want us to believe the new GC prefers settling more lawsuits and scaling back on the number of cases that go to court."

"But that's not what you think."

Her chair creaked again. "The math doesn't make much sense. Why call it off on the eve of the trial, especially if the resources they put toward building a case are already a sunk cost? And offering more than a client is asking as part of a settlement? That's unheard of for an insurance company. I think something else is going on."

"Something else?" I parroted back, still fighting to achieve articulation. "What do you think they're playing at?"

"I think if they're offering above your ask, they think your case is worth more than the face value of the policy."

I shook my head, incredulous, now robbed fully of the power of speech. What card in the world could they think we had that we hadn't already played? This was an appeal. We'd already revealed our arguments in the earlier proceedings. Our best hope was to win with a different—and more sympathetic—judge.

"It's just speculation, but here's what might be going on," she continued when I didn't answer. "They think we've got new evidence—something that would cause the judge to determine you're entitled to more, possibly a lot more than half a million dollars. They're offering that amount now, hoping it will sound like so much money to you that you sign without asking questions."

"Half a million dollars *is* a lot of money to me." I found my voice again. "I could pay off my house and my car. I could put money away for the kids to go to college. If I have no mortgage to pay, I can work less and spend more time with my kids. Half a million dollars is a lot for most people, especially a single parent."

No, you're a widowed parent. And there's a difference, a voice inside me said. It was true. Raising children on your own was difficult, no matter the circumstances. But raising children on your own when their dad was never, ever coming back...now that was next-level. Most days, I felt like I was failing—

tired from trying to juggle so much and stretched too thin to be there like I wanted to for Bri and Trey.

"What do you think I should do?" I finally asked.

"Obviously, it's your choice. But my advice is, we don't do anything yet. Let me investigate whether they're telling the truth about the new general counsel. And let me try to figure out what new claim they might think we have. It could be anything—even a technicality of some law that's changed.

"It's my job to keep you informed of things like these, and that's why I'm calling you now. But it's also my job to protect your interests. My professional opinion is, there's more than meets the eye. Let me start fresh with a different investigator—see if I can turn up new information about the case."

* * *

I wasn't surprised when I woke up at 4 a.m. the next morning in the middle of a panic attack, my heart pounding and in a cold sweat after being jarred from a dead sleep. Anxiety about the case liked to mess with my head. Not just stress about the outcome—but the heavy dose of heartbreak it dredged up.

They'd started out as nightmares back when I was getting up with Trey, back at a time when he nursed in the middle of the night. I'd been drowning under the weight of taking care of a newborn and a toddler. I had a legal battle ahead of me. My hormones weren't right and, on top of it all, I was grieving.

What I'd needed more than anything at that time in my life was sleep. There were times I was so tired, I fell asleep standing up—times when I was afraid to sleep with Trey next to me for fear I might roll over on him.

What sleep I *had* gotten hadn't been peaceful. It felt like every time I closed my eyes, I would imagine Todd in that burning forest. The worst were the funeral dreams—the ones where I went to the front of the church and saw him in his casket. For his real funeral, we'd had to keep it closed.

Two years later, the nightmares had stopped, but the terror itself hadn't. Instead, I would wake up with panic attacks in the middle of the night. It was like waking up from a nightmare without remembering the nightmare itself— knowing something terrible was haunting me all the same.

It had been a solid year since the panic attacks had subsided. It had taken ther-apy, some supplements, and a formal sleep plan. Returning to a healthy state of sleep had been hard-earned. A middle-of-the-night panic attack was now a sobering reminder of how precarious my sense of peace was.

I can't go back to this.

I thought it as I stood in my kitchen setting my kettle to boil. After breathing through the aftermath of my rude awakening, I'd ventured downstairs. The tea that helped you fall asleep was in the back of my cupboard and I'd had to turn on the light to dig.

I can't go back to this. I can't do this for another minute.

Intrusive thoughts wouldn't stop running through my head, thoughts that made me want to take the money and walk away. But the part of me that just wanted it to be over—that wanted to close that chapter of my life—felt like giving up was the same as dishonoring Todd.

That wasn't all that had me rattled. Earlier, I'd told Chase. I'd tracked him down on the farm—actively sought him out for advice. But, when I'd told him about it, he'd looked strangely pissed off about the whole thing. Chase usually had a way of talking me through every side of an issue. But he'd hardly said anything at all.

All of it had thrown me. Confusion on top of confusion. The kids had picked up on it, too. Five minutes after I'd gotten her from school, Bri had asked what was wrong. I didn't know anything but for the fact that climbing back onto an emotional roller coaster wasn't an option. I could not afford to go off the rails.

Chapter Nine
CHASE

*W*e *need to talk.*

No sooner had I dropped Violet off at the events barn than I took out my phone and texted Forrest.

Violet dropped a bomb.

I'd done my best to contain myself while she was telling me about the settlement—had tried to remain neutral and offered balanced advice. But it had been all I could do to keep from punching something.

We need to talk about this investigation.

I texted Forrest again. The insurance company making her an offer like that was more than a little suspicious. Waiting to talk about it was making me want to crawl right out of my skin.

I'll call you in five, came Forrest's answering text.

Good. It would give me time to get back to my house. I didn't want to say what I had to say out in the open. And I really didn't want what I had to say to be true, even though the more I thought about it, the more I felt in my bones it was.

"I think you're right," I said the second my phone rang. I didn't bother to greet

Forrest. "There was something suspicious about Todd's death. Somebody tried to cover something up. And more than one somebody figured it out."

I was out of breath as I said it, not just from hoofing it back to my house to have some privacy, from the weight of emotion crushing my chest.

"Start from the beginning." Forrest's voice was grave.

I gave him the whole shebang. Violet's upcoming court date. The strange timing of the settlement offer. The puzzling amount. The story the insurance company fed her attorney. Violet agreeing something wasn't right but wanting it all to be over. Her not knowing what she ought to do.

"The insurance company knows something," Forrest concluded when I finished my story.

"That's what I'm thinking," I said. "You remember the way their lawyer, that asshole named Morone, laughed at me—*laughed at me*—when I told him we would appeal? I still remember the exact words he said."

I clenched my jaw, nearly too mad at the recollection to get it out.

"He said we would never win because we would never have a case. Then, he looked at Violet and preached to her. Said she should have taken the settlement they'd offered her on day one. Said now, they would never offer another dime."

That moment was emblazoned in my memory as one of only two times in my life when I had to be physically restrained from fighting.

"Do you remember what that day-one settlement offer was?" Forrest wanted to know.

The insurance company had offered her a token amount when they had first taken the case; an incentive for her to walk away so that all parties could avoid a protracted trial.

"Thirty-five thousand dollars." My throat tightened to even have to say it. "That's what they said Todd's life was worth."

The other side of the line was quiet as we both let that sink in. Not that you could put a value on a human life, but half a million dollars was a lot better. It would get Violet on solid financial footing and give her a degree of closure that most life insurance beneficiaries had from day one. Still, it didn't sit well with me.

For three weeks, I hadn't wanted anything to do with Forrest or the investigation or unrestricted access to Todd's case file. If I was honest with myself about it, I'd been scared. Scared that it would open old wounds, and that the evidence would prove my worst fears—that I was responsible for his death. But now—for Violet's sake—I needed to know everything about that day.

"I'm in," I told Forrest definitively. "When do we start?"

"Now, hold on." Forrest put on the brakes. "Just what is it you're planning to do?"

"Find out what the insurance company knows. Help Violet with her case."

"Not possible," Forrest replied with finality. "Everything we'll be privy to is classified. When I tried to entice you with access to Todd's file so you could finally have some closure? That was supposed to be just for you and your own edification."

"They're trying to screw her, man." Now, I was talking louder. "They already did it once. They're trying to do it twice. If they're offering her half a million dollars to walk away, her case is worth more. I don't know about you, but I sure as shit don't want her to miss out on a single ounce of justice."

Forrest was quiet for a long time. I had half a mind to tell him I would help Violet anyway, with his blessing or without it. I could have reminded him that he had already given me the file, and that he was already an accomplice. But I'd known him long enough to anticipate that a lack of protest was a good sign.

"We need to talk about how we're gonna do this." Forrest finally spoke. "But we won't do it on the phone. Face-to-face meetings in secure locations from here on out."

"We'll be careful," I promised. "Whatever we need to do, I'll do it. I can't let her down twice."

After Forrest and I hung up, I realized I'd been shaking. My hand trembled as I threw down my phone. I was in my living room, not seated, but pacing. I ran a hand through my hair. That's when I realized I was sweating. I pulled off my shirt, still breathing hard.

You need to go for a run, a wise voice in my mind said.

You need to read that file, said another.

My gaze darted to the papers Forrest had left—the ones I'd stared at every day, but had never been able to bring myself to touch.

But it wasn't about me anymore. Now, it was about Violet. Now, it was about Bri and Trey. Now, the time had come. I sat on my sofa and opened up the file.

* * *

"Sorry I'm late," I called up to the event barn loft as I jogged up the stairs. I'd seen Violet's form sitting at the conference table when I came in. Punctuality was a virtue my mother had instilled in me as a child. I'd grown up knowing when you're early, you're on time, and when you're on time, you're late, and when you're late, you're in big trouble.

"I overslept," I said by way of explanation, keeping it short and sweet. I'd also been taught to avoid excuses, to apologize proactively and never slink away from taking blame. "I'm sorry. I know how busy you are."

"You *overslept*?" Violet gave my explanation the disbelief it was due. Farmers were early risers. Most days, I was up and out in the orchards hours before she came.

"Late night." I said it, then I realized how it sounded. "I was up reading. I should have gone to bed, but I couldn't put it down."

If Violet wanted to assume I was talking about a book, I'd go ahead and let her. But the thing I'd been reading hadn't been a book—it had been the incident report for Todd's deadly fire. I'd been chipping away at it for three full nights and had barely made a dent.

"I actually don't have much today." Violet looked distracted.

She, too, seemed underslept. Because I knew better than to ask a woman why she looked so tired, I said nothing. The numbers meetings were once a month, and that one had been last week. The ones in between were just downloads on all that was happening on the farm.

"People are calling wanting to know when reservations will open for The Noble Pig, and what the season dates will be for next summer. I wanted to ask whether you had any preferences or conflicts."

"Forrest and Sierra's wedding is scheduled for next summer. I'll see if I can get him to let me know the date."

"Plans for their engagement party are going well," Violet replied. "They're coming to the farm this week for a walk-through of our spaces."

"Make sure to let me know when. I'll join y'all on the walk and have lunch ready for the four of us. They're redoing their kitchen. Sounds like it's been a while since they've had a good meal."

Violet nodded and made a note, then moved on to the next thing. We both seemed worse for wear. Maybe I could find a gentle way to tell her to take the day off. Before I knew it, she'd run through most of her list and we were close to the end of the meeting.

"Final item," she began. "I'll need you for interviews week after next. I'll be screening a few candidates for the events manager position. After that, I'll want you to meet all the finalists."

"If you want me to, I can," I said. "But, Violet, you know it's your decision. They won't be working for me—they'll be working for you."

A potently uneasy look took over Violet's face. She was funny, the way she made a big production out of our weekly meetings and having me approve a bunch of things. Violet had built the event business at Noble Farms from nothing. Violet was the boss of all of this, even if she didn't act like it yet.

"Also, you should know," I continued rather than say any of this. "I'm gonna be around a lot less. Me and Forrest…we've got things to do. I need to go with him to Washington for a couple days, for a meeting."

"He's got you doing things for the wedding already?" she speculated. "I take it you're the best man."

"It's not related to the wedding. I told you. He's trying to pull me back in. Cody's going to help me with the orchards and I'll be back in the service part-time."

Violet looked like she could hardly believe the words I was saying. I could hardly believe them myself.

"You're going back to the fire service?" she practically sputtered. I was sure she thought she'd never see the day.

"I'm dipping my toes back in." I kept it deliberately vague. I absolutely could not tell Violet I was trying to get to the bottom of Todd's death, or that I suspected anything strange. I couldn't tell her any of this until I knew something. Because the only thing worse than grief was hope. I didn't want her to hope I could get to the bottom of things because what if it turned out I couldn't?

So many emotions passed over Violet's face that I didn't know what to say. I hadn't anticipated that telling her would affect her like this.

"When are you back from DC?" she asked abruptly.

"Next week. I can meet with events manager prospects eventually, but for the next few weeks, I'll be juggling. It can't be that urgent to hire somebody… right?"

It should have been an easy answer. But when Violet's brow furrowed and her eyes got shiny, I was alarmed.

"It *is* that urgent." Her answer came out in more of a whisper. "It needs to happen soon, and I need you there. And I need you to really, really care about the person we hire."

"What's going on here, Vi?" Wherever this was going, it had my hackles up.

Her eyes became shinier. "Chase. There's something I need to tell you."

Then, tell me already. I managed to keep my impatient voice at bay, even as my heart began to thunder.

"After I train the new events manager, I'm leaving Noble Farms."

PART II

Chapter Ten
VIOLET

The ringing of my phone woke me from a cozy noontime sleep. I was upstairs in the event barn, on the feather bedrolls in the loft. Jameson snoozed at my feet. It was the space Chase had built for me back when I'd been bringing the kids to work. I'd spent precious hours in this bed, nursing Trey when he was a baby, reading Bri to sleep, and catching some winks myself.

Chase had wisely built it in the warmest place in the barn, which made it pleasantly toasty. Its thick feather bedrolls let me sink down in the most delicious way. Given how badly I'd been sleeping at night, daytime naps were saving me. It felt so nice, I was reluctant to pick up my call. A second before I did, I looked at the caller ID.

"Hey, Katrina." I stifled a yawn.

"I'm glad I caught you. I've got new information about your case. The story they fed us about the new general counsel? It doesn't add up. At all."

I nodded in groggy understanding, then said "Right" because body language wasn't audible. Shimmying forward, I swung my legs off of the bedroll and onto the floor.

"The GC's name is Don Rutherford. They poached him from another big insurance company. People at that level only get poached when they're delivering results."

I asked the half-a-million-dollar question. "So how is he winning his cases?"

"Turns out it's the opposite of what they told me. He doesn't have a track record of settling—he has a track record of winning in court. He's notorious for taking cases to trial. Rumor has it, he's so obsessive, he drives the defense attorneys who work under him so hard, a fair number of them quit. He's even got a nickname: Donnie Darko."

I frowned. "If he's notorious, why would they feed you an obvious lie?"

"Classic underestimation." She didn't miss a beat. "Attorneys are trained to size up the opposition. They look at you and see a Black woman without a college degree, who lives in a small town and married a working-class man. They're betting that 500,000 dollars is enough money to buy you off. They look at me and see a Black woman attorney who didn't go to a fancy school and doesn't work at a big-name firm in a big city. They think I'm not going to do my research."

"Yeah, that tracks." I wasn't surprised now that she'd laid it all out.

"That leaves us with two plays," Katrina concluded. "Option one is to agree to a settlement and negotiate a higher amount. But without knowing what they think we have, we'd be taking a shot in the dark."

"What's option two?"

"We let the case go to court as scheduled and work like hell to figure it out. If we're successful, we bring in the new evidence; then, we win based on what the case is worth."

"But we might not ever figure it out," I observed aloud.

"That's right," Katrina confirmed. "If we go back to trial with no new evidence, the best-case scenario is a better judgment from a different judge and jury. A group that is extremely sympathetic could award you the 400,000 dollars—the maximum amount named in the policy. The worst-case scenario is, you get nothing."

"A bird in the hand is worth two in the bush." By now, Jameson had awakened and repositioned himself to set his head on my lap. Petting him held the added benefit of helping me soothe myself.

"Sometimes it is," she agreed.

I thanked her for her thorough due diligence. She told me to think it through. I was about to hang up when I remembered what I'd been meaning to ask.

"Hey, do you happen to know any attorneys who handle incorporations?"

"What kind of business are you looking to start?"

"An interior design and event planning business."

"You're leaving Chase?" The degree of surprise—and interest—in her voice was unexpected. She knew Chase well, from the initial trial. He'd been there every single day in the courtroom for moral support.

"Not in any absolute sense." I made a concerted effort not to sound defensive. "More like, I've overstayed my welcome. And now I'm moving on."

"Alright...well, I guess congratulations are in order." Katrina didn't sound convinced. "And I do know an attorney who could help. I'm in meetings all afternoon and in court tomorrow. But I'll send you a warm intro. Give me a couple days."

* * *

MAN ENOUGH WAS on but I could barely pay attention. It wasn't often that I felt uncomfortable in my own house. Then again, it wasn't often that Chase and I were fighting. "Fighting" was a fluid concept—a word that meant different things to different people. For us, it meant short fuses and working each other's last nerves. Things had been chilly since I'd told him I was leaving.

"Thanks, Chase." I tried to be the bigger person as he handed me a drink. Tonight was peach martinis made using a special batch from Marly's Moonshine. She was the only distiller who Chase would sell to. He liked to brag that his Octoberfest peaches were the secret weapon to her award-winning spirit. For those of us who didn't have to drive home, he'd made a second round. I was already feeling the effects of the first.

He answered my gratitude with a wordless nod and took his usual place next to me. Tonight, I wasn't feeling the love. Neither was anyone else in the room, apparently. Unlike most Thursday nights, when we supplied wisecracking comments while watching the show, all the adults—and even the kids—were silent.

"Looks like Marcus is being his normal self," I said by way of getting our snarking started. I could not allow things to go on like this. So many things were in flux for me, I needed Thursday nights to feel good. Marcus was the suitor who Jules loved to hate, so I'd targeted him deliberately, hopeful that she would pile on.

Moments earlier on the show, Marcus had insisted that he and Chelsea skip their circus date so he could check in about their last conversation. She'd begun to share some serious things about her past on their last one-on-one, but Eric had crashed the party and rudely cut them off. Most other suitors would be eager to woo Chelsea on their next date—to ingratiate themselves to her and notch up the romance. But Marcus had put on the brakes.

"Can someone please tell me what he's still doing in this game?" Like clock-work, Jules took the bait. She had a mean sense of humor, but she was funny. If anybody had us laughing, it was her.

"Marcus is sweet," Tatum defended.

"Marcus ought to keep a hankie in his pocket," Nikki quipped.

"To dry all those salty tears," Jules joined in.

Bri giggled. Jules fist-bumped Nikki. Trey just looked confused. And Chase looked absolutely livid.

Watching his face redden, my own blood began to boil. Why didn't he want us to go back to normal like I did? Why was he hell-bent on us not having fun?

"Maybe Marcus is the only suitor on this whole damn show who's man enough to truly be there for Chelsea." His tone was acerbic.

"Maybe Marcus needs to learn to let things go," I bit back.

He looked at me accusingly. "Maybe Chelsea should quit trying to be a hero and shouldering everything alone."

"Maybe Marcus should quit feeling like she owes him an explanation." I lifted my chin indignantly.

"Maybe Chelsea should quit acting like she doesn't."

Now, Chase and I were scowling at each other.

"Kids, time to brush your teeth," Nikki said. "It's time to get ready for bed."

I broke my death glare at Chase long enough to see Nikki spring up from her seat. It didn't take long for the others to make their excuses. Tatum pulled Jules to her feet, claiming a need for a companion in catching some fresh air. On her way out, Tatum cast Chase a sympathetic glance as Jules gave him a dirty look.

"Mommy is too mad about Marcus," Trey said plaintively to Bri as Nikki shooed them out of the room.

"I don't think they're talking about Marcus," Bri responded.

Shit.

Now, I had as much of a hand as Chase had in ruining girls' night in, and I'd scared my children to boot.

Once they were all out of earshot, I sprang to my feet, crossed my arms, and glared at him even harder. "We can't do this, Chase. Not in front of my kids."

He sprang up just as quickly. "You're right. We can't. So, let's settle this—right here and right now. I'll make myself clear. I do not accept your resignation."

I brought my fingers to my temples and closed my eyes. "You're only making it worse."

"I will consider your resignation when you state your reasons." He doubled down. "It's reasonable for me to want an explanation as to why you're bent on abandoning the house you built. Until such time as you provide one, you're mine."

My body's reaction to him staking a claim was involuntary and traitorous. He'd said it more like a jealous lover than a pissed-off boss. I'd never known what it felt like for a man to want to possess me. And this was turning into one of those times that I couldn't *not* think of Chase as a man—not with him standing tall over me, looking like he wanted to throw me over his shoulder and drag me off to his cave.

I expected some reaction from him—some sudden realization of what he'd just said, but his eyes didn't relent. Chase had always been protective of me, even before Todd. And he'd certainly been persistent, the way he'd cajoled me to accept his help. But the way he was acting now? He wasn't a man bent on protecting my interests. Domineering Chase was a first.

"Last time I checked, this was a free country." I wouldn't back down, either. "You can't lock me up in my tower like Rapunzel."

"Maybe not," he seethed. "But, last *I* checked"—he threw my words back at me—"you were the most important person in my life."

This time, he did look like he knew what he had said. I was speechless, and aghast, and entirely too flattered by his words. My schoolgirl crush on him was playing with my mind—it was reading into things he said and giving me the most dangerous thing of all: Chase telling me he needed me was giving me hope.

Now his eyes were pleading. "These past three years, we built something. I know it was mostly you. But I like to think I had a hand in giving you space to create a job you love. I thought you were happy. And thanks to those reports you show me every month, we both know the events business is thriving. You can't leave me high and dry without an explanation."

"You know I would never leave until I trained my own replacement." My voice was weak. "You know me better than that."

The other thing both of us knew was that I was deflecting his question.

"Violet." His voice broke a little when he said my name and it nearly broke my heart. "I just need to know why you're walking away from something good."

Don't cry. Don't cry. Don't cry.

For the briefest moment, I considered telling him the truth: that continued proximity might mean I'd never get over him, or that I'd do something stupid to mess up what we had; that to see him every day would doom every man I dated to comparison; that I couldn't take his charity anymore.

"Chase…" Now my voice broke. "You gave me so much more than I deserved. You gave me exactly what I needed at the moment I needed it most. But the plan was never to work for you forever. All these years, I've been building your business. All these months, I've been earning my degree. The plan was always for me to find my own way. And to give you back a fraction of all you gave me."

I said it earnestly, with sincerity and passion, because none of what I'd said was a lie. It was only a half-truth.

I saw the moment the fight went out of him—the moment it was replaced with fatigue. "You don't have to pay me back."

He repeated what he'd said to me a thousand times. So I let him think what I needed him to—that this was just a bigger version of the same fight we'd been having for years.

"I know." Tears blurred my vision. "But I want to."

Chapter Eleven

CHASE

"You're a jackass."

"I don't want to hear it, Jules."

She'd wasted no time saying her piece the second she got in the car. I regretted the agreement I'd made months ago to be her Thursday-night ride. Most of our time together was spent listening to a radio station neither of us actively hated. Other times, she liked to tell me her *opinions*.

"This is truly asinine, Chase. Even for you."

Jules being Violet's best friend meant I couldn't afford to alienate her. I clenched my jaw against saying something I would regret. I was fired up enough that I just might.

"I mean it. Not tonight," I warned.

"Why? You planning on growing some sense by tomorrow?"

Now, I was getting angry. "She dropped a bomb on me. I think I have a right to ask her why."

"You even saying that proves what an idiot you are," she spat.

"I consider 'idiot' to be an offensive term."

"*Fine,*" she came back angrily. "You're a goddamn fool."

What did I have to say to prove to this woman that I was not in the mood? "Don't make me leave you on the side of a dark country road and call you an Uber."

"Someone's got to tell you, even if Violet won't."

There it was. The gauntlet. Proof she was not going to let this go; proof that she knew my weakness; proof that she knew that I knew there was something more at play. What I needed was information. I'd gone to the source, but Violet wasn't budging. I hated that I was going to take the bait.

"So quit insulting me and tell me," I demanded, my hard glare that was meant for her trained on the road.

She leaned up in her seat, turning to me more fully. "You're so focused on the bomb she dropped on you, you aren't asking yourself how she's doing. Or thinking about the bomb you dropped on her."

"What bomb?" I was defensive—resentful of how she was picking at me.

"The one where you're going back to the job that killed her husband. *You.* The most consistent father figure her kids have ever known. Trey wasn't born when he died and Bri only remembers Todd from pictures. You told Violet you'd be there for her, no matter what."

Fuck.

I let what Jules was telling me begin to sink in—let myself imagine what hearing that must have been like. It dawned on me that Violet quitting seconds after I'd told her hadn't been a coincidence. Maybe Violet didn't want to leave me. Maybe it was the ultimate act of self-protection—her leaving me before I could leave her.

"Now, she's got to think about whether you're gonna run into a burning forest and never come out again." This time, I didn't blame Jules for the contempt and sarcasm in her voice. "I wonder why something like that might have her rattled."

"Fuck." I banged the steering wheel as I yelled the word out loud. I'd given up on exercising a filter.

"Yeah. *Fuck*," Jules bit back.

I gritted my teeth against all I couldn't say. Neither Violet nor Jules could know my real motivation for returning to the fire service. They couldn't know that I was investigating Todd's death, or that I was flirting with breaking the law. I *would* find a way to leak whatever information was needed for Violet to win her case, but there was no coming out and saying that. So I defaulted to what I could say, however vague.

"The job's not what she thinks. I won't be running into that many forests."

"*Not that many?*" Jules looked at me like I'd lost my mind. "Well, I guess that changes everything. Let's call Violet right now and tell her you won't have *that many* chances to be killed."

I shut my mouth again. I couldn't guarantee anybody I wouldn't be called to a scene as part of the investigation. And reaching my goal meant maintaining my cover, and playing my part.

"Look," I said finally. "I don't want to run into a burning forest, either. Violet knows how much it fucked me up when Forrest asked. She also knows how many other people have asked and how many times I've turned it down. Do you honestly think the idea of being on the ground during a fire doesn't scare the shit out of me? I spent two years in therapy for PTSD. I'm an investigator now and I'm going to do my damndest to stay out of the fire."

Jules sighed and shifted her body somewhat, looking out the window again. Maybe our conversation was over and maybe it needed to be. But Jules was right. I should have seen the obvious. I should have gotten past my own insecurities long enough to realize how all of this might scare Violet, and the kids.

Soon enough, I pulled onto Jules's street, up to her house, and into her driveway. I was on the brink of humbling myself—to thank her—when she spoke.

"What's done is done." She looked at me pointedly. "Now you have one job only. Don't make her any promises you can't keep. Don't write her a single check she or those kids might not be able to cash. And, for the love of the Lord, do *not* try to get her to stay with you on that farm."

That last one walloped me. It felt like a punch in my gut. But there was nothing I could say on my own behalf. I couldn't explain to Jules how not making Violet any promises was exactly what I was trying to do. I couldn't say how I was protecting her by not giving her hope that I could help her case. I couldn't confess that all would be explained, but not until I had something substantive. I couldn't prove that I only had Violet's best interests at heart.

"I mean it, Chase," Jules dug in. I'd never seen her more determined. "Don't make this about you for once. Quit interfering and just follow her lead. Let her prove to herself for the first time in her life that she can be on her own."

* * *

"WELL, THAT WAS INTENSE."

I squinted into the sunlight as Forrest and I exited the distinguished building and found ourselves on a busy Washington street. I'd been inside the headquarters of the Department of the Interior for hours. Forrest and I had flown in that morning to meet with the Secretary herself. We'd gone there straight from the airport. I'd also needed to get my security clearance and learn the protocols.

"Monica doesn't play around." Forrest was on a first-name basis with the Secretary, the head of the agency who was two years into her role. Secretary of the Interior wasn't an elected position—Monica was an appointee, selected personally by the President of the United States.

"So let me get this straight…" I cast Forrest a sidelong glance. "You're a special attaché to the Secretary, which makes her your direct boss. But her direct boss is the President. That makes the President your grand-boss."

"That's right."

"And since you're the head of the Council on Wildfire Prevention, and I'm a council member, that makes me your employee."

Forrest chuckled. "Technically, yes."

"That means the President of the United States of America is technically my great-grand-boss," I concluded.

Forrest nodded. "It surely does."

"Hot damn," I muttered, still disbelieving as I followed Forrest to wherever he was leading us down the street.

He lived in Tennessee, but DC was one of his stomping grounds. Once upon a time, he'd been the federal fire marshal assigned to Great Smoky Mountains National Park. It had been a prestigious job to begin with given the park's status within the system. But Forrest hadn't stopped there. He'd climbed his way up the ranks. Every firefighter who worked for a federal agency had heard the name Forrest Winters.

After he left Great Smoky Mountains, he'd managed to get himself assigned as the head of a special commission based on a big grant he'd won. Its charge was to investigate wildfires nationwide, and develop an early detection system using drones. Now, he'd been tapped to lead the council. I'd known before that he was a mover and a shaker, but after all this, *I knew*. I was just beginning to truly grasp the council's visibility, and was blown away by being here now.

Forrest had tried to tell me this "wasn't some rinky-dink council" and he was right. They hadn't just checked my ID and handed me my badge. They'd asked for my birth certificate and my passport. They'd taken my fingerprint and scanned my retinas. They'd asked me intrusive questions. They'd proven to me how seriously they were taking all of this.

"So now you know our charter." Forrest stepped off of a curb to cross the street. "You heard what Monica said. The three wildfires we're investigating aren't the three deadliest from the past ten years—they're the three most suspicious. We're looking at the ones where there shouldn't have been loss of life. Given Violet's *situation*, we're starting with the one that killed Todd."

"I've read the case file," I told Forrest then. "End to end. Top to bottom. I've read it over three times."

"That's just the assembled case file—the conclusions drawn by the State of California. The goal of that investigation was to determine the cause of the fire and to establish whether the agencies involved followed procedure. Our job now is to treat this as a new investigation. To figure out why—if everything was on the up-and-up—three men had to die."

I frowned. "You think maybe I shouldn't have read the case file? That I biased myself?"

"Maybe," Forrest hedged. "But that's just the tip of the iceberg. Now, we need to look at the feeder reports—official findings from the smaller agencies; we'll review documentation from dispatch and incident command; documentation from the captains on the ground, including our own; and exit interviews from the men who fought the fire."

The question I might have asked next flew from my mind no thanks to a distraction.

"Is that the White House?"

Forrest didn't need to answer. It was across the street on the next block, behind tall wrought-iron fences and set way back from the photo takers and onlookers who lined the street. My first instinct was to whip out my phone and take a selfie with Forrest. Easier said than done to frame it up. Then, I remembered. Violet and I weren't right. The only reason to have taken a selfie would have been to send it to her and the kids. I needed to smooth things over when I got back to Tennessee. I needed to sort myself out and figure out how.

There was nothing in the world I hated more than fighting with Violet. It was unusual for us to be at odds, which made the times we were that much more painful. We had mostly locked horns over me offering her help. I would never forget what happened after the guys took up a collection when we found out the insurance company wouldn't pay. When I handed her the check, she'd yelled at me through her tears for ten solid minutes. At least then, I'd understood why we were fighting.

Every bone she'd ever had to pick with me had been about something like that —me giving too much; her wanting to do things on her own. But Jules was right about this one. For once, this wasn't about me and my stubbornness or Violet and her pride. Her being scared for me? I didn't know what to do with that.

"How much will I have to travel?" It was time for me to plan. The clock was ticking. Violet's retrial was in seven weeks. That gave me fifty days to crack her case, all while simultaneously letting her go and reinforcing a sense of presence and security for her and her kids—all while running a working farm.

"We'll start with the reports from the smaller agencies. After that, we'll knock on some doors. A lot of those doors will be in California."

I didn't like the idea of more days away from home, or being a plane ride's distance away from her.

"You gotta try the restaurant here," Forrest said as we entered the lobby of the Hay-Adams. Of course I'd heard of The Lafayette. Any other day, my mouth would have been watering for long meal. But I just wanted to get to my room, and to my desk.

He must have sensed my disquiet. "I know you're wanting to get started. Trust me—I am, too. But nothing good ever came from an empty stomach."

* * *

IF YOU HAD TOLD me a month ago I'd be sitting in my living room reading classified incident reports, I wouldn't have believed you. If you'd told me it energized me, I wouldn't have believed you twice. Nowadays, I fell asleep with my laptop on my chest. And something about being around this again—I liked it.

Thinking about safety protocols and incident leadership would bore most people to tears. I'd been telling myself I was only staying up so late out of a sense of dedication. But there was more to it than that. This didn't feel like work. Time flew and I was in my flow.

Cooking was like that for me. It hadn't escaped my notice that running a kitchen was a proxy for the excitement I had missed. Some part of me thrived in fast-paced environments, and being around highly trained people doing what they did best. In just two days of being an official investigator, the process had proven something I'd been denying: there were parts of the fire service I missed.

During an actual incident, information dashboards were digital and changed second by second—they showed the most pressing needs within the system at a given time. Reviewing reports after the fact was a lot different. At the moment, I was looking through incident severity data that had been pulled out at one-hour intervals. It contained far more information than would have been feasible to review on the day of.

Wildfires were rarely single, contiguous blazes. Multiple blazes could be active within a single fire. But it could also be the case that multiple fires in proximity to each other were named separately. Separate fires were what we'd been dealing with on the day that Todd was killed.

Cranston Fire. Population Threat Level 6. Status: 34% contained.

Rutland Fire. Population Threat Level 9. Status: 18% contained.

Pomona Fire. Population Threat Level 2. Status: 58% contained.

Artville Fire. Population Threat Level 4. Status: 76% contained.

The basic logic of fighting wildfires was to keep them away from populated areas—to let a fire burn a forest sooner than we would let it burn a town. The environmental trade-offs could be argued, but the economic and human stakes were clear. It was also a priority to fight fires that could be contained, rather than ones that would be resistant to our efforts. The information was all here, but in tabular form. I would do better graphing it all out.

This doesn't look right.

No sooner had I set parameters for my chart than I found three lines that trended the wrong way. If procedure had been followed, the chart ought to look like a waterfall cascade. The fires with the highest population threat levels should have appeared highest on the y-axis, with the x-axis indicating time. Each line curtailed itself once a crew had been sent. But two lines close to the bottom were misplaced, an indicator that crews had been sent in earlier than they should have been. One of those crews had been ours.

Something doesn't feel right.

I looked at the data again. Then I went back to the source data and reran it. Frantically, I went back and triple-checked the source. From there, I went into two different databases and looked at the sources that fed the sources. When I knew for sure there was no mistake, the rage came fast.

I didn't realize I'd thrown my full coffee cup against the wall until I heard the smash. Now it was shattered, just like me.

I squeezed my eyes shut, willing it all away—trying to shut down the part of my brain that wanted to take me back *there*. My eyes burned, maybe with tears, maybe from the sweat I had broken into seeping beneath my eyelids, maybe because I was back in that forest and it was the smoke. For minutes, I held on to my breath like a lifeline, some corner of my mind trying to measure it out.

I had the presence of mind to reach into my memory for tools I'd learned in therapy. I remembered something about my five senses—rooting myself in each one in order to ground me. I remembered to make my exhales longer than my inhales. It took everything I had in me to pry my eyes open and speak aloud five things I could see. By the time I finished four things I could feel, I was outside. By the time I'd listed the three things I could hear and two things I could smell, I was feeling more in control. As a final measure, I tasted a blade of grass.

The dark sky told me how late it was, probably the middle of the night. My hands trembled enough that I didn't want to look at my watch. I shivered from the coolness of my sweat as it changed in the night air. When I regained my faculties, I texted Forrest.

Chapter Twelve

VIOLET

I'd slept so badly the night before, I'd circled back home after dropping the kids off at school. Another couple of hours had done me good. Nothing pressing had awaited me at the office in earlier hours, though the afternoon was a different story.

Forrest and Sierra were coming on-site to look at engagement party spaces. I didn't want to be dragging when we met. They'd be getting a lot more than the ten-cent tour of our entertainment venue. I wanted to be alert—and social—during lunch.

It was 10:20 before I rolled in to the office—time to ready a pitcher of sweet tea and put out glasses in preparation for their arrival. They would come straight to the events barn, where I would walk them through showroom decor. I was also prepped and ready for my weekly check-in with Chase, which was slated for 10:30. Scratch that—I was prepared to walk through the agenda. Seeing Chase would be a different story.

For the first time since I started school, Chase had missed coming over on Saturday. All weekend, he'd been working with Forrest. It brought back all kinds of things I didn't want to think about. Chase had been as steady as a rock in our lives—been there for us like clockwork. Now, going back to the fire service, he would surely return to working odd hours.

That wasn't all I was dreading. Now, he would come home with a different kind of shop talk altogether. Less about the orchards and the supper club; more about the calls and the guys. The part I struggled with now was my own resentment. But resentment of what? Chase owed me nothing.

You owe him an apology.

I heard the scolding of my inner bossy voice as I slid open the door to the barn. Then, I saw that something was amiss. The lights downstairs were on, including the spotlights that illuminated the model tables on display. A light was also on in the loft, but only one—the lamp on my desk.

Curious, I made my way forward, across the showroom floor, and up the stairs. As my desk came in to view, my stomach flipped. Sitting upon it was one of the largest bouquets of flowers I had ever seen. The winsome array was rich in my favorite color, which Chase always joked was a bit on-the-nose given my name. I was underwhelmed by actual violets. But I loved the smell of lavender and purple roses, and I adored the look of snapdragons and bells of Ireland and green button spray mums.

These could only be from one person. If I had any doubt as to his identity, the plate of cinnamon rolls next to the vase gave it away. No one had ever sent me apology flowers and it stole my breath a little. As did the handwritten note propped up on the vase. On it were written the two words I had felt deeply myself. Seeing it released fears I'd been holding on to—fears that things would never be the same. I didn't like fighting with Chase and we didn't do it often. I just wanted us to be us again.

The rolling slide of the same barn door I'd just recently walked into sounded from downstairs, along with the jingle of Jameson's tags. My heart lifted to see that it was Chase. He stopped in the middle of the showroom floor and looked upward, catching my gaze.

"You found your flowers?"

I nodded. "And your note. Chase. I'm sorry, too."

He came up the stairs hastily, taking them two at a time and greeted me with a hug that didn't feel customary. This one lasted longer, with him holding me tighter and sighing into my hair. I didn't know how much I'd needed this comfort—needed to feel the energy to flow between our bodies to tell me it would all be okay.

We pulled back after a long minute and he offered an impish smile.

"You sharing those cinnamon rolls?" he asked.

"You mean my favorite ones that you baked?"

"The ones that are still warm from the oven."

I smiled slyly. "I think there's milk in the fridge."

I liked mine with coffee. He liked his with a cold glass of two percent.

"I think there's cold brew in there, too."

Cold brew that hadn't been there yesterday.

"You know me too well."

It came out sentimentally, so much so that he held my gaze. "We've been through a lot together."

Jameson, who had followed Chase upstairs, suddenly turned tail and dashed back down. Before another word could be said, the heavy barn door slid open. I swung my gaze toward it in time to see Forrest and Sierra step inside with Everest, their Bernese mountain dog. They laughed at the sight of Jameson rushing them.

"Hey, we're up here!" I called from the loft, smiling down at our friends. "Come on up! Chase made cinnamon rolls."

Forrest wasted no time heading toward the stairs. "Don't mind if I do."

* * *

"So tell me about the proposal," I implored Sierra as we strolled, elbows linked, twenty feet in front of Chase and Forrest. Eager to walk off our cinnamon rolls, we'd decided to start with the tour. They already knew the scenic orchard road where we served dinner at The Noble Pig. Weather-wise, that would be risky for late fall, which left us mostly with indoor spaces, or a few outdoor ones that could be set up with heaters and tents.

Out of all the firefighter wives, I liked Sierra the most. By day, she was a ranger at Great Smoky Mountains National Park. Being a uniformed official herself, she knew how to wrangle the kind of men who she and Forrest worked with. Watching her take down unworthy opponents was a true delight.

"He proposed to me on our meadow…" Sierra was starry-eyed.

"The two of you have a meadow?"

Sierra nodded. "It's a secret meadow in the park—a place where we like to go, you know, for picnics. We'd been there for a while, on our picnic blanket, just lying down and relaxing. Then, he told me Everest was getting restless and wanted to play fetch. He tricked me into standing up to throw her a ball. When I turned back around, he was on one knee. He even got Everest in on it. When she came back, he said, 'Come on, girl. Ask Momma.' He'd taught her to lift up one paw and cock her head."

Both of us erupted into giggles.

"He sure knows how to pick a ring." I'd been admiring it since she'd walked in the door. It was hard not to notice: at least two carats—cushion cut—set up high on a simple platinum band. Smaller pavé diamonds elevated the crown and flattered her slender fingers and elegant hand.

"Honestly?" She gazed down at it. "I didn't think of myself as the kind of girl who was into fancy jewelry. Now, I hate taking it off."

"I wouldn't want to, either." I threw her a knowing glance.

She returned it with a softer one. "Was it hard? Not wearing your wedding rings?"

That was another thing I'd always appreciated about time I spent with Sierra. She never walked on tenterhooks around me, or avoided asking questions about Todd.

"Todd and I didn't have real rings." I smiled at the recollection. "We just eloped one night. In Las Vegas while we were already there. We flew in for my friend's wedding. By the time we left, we were married ourselves."

Sierra dropped her jaw in a way that made me smile more widely at her response. "Please tell me you did not let Elvis marry you."

"I did not let Elvis marry me," I parroted back.

She narrowed her eyes, as if suspecting trickery. Forrest called from behind us, "She's lying!"

Sierra stopped short and looked at me with wide eyes. "You got married by an Elvis?"

The guys caught up to us and Chase chimed in. "It would all make sense if you'd known Todd."

"He was the life of every party." Forrest slung his arm over Sierra's shoulder. "He came up with the wackiest schemes, and he'd somehow convince you to do them. Brought fun with him everywhere he went."

"And you were never mad about it," Chase said. "You never woke up the next day like, 'why the hell did we go along with Todd last night?' He was just charismatic, and a shitload of fun."

"So, wait…" Sierra turned to me. "You're telling me you never had a big wedding and you never had a big ring, and now you're a wedding planner?"

"Technically, yes." No one else had ever said it out loud, but there was no point in denying it.

Sierra looked stricken. "And you never wanted one yourself?"

I didn't know how to answer. My wedding had been spontaneous, and romantic, and the two of us had been in love. It had held its own perfection. But Forrest was right about how Todd had been. He'd had a special kind of charisma that made people want to follow his lead. And I'd been more vulnerable to his charm than anyone else.

"Maybe," I hedged, relieved that we were nearing the venue we called the red barn. "But that doesn't diminish how much I love doing what I do. If I did, how would I create this?"

I opened the door with a flourish to reveal the setup space inside. This afternoon, we were hosting a small wedding—one with a similar number of guests as Sierra and Forrest planned to host. Showing them this space now would let them see what it looked like fully decorated, with tables, and finishes, and florals.

Raising kids and working odd hours didn't exactly go together. My event setup process was a well-oiled machine. Over the years, I'd come to rely on a small handful of trusted vendors who knew the ins and outs of every space. I also had an hourly employee who came in before each event to check that everything was right—that it met the high standard I expected. As usual, it did.

Sierra actually gasped as her gaze began to wander. "Vi." She shook her head. "This is exquisite."

The room had been set up in the style of a banquet, with connected tables forming long rows. White bunting draped airily from the rafters to create a sense of magic in the space. In place of centerpieces, a wide path of flowers ran down the middle of each table—runners made of lilacs and white roses and green leaves the color of sage. Light, wooden cross-back chairs painted rustic white gave it an air of country chic, as did the heirloom plates and flatware. Small crystal chandeliers had been dropped from the ceiling at intervals over the table. It was amazing what a little lighting could do.

"Engagement parties are more understated than weddings." My voice went quiet, honoring the sacred feeling of the space. "If this seems more formal than what you need, don't worry—it can be toned down."

Forrest and Sierra pushed farther inside, volleying ideas as they continued their slow stroll. As usual, I gave the couple space to discuss their vision.

Chase fell in next to me and remarked without confrontation, "See why I don't want you to quit?"

* * *

LATER THAT DAY, staring out my office window, echoes of the visit stayed with me. Sierra and Forrest had chosen the red barn for their affair. I met with couples in love every day, but touring with them had been different—it had taken me down memory lane.

Chase being there had snapped things into a different focus. With every venue we'd viewed, he'd described how I had transformed the space, adding my design sense to defunct areas of the farm and "making magic." Chase had always liked to flatter me, but it felt like more than that. I couldn't deny the reverence in his voice.

And it wasn't just the way Chase talked about me that gave me all the feels. Now that I was leaving, it was bittersweet to look back at all I'd done—to be reminded of how little of this had been here three years ago when Chase had given me a job. I was firm in my decision to strike out on my own. But it was only just starting to dawn on me—how hard it would be to walk away from all I'd built.

And then there was Forrest and Sierra, taking us through their own memories of the farm—how they'd come to The Noble Pig as their first official date; how they'd listened to bluegrass music while Sierra had leaned in to Forrest and he'd held her with his arm around her shoulder; how they'd seen fireflies by the lake and shared their first kiss.

All of it was messing with my mind. It made me want what they had. Our slow, strolling perusal made me remember all the beauty of the farm and how much I would miss it once I left. Us not fighting anymore made me not want to leave Chase. It had been nice, walking next to him, our friends and the two dogs our companions as we shared our own stories of the farm. In the sweetest moments, it felt like ours.

Except it isn't ours.

That was what I had to keep reminding myself. Wanting it too much was why I had to leave.

Now, back in my office, it was time to close up shop; to walk Jameson back up to Chase's house; to go home and play with my kids and help them with their homework and—after I put them to bed—to take out my planner and start working on my business. I had just zipped my phone into my purse and started down the stairs when it began to ring and buzz. No matter how recently I had put away said phone, finding it again was always a fishing expedition.

"Hello?" I managed to pick up on the last ring before it would have been sent to voicemail.

"Well, hello, gorgeous. It's Rodney. I just got back from my trip."

"Oh!" I hoped I sounded more excited than astonished. "How was it?"

With all the changes that were happening on my end, I had all but forgotten about him. Had it already been two weeks?

"Transformative, as usual. When you're in the bush, it's hard not to feel the pulse of life. I never mind giving over my time in service of those gorgeous creatures. We poached the poachers, if you know what I mean."

I did not know what he meant, and I wasn't sure I wanted to. But more pressing matters were at hand, like the fact that the guy who I hadn't expected to hear back from was actually calling.

"I thought about you." His voice lowered a little. "I'd like to take you out again, maybe something more traditional. We could go to Knoxville and grab a beer."

I hadn't given too much thought to whether I wanted to see Rodney again. I didn't dislike him, but I didn't feel a spark.

For one, he talked a lot and seemed pretty into himself. But a lot of men were like that. Maybe this was just par for the course. And I wasn't even really looking for a relationship, so maybe I didn't need to like him. Maybe I just needed to remember how to put myself out there—to make conversation and get to know another person.

There was one thing I knew I liked: he hadn't been all over me physically, or looked at me in that wolfish way men sometimes did. I liked that he seemed to want to take things slow. That was what I had to keep reminding myself: I wasn't looking for a new husband, I was looking for a path forward in my own life.

"I'd love to," I blurted, before I could think about it too hard. There were other reasons why I had to do this. It was like Jules said—I couldn't just keep on canceling dates. And I'd never have what Forrest and Sierra had if I never put myself out there. Fake it 'til you make it had to be my new M.O.

"Perfect. I made reservations for Saturday."

Jeez. Presumptuous much?

"Saturday sounds great." I kept my voice light and chided myself to give him a chance.

"I can't wait to see you, Violet." Rodney said my name with affection. "I'll pick you up at six."

Chapter Thirteen
CHASE

"Thanks for tagging along." Forrest said it to me but looked into his rearview mirror as he pulled away from the curb. We'd met in town and I'd just gotten into his truck. We'd spent the majority of yesterday together—on my farm, with engagement party planning—but we'd had neither the time, nor the privacy, for shop talk.

"Looks like Sierra's got you running." I cast a glance in the backseat, where Everest sat securely in her crate, going to town on what looked like a real meat bone. The plan was to take her to the groomer. Best as I could guess, the bone was a bribe.

Everest was a smart dog, just like Jameson was. Everest was also a chowhound, just like Forrest, so he understood the assignment. If she had to go to the groomer, she'd better get hers.

"Just helping her out." Forrest merged into traffic. "Sierra's up for another promotion at work. With all the wedding planning, this is the least I can do. Everest's grooming will take about an hour. We can take a walk."

Fifteen minutes later, Forrest had checked Everest in and we were starting down a local hiking trail. It all felt very cloak and dagger.

"I've been over and over the data," Forrest said. "It wasn't a mistake. There was no way to reprioritize the list without a manual change. And it would have had to be changed in multiple systems."

"Someone wanted the Cranston Fire prioritized," I concluded. "Someone powerful enough to make it happen."

"That's where we need to go with this," Forrest replied. "Motive, means, and opportunity."

"I've started looking into that." I'd been thinking much the same. "The area was remote. Mostly unincorporated. Damage to developed property was mostly to luxury vacation homes. Do we know anyone up there?"

"Sierra used to be a ranger at Shasta. She still knows people she can trust at Cal Fire."

Forrest and I had already talked about the implications of going through "proper channels." We were drawing closer to territory that had the potential to draw suspicion if people knew we were sniffing around.

"Once we get a list of landowners, we can move on to means," Forrest continued. "Find out who had the kind of money or power, or access that would let them tamper at that level."

I nodded. "And we also have to look at the personal connections of anyone who was on duty."

"That gets to opportunity," Forrest continued. "Not only would the person who set all this in motion have needed enough power to influence things—he would have needed one of his own boys on shift. Suspicious shifts in personnel or chain of command is another logical place to look."

"This shit's gonna take us at least a week."

"Could be longer." Forrest's voice was grave. "Chances are, we'll still need luck to piece together the connection."

We'd walked a ways down the path and were coming upon a clearing. I paused, facing Forrest now, my chest proactively tightening with familiar rage. I had to tell him the other thing I figured out.

"I know what the insurance company's afraid of," I began. "The current cause of death is accidental. If we were ordered to fight the wrong fire, that all changes. If we can actually prove we never should have been put in that situation…" I waited for Forrest to piece it together.

"Then the case isn't about whether they're obliged to pay for an incident that took place across state lines—it becomes about wrongful death. Shit." Forrest now looked as incensed as I felt. "Shit," he repeated after another few seconds.

I gave him time to let it all sink in.

"Now, we know what we could be dealing with. This could be a multimillion-dollar case. And they'll have to pay it out times three. Once the other two families catch wind, they'll file suit."

"This is getting serious," Forrest said. "And messy as hell."

"Violet's lawyer needs to know."

* * *

LATER THAT MORNING, after stopping home to gather documents that could serve as clues, I cased the parking lot of the building where Katrina worked. It was housed in a seventies-era office park that was just dated enough to possess its own charm. The building was well-kept and clean, if not a bit quiet walking down carpet-lined halls. The door plates on most other offices seemed to be for therapists or other attorneys.

I didn't have any qualms about showing up unannounced. Katrina's approach was to work alone but to work with a small number of clients, giving her real time to focus on each client's case. She was in her mid-forties, liked to wear bright colors, and wore her hair in long, shoulder-length locs that lightened to russet at the ends.

"Chase Greenleaf. As I live and breathe. To what do I owe this distinguished visit?"

I grinned. "Kat Stephens. It's been a while."

"Seems like your pun game hasn't gotten any stronger."

I threw up my hands in the universal sign of peace. "Hey. Don't blame me if your momma and daddy have a sense of humor. I can think of worse folk singers to name your kid after."

Kat rolled her eyes in a way that told me she wasn't going to explain to me again that her parents hadn't named her after *the* Cat Stevens, and that I was welcome to call her Katrina like everybody else.

She shooed me into her office and closed the door behind us. "Tell me, Chase. What can I do for you?"

Katrina walked around her desk to sit behind it, then motioned for me to follow by sitting in the guest chair across. I took the invitation and shed some of my playfulness in preparation for what I was about to say.

"I have some information that may be useful to Violet's case."

"Fantastic." She trailed off with caution, giving me the side-eye I deserved. She was right to be suspicious of why I would be coming to her instead of going directly to Violet.

"I'm here because I'd like to tell you about it," I continued as if such visits were perfectly natural.

"You mean tell *us* about it," she corrected. "Let's dial Violet in."

"We can't call Violet." I knew better than to bullshit her. "Not in this exact circumstance. I need what I have to say to stay between me and you."

Katrina didn't hesitate to answer.

"I'm afraid that's not how it works. Violet is my client, which means that my obligation is to work in her best interests."

"I can assure you, everything I'm about to tell you is."

"Part of acting in her best interest means disclosing everything I know about the case and how I know it. I am not at liberty to conceal my sources from her."

"Well, what if I hired you, then? Wouldn't anything that you and I discussed be protected?"

Katrina shook her head. "Not automatically, no. If I suspected that something you had to tell me posed a conflict with an existing client, it would be my duty to refuse to take you on."

I quieted, thinking of the thumb drive in my pocket—of the set of documents that could make Violet's case—of whether there was anything in the world I could say in this moment to convey some of that information. The drive contained enough clues for an investigator to find the right tree to bark up. It contained only reports that were a matter of public record. Best-case scenario, Katrina's investigator would figure it out and request that other reports be unsealed. But none of that would happen if Katrina wouldn't take it anonymously.

"Looks like I'm out of luck today."

Katrina gave a half-rueful smile, as if she empathized with whatever I was trying to do. "Yeah, that's kind of how it works. Based on the way this conversation is going, I should advise you that anything more you say about Violet's case is something I'll have to disclose to her."

"Understood." I rose from my feet and extended my hand. Even though the meeting hadn't gone the way I had hoped, I respected her professionalism.

"Can I give you a word of nonlegal advice?" she asked before I could leave.

It was my turn to nod. I had a feeling I knew what was coming.

"I know how much you care about her. You were there every single day of the first trial. Whatever's going on here, find a way to level with her and do it quick. You and Violet are too good of friends for you not to tell her the truth."

* * *

KATRINA'S APPEAL weighed heavily as I drove back to the farm, seeing no way out of my own pickle. I was trying to protect Violet on all fronts. I wanted to spare her every ounce of rage and grief and revenge that had begun to consume me, or to at least delay telling her until we knew the whole truth. Because the only thing more tortuous than the truth itself was the questions.

But I couldn't be so focused on handing her a neat little package that I deprived her attorney of information, possibly sacrificing her ability to win the case. And she would have found out sooner rather than later if I'd successfully executed my leak. And maybe this was all just me protecting myself. Maybe I loved Violet so much, I couldn't handle breaking her heart. Maybe I was still all messed up.

"Mornin', darlin'." After my trip to Katrina that morning, it was barely that anymore.

Violet and I had needed to reschedule our weekly meeting given Forrest and Sierra's visit. When I'd come up on her at her desk in the loft, she'd been deep in concentration. Upon hearing my voice, she looked up at me.

"Oh, hey, Chase. I didn't hear you come in."

Her reaction to me was instantaneous—her eyes softened and brightened all at once and her lips melted into a smile. It triggered persistent thoughts that had been running through my mind since she'd tendered her resignation to come back in full force.

Violet was the most important person in my life. She was the glue that held me together. The very best thing that had ever happened to me and this farm. I loved her and I couldn't let her go.

I love you, Violet. I always have.

If only I could say it out loud. But I'd never been able to do that, either. So, I pulled her up into a hug that I sorely hoped was neither too tight nor too desperate, no closer to answers about what I was going to do.

Chapter Fourteen
VIOLET

"Mommy, can we go on the slide again?"

Both of my children tugged on my fingers, Bri on the left and Trey on the right. They had rushed me like tiny football players, tackling me where I stood. Tatum and I were in line for hot chocolate—something to take the cool edge off the breezy fall evening air. Chase had insisted on a trip to the pumpkin patch.

He may have been chaperone to four young children, but Chase was the biggest kid of all. He'd already spent $100 on tickets, and taken my and Tatum's kids on every ride twice. In reality, Moore's Pumpkin Patch was more like a Halloween village. Apart from pumpkins, there were bouncy houses, a corn maze, a haunted hayride, a house of mirrors, and a lit-up, extra-tall slide.

"Does Uncle Chase want to go on the slide again or does he need a break?" I looked between my children.

"He wants to go on the slide!" they both practically screamed.

Since they'd run ahead of him to beg me, the man himself was just arriving. Chase held the hands of each of Tatum's five-year-old twin boys who had been born the year before Trey.

"You want a break?" I asked Chase in earnest. "Buy snacks with Tatum while I take the kids?"

"Drinks are for quitters," he ribbed. "Only reason we're back is 'cause I told you I'd check in by six thirty."

I looked at my watch to find it was six twenty-nine. Chase had taken all the kids for a full hour. Tatum and I had walked around the pumpkin patch and shopped for home goods and decorations in the attached crafts store. I'd felt relaxed and unencumbered by the passage of time, and too distracted to think about all that troubled me. I was living the parental dream.

"Do you want me to get you anything?" I asked, tipping my head toward the snack shack menu.

"A candy apple!" Bri shouted at the same time as Trey asked what kind of food they had.

I ignored my children and kept my gaze on Chase. They didn't need any more sugar and I'd been talking to him.

"Hot cider?" he asked.

I nodded, then reminded my children that dinner was at home and they would not be eating more snacks. Ten seconds later, Chase was throwing a "thank you" over his shoulder and my children were tugging him back into the crowd, with Tatum's far more well-behaved children in tow. I smiled, forgetting all my worries for a minute in the way I often did when I got swept up in my children's joy.

On a contented sigh, I turned my attention back to Tatum, who looked after them with a soft smile on her face. Like me, she hadn't had an easy go of things. We'd known each other vaguely online when we'd been in the same private group for firefighter wives. Then, her husband had died of cancer the same year that Todd was killed. That's how we'd found ourselves together in a grief group for survivors.

"It seems like you really like Rodney."

Before our kids had paid us a visit, we'd been on the topic of dating and men.

I shrugged. "Too early to call."

"Well, it seems like you're really making moves. You're dating a guy, you're starting your own business, and you're graduating at the end of the year. Honestly? You're a different person than you were back when I met you."

"Girl." I gave her a look. "When you met me, I was a mess. All you're seeing is me finally getting myself together. It's only been going on four years."

She didn't crack a smile at my self-deprecating humor. It was hard to imagine why. Tatum was one of the most optimistic people I'd ever met. She liked to see the good in people and situations. She was always ready with a kind word. Even after all she'd been through, it was rare not to see her smile.

"Is there anyone else you're interested in? Anyone else you'd consider dating?"

I smiled playfully. "Why? Have you got a cute cousin you've never told me about? Are you trying to set me up?"

She laughed a little too hard, waving away my comment in a way that made me suspicious. Then, something different came over her expression. I couldn't fathom what was up with her.

"Actually, I'm trying to set myself up. I was wondering how you might feel about it if I went out with Chase."

Tatum wanted to go out with Chase? Or did Chase want to go out with her? And how had I not seen this coming? Whenever we watched *Man Enough,* she agreed with him a lot. She was always laughing at his jokes and offering to help him in the kitchen. I'd chalked it up to her being so nice. But now I saw it: she'd been flirting.

"Oh!" I tried to keep my voice light, well aware that I hadn't answered her question. "You didn't tell me Chase asked you out."

I was about to get to the bottom of this. I needed to know who liked who, and whether both of them liked each other and I'd been too distracted to see it. Not that Chase was shallow, but Tatum was kind of gorgeous and oozing with Southern charm. She was always composed and put together. Her children were always impeccably clean. Unlike me, she never seemed stretched thin, like she was barely getting by. She wasn't needy like I was. And she was as sweet as pumpkin pie. Honestly, I could see the appeal.

"Oh, he didn't," she was quick to say.

The magnitude of my relief was frightening. It had taken only seconds for my mind to spin up real concerns, like how could I pretend to be happy for one of my best friends if she was dating the one man I secretly wished I could?

"I mean, not yet," she continued. "I guess I just wanted to be sure I wasn't stepping into the middle of something complicated. You and Chase...you're really...close."

"Close in a platonic way," I replied, quick with my pat answer. "I mean, he and Todd were best friends. It's not like me and him could ever..." I didn't finish the thought. "Me and Chase are just—" I searched for the right word to describe it. "—in it together. He feels obligated to me because of Todd. On top of that, he's my kids' godfather. And I see him every day 'cause he's my boss."

Tatum didn't look convinced, but she also didn't push it. Having her back off was a relief. The sooner this conversation was over, the sooner I could breathe again. I'd been so busy defending my decision to quit my job—so staunch in my belief that I had to move on—that I hadn't thought ahead to what it would feel like to let him go.

I wasn't stupid. I knew what some people thought of me being all up in his life and him being all up in mine. I knew we had an intimacy that may have been hard for some folks to understand. But how many people had been through what we'd been through together?

Don't forget how good it feels every time he begs you to stay, a little voice inside me said. I took it as validation that certain things between us were real, even if those things didn't have a place or a name. But for Chase to actually date somebody—that would drive it home. My head knew that all of this was antithetical to my genuine wish for Chase to have normalcy. But my heart clenched at the idea of him moving on.

"Alright, then." Tatum said it on the end of a deep breath, her voice lighter now, with relief.

"Alright, then," I repeated back.

By the time we had settled things, we'd gotten to the front of the line. I reached into my pocket, still dazed as I fished for money to pay for our drinks.

"Don't worry." Tatum smiled. "I've got this one."

* * *

"Boo!"

I nearly jumped out of my skin when someone came up behind me in the House of Mirrors. My kids had convinced me to come in. I'd agreed to enter the labyrinth only once. They'd been in at least five times, which meant they'd already memorized the way. Seconds after we'd stepped inside, they'd left me in the dust.

That had left only me and my addled brain in the dark, repeating corridors, wishing I'd never seen the movie *Us*, and that I'd made more of an effort to keep up with my children. I was neither clear-headed nor good at this—a terrible combination if I ever wanted to get out of this thing.

Speaking of which…

I whipped around, acting purely on instinct, ready to surprise whoever had decided to come up on me with a swift kick in the pants. It was probably just teenagers having some fun. But it wasn't a teenager—it was Chase. I'd been so deep in thought, it hadn't registered. When I pushed him in protest, he didn't budge.

"Chase," I scolded. "Never scare a Black woman in a haunted house unless you're trying to get yourself killed. I was about to fight you."

He put his hands on my shoulders and squeezed them in brief massage, something he'd done in other situations to get me to calm down.

"Oh, I'm sorry. I was just playing." He used a voice he knew would appease me and gave me his "I'm too cute not to be forgiven" puppy dog eyes.

He turned me back around and put his hands on my shoulders, guiding me forth. By now, he'd been in here as many times as the kids. It meant that, just like Trey and Bri, he knew the way to the exit. I tried not to dwell on how much I enjoyed his touch.

"You having a good time?" he asked in a low voice. "Tatum said the two of you went shopping for decor."

I wonder what else Tatum had told him, whether she'd already mentioned they ought to go out. Then I stopped myself, because I was being ridiculous.

"Actually," I replied. "Everything I bought is for you. Trey says your house needs to be more Halloweenie. While you're out one day, we'll decorate. But you're not supposed to know about it. When you come home, act surprised."

Chase chuckled good-naturedly, unaware of my errant thoughts. "Every kid has a holiday. Halloween is definitely his."

I rolled my eyes. "Don't front. Halloween is your favorite holiday, too. So don't you go buying him more decorations. I've already cut him off. And I know the two of you are in cahoots…about a lot of things."

"Every little boy needs a dog, Vi."

"You're his godfather. He has a god-dog."

Chase chuckled. "God-dogs aren't a thing."

"Neither is a four-year-old who's responsible enough to take care of a puppy."

"Bri mentioned something to me," he casually changed the subject as he walked us around yet another corner. Man, this maze was getting pretty long.

"What is it?"

Chase's hands weren't just sitting on my shoulders. I liked the way he squeezed them as we walked. As always, when we were someplace quiet and dark together, I noticed how it felt for him to stand close.

"She said something about a dance, and needing a date for it. But I figured, that can't be right. She's seven years old. Unless things have changed vastly since I was a kid, she's about five years too early. But she was kind of shy and vague about it, so I figured I'd just ask you. Did I misunderstand?"

"No, you heard right," I said on the tails of a heavy sigh. This night was not getting better. "She was talking about the daddy/daughter dance."

I'd been spitting mad when Bri had brought home a ticket order form that afternoon. So much that I'd given the kids weeknight screen time—which I never do—so I could call the school. With their headphones on and their eyes on their games, my children had remained blissfully unaware when I'd given that elementary school principal a piece of my mind.

Chase stopped me and spun me around to face him once again.

"Now don't you worry." His eyes were serious and his voice matched his eyes. "First thing tomorrow, I'm gonna call that two-bit school. Tell them more than they ever wanted to hear on sensitivity. Bri can't be the only kid who's ever lost her dad. And whose bright idea was it to hold an event that's so audaciously gendered? I'll give them a map, so they can find their way out of the dark ages."

Chase with a bee in his bonnet often made me laugh, but I couldn't laugh about this. Bri had put on a brave face, but she'd been crushed. I'd wondered what the other kids might have said to her or—possibly worse—what sad thoughts she might be having herself. I knew I couldn't talk to her about it until I was calm, or at least until I had processed my own emotions. Chase coming so fiercely to Bri's defense was more than I could handle.

I sniffled, fighting vainly to keep my wave of emotion at bay. It came at exactly the wrong time. People were catching up to us. I could hear them.

As if no one else existed, he engulfed me in a tight, warm hug. I couldn't help but to lean in. As soon as I did, I realized this was what I had needed all along.

"Let's go somewhere and talk," he finally said. We meandered our way out of the maze seconds before another group caught up to us. When he spotted Tatum, he called, "Hey! Would you mind taking the kids in again?"

Tatum gave the thumbs-up and the kids gave a little cheer. Once they were out of sight, he steered me to sit on a hay bale off to the side.

"What's our goal here?" he asked me gently with soft eyes. "Do we want to get them to call it off? Force them to do away with the tradition? Or maybe smoke them out? I can hold a competing event at the barn. Invite all the families. Call it a special dinner for The Noble Pig..."

I shook my head. "I don't think any of that will fix it for Bri. I think she just wishes she had a dad."

Chase put his arm around me now, offering more comfort. After all the strangeness between us, Chase still had my back.

"I'll take her to the dance. I'd be honored if she let me. With your permission, of course."

This time, my regular protests died right in my throat. Depriving myself of his help would be one thing if it was just me, but this was Bri we were talking about.

Instead of responding directly, for a long moment, I squeezed him back, that gesture conveying more than I ever could in words.

"Let's give it a few days. Find out what she really wants. Let her process through it all. If she decides she wants to go, I'll tell you and let you do the asking."

Chase nodded and kept his arm around me while we waited for the others to make their way through. At some point, he dropped a kiss to the top of my head. When I finally felt I could breathe again, and had melted into him a little, I heard him murmur, "I'm still gonna call that school."

Chapter Fifteen

CHASE

Genie's Country Western Bar was as good a place as any to meet up with a friend for a burger and a drink. Living out in the country, I didn't mind coming to town. The farm wasn't a lonely place in the daytime. But, at night, I was just alone.

Sure, if I wanted to, I could always head down to Cody's trailer for a beer. But Cody often had company, and by "company," I meant a different woman every week. Even if he was alone, the problems of a thirty-four-year-old man were different from those of a twenty-two-year-old. Craving companionship was how I ended up at Genie's that night with Forrest.

"How's Cody working out?" Forrest knew how Cody had stepped into my farm duties now that I was working the case. It was the off-season for the orchards, but it was still a lot of work. The trees needed grooming; the grounds needed keeping; equipment needed repair. Cody was happy for the extra money and I was happy for the help.

"You know? It's working out all right. Makes me think I might actually be able to take a vacation one of these days."

Forrest shook his head. "Man, you work too hard."

"Most days, it doesn't feel like work. Not that I wouldn't mind some time on a beach in the Caribbean. But after a week, I'd be itching to come back."

Forrest gave me an assessing look. "I think your momma was right about you. She always said you'd end up a farmer. Said you had it in your blood."

"I like it better than I thought I would."

I would never cop to it in front of my mom, but I could admit this to Forrest. In my twenties, I'd sought adventure—something different from what I'd always known—and in the fire service, I'd found it. Now that I'd seen how much more there was to life, how much a man could have and how much he could lose, I could no longer take the life I'd been born into for granted.

"Maybe once this is all over, you can finally…"

Forrest trailed off and I raised an eyebrow. He could only be talking about the investigation, and the case.

"Be happy? Move on?" I finished his sentence for him.

"Find some peace, for starters. Forgive yourself for losing him under your command. Give yourself some credit for everything you do for Violet and those kids. The best you can do with shit like this is let it teach you how you want to live your life."

"Knowing how I want to live isn't the problem." I let loose a thought I would've kept to myself if gin hadn't loosened my filter. It wasn't as good as the small batches of the spirits I distilled on the farm, but it would do.

"What *is* the problem?"

I briefly considered brushing off the question or feeding him a line. But a deadly combination of self-pity and despair had me bursting with it.

"Violet's leaving the farm."

Forrest frowned like he didn't believe it. "To go where?"

"She wants to start her own thing," I explained miserably. "Even though what she started on my farm *is* her thing. I can't tell you how I'm gonna do any of it without her. She's the heart of Noble Farms."

Words I'd never said out loud couldn't have rung truer. She'd done more than just start an events business. She'd gotten us into farmer's markets, started the supper club, and created a program for school children to tour. She'd taken us from being an anonymous wholesaler to a part of the community. She'd given the farm life. And she'd given a hell of a lot more to me. Last night at the pumpkin patch had scared me to death. Because how could I know if something was wrong with her if I couldn't see her? How could I be there for her if I literally wasn't there?

"So ask her to stay."

I looked at Forrest like he'd lost his senses. "Do you honestly think I haven't tried? I practically begged once she told me. Gave her a raise which, by the way, she fully deserved. Hell, I'd offer her the deed to the farm if I thought she would take it. But Jules told me to stop trying. And you've met Violet. She's as stubborn as they come."

"It's not like you'll never see her again. Y'all are together all the time."

"Not if we're not working together. Not if I'm not watching her kids on Saturday while she's in class. She graduates this semester, which means she won't be needing me anymore on Saturdays. That leaves me one night. One single night a week. And you know how that shit goes. It could dwindle to nothing, just like that."

I'd done the math. With everything else out of the equation, that left me girls' night in—the only day of the week I was guaranteed to see Violet. And what if even that changed? What real standing did I have in Violet's life? What if I was reduced to the guy who gave her a leg up when she needed it? I knew we were more than that, but I was also realistic. There was no way not working together every day wouldn't jeopardize our relationship. Out of sight, out of mind and all.

"This doesn't seem like it's about the farm."

"What?" I was busy spiraling in my own thoughts.

"You said the problem was that Violet was leaving the farm."

"That is the problem."

Or at least half of it.

"And I'm saying it doesn't seem like that's the problem. You can get a team of people to run things. Sounds to me like you don't like the idea of Violet leaving *you.*"

There was no point in denying what Forrest was already figuring out. And I didn't have the energy tonight. The whole thing had me restless and out of sorts.

"Maybe I don't."

I braced myself for his judgment, but something about him was kind. "You got something you need to tell me about you and Violet?"

The second he asked, I knew he knew.

"I'm in love with her."

He quieted and there was nothing more to do than sit with it—the shame and the awful truth.

"You really think you're losing her?" Forrest asked before long.

I sighed into my drink. "It's complicated."

Forrest quieted again. I couldn't imagine what he was thinking. I didn't know that I wanted to know.

"I have *thoughts* on the matter," Forrest finally said. "But I'll save them for the appropriate time and venue. In the meantime, clear your calendar on Wednesday. You're coming with me to secret poker night."

* * *

THE SECRET POKER Society of the Green Valley Fire Department was not as cloak and dagger as it sounded, though its location in the basement of the county sheriff's office had panache. Deep in the bowels of the basement sat a round table in a small room with rack after rack of stacked boxes. Rumor had it, it was deep storage for evidence lockers dating back thirty years.

Despite the secret nature of the location, I entered without ceremony, following Forrest's instructions to a T. The front office was dark, but the door was unlocked; a single deputy sat at the front desk, seeing by lamplight that couldn't be detected from the street. He nodded cordially when I came in, then gave directions for where I could find the back stairs and wend my way down labyrinthine halls to find the secret room.

"Chase!" A chorus of enthusiastic voices met me as I entered. I'd been looking forward to seeing the guys. Jed Lawson and Sebastian Kirkwood were still firefighters with Green Valley. Captain Grizz Grady was about to be promoted to chief. Forrest had brought some of the newer guys—Lieutenant Buck Rogers and firefighter Dan Means, around the farm.

Even though I'd left the agency, a lot of guys were regulars at The Noble Pig. Any firefighter could come to my table any night and I could always accommodate more. That had been one of the silver linings of opening the place. It helped me stay connected and reminded me just how much I loved these guys.

"I come bearing appetizers," I announced after hugs were shared all around. I knew better than to not show up with food. Before culinary school, I'd loved cooking for the guys at the house. I'd ended up at the National Forestry Service but I'd started at Green Valley Fire. Not knowing about secret poker night was proof of all I'd missed.

"So I've gotta ask the question," I started once we were seated at the poker table —after we'd spent a solid twenty minutes eating and catching up. We had drinks in front of us now and Grizz looked ready to deal. "Why a secret poker night at the sheriff's office? It's just poker. Why not play down at the firehouse, in the open?"

"Open play is for Tuesdays," Grizz explained. "One Wednesday a month, we need time away from *the women*. That's why secret poker exists."

"Since when do women come to poker night?" That definitely hadn't been a thing when I'd been with Green Valley Fire.

"Since Forrest invited Sierra."

"Sierra comes to poker night?" I was incredulous.

"Sierra's a total shark," Grizz said a bit sourly. He didn't like to lose. I was surprised they were even letting him deal. Everyone and their momma knew Grizz cheated.

Forrest looked at me levelly. "To not invite women from our agencies in Tuesday night poker would be sexist."

I looked around the table. "And this right here isn't sexist?"

Buck responded, "Oh, it definitely is. But we don't do it to be exclusionary."

"We do it in service of the brotherhood," Forrest added. "Creating space for men to help each other with their woman troubles. Men such as yourself."

That comment garnered everybody's attention. It reminded me of my desperation, and my fear. Maybe admitting to a room full of firefighters that I was in love with my fallen buddy's wife was a bad idea. Maybe in spite of Forrest's pep talk, my first instinct—to stay away from Violet—had been right.

Suddenly, it seemed very possible that I could take heat for loving her. Maybe if I did, it was nothing less than I deserved.

"So what's going on?" Grizz asked bluntly. Usually, he was all smiles, but when something was up, he was all business.

"There's a woman I've known for a while, and she's—" How could I describe her? "She's fucking beautiful. I mean, everything about her is magic. She's sweet, and smart, and every single thing she touches, she makes it glow. These past few years, life's thrown her a big, hot steaming pile of shit and she's managed to keep her head up."

"You're in love with her," Grizz concluded. "So what the hell's the problem? She doesn't feel the same way? Or—let me guess—you're too scared to tell her how you feel?"

"Stop interrogating the man," Forrest scolded, then turned to me.

"Don't let him intimidate you, brother. This is a safe space."

I nodded and decided to answer Grizz's questions in order. No sense in delaying the inevitable.

"Yes—I'm in love with her. But I'm not supposed to be. It doesn't matter if she feels the same way. And I can't tell her how I feel. That would break the only rule."

"What's the only rule?" Jed wanted to know.

"To keep things between me and her platonic."

Grizz seemed offended. "Why would you make a rule like that with any woman?"

"What is she? Your stepsister or something?" Buck asked.

"He doesn't have a sister," at least three guys chimed in.

"Your cousin?" That was Grizz.

Forrest shot him another reprimanding look. "*Safe space*," he warned again.

"Naw, man. It's nobody in my family." I braced myself to just say it out loud. This guessing game was stupid. I squeezed my eyes shut. "It's Violet. Violet LaRue."

The room went deadly silent. Seconds passed and I knew I had to face their reactions. I pried my eyes open and was not surprised to find incredulous faces staring back. The expressions of the men who had known me a while sported predicted looks of horror. Then, they did the last thing in the world I ever expected—they laughed.

It wasn't nervous laughter or "you must be joking" laughter—this laughter was mocking and raucous, as if I'd just said the funniest thing any of them had ever heard.

"Quit it, you shitheads." Forrest's admonishment was the third of the night. He said it at the same time I asked, "Why the hell are y'all laughing?"

"Chase." Grizz cackled through sweeping breaths. "You've been in love with Violet for damn near ten years. You were in love with her while Todd was dating her and everybody knew it. Hell, you were in love with that woman before they even met."

"Nine years," I grumbled miserably, still not seeing how any of this was funny. "Me having feelings for her for so long makes it even less of a joke. And it's even worse given the way it all turned out. So if any of y'all have had the grave misfortune to be in love with your best friend's widow, you let me know what I ought to do."

Referencing Todd's demise finally led to quiet.

"Honestly, man?" Jed spoke for the first time. "You need to tell her how you feel. And tell her the truth—that it ain't even about Todd. Tell her how you saw her for who she was from the beginning."

"You think—" I could hardly speak the words out loud. "You think it's okay for us to date?"

"It's not like you're just trying to hook up with her." Sebastian put down his beer. "You're in love with her—now that's another level."

"One question…" Buck began haltingly. He looked a little young to be giving love advice. I knew he was married, but still. "If you've been in love with her for nine years and said nothing, why would you tell her now?"

I swallowed thickly. "Because I think I'm losing her."

"How does she feel about you?" Grizz wanted to know.

I'd never said this aloud. "The way she looks at me sometimes, I think she might feel something, too."

"Y'all should've seen them a few days ago at the farm. It all seemed rather… domestic," Forrest chimed in.

The room quieted for a long moment. All poker activity had stopped as every man in the room paused to think.

"I know a few things about loving a woman who wishes she didn't love you back." Buck was the next one to speak. "I had it bad for Loretta, but she thought I was too young."

"Sierra straight-up hated me at first," Forrest admitted. "It took me a long time to get into her good graces. Once I did, she spent weeks trying to resist my charm. Point is, strong women don't like to admit defeat."

"Sounds to me like she likes you back," Jed offered. "So make it easy for her to come to you. Give her the one thing she thinks she doesn't have— permission."

"There's this guy she's dating." I began to voice my other worry. "He's nothing like me. Honestly, neither was Todd. Sometimes I just don't think that I'm her type. Both of them are kind of big talkers, you know? Real in your face about who they are. Sometimes, I think Violet doesn't see me as a man."

My comment was met with furrowed brows and confused blinks. Grizz looked scandalized. "You're a firefighter. That makes you a beacon of masculinity."

But I wasn't so sure.

"Most of the time when she sees me, I'm wearing an apron in her kitchen cooking dinner, or decorating cupcakes for the bake sale, or letting her kids dress me up; hell, every Thursday night I go to her house for girls' night in. Half the time, I'm driving her minivan. Meanwhile, the guy she's dating drives a Hummer."

"*That* guy's compensating for something," someone muttered under their breath.

"Thank you." I felt validated. "At least *we* know what that means; meanwhile, she's falling for it. Trust me, I've got his number. He doesn't even come close to deserving her. But—right now—the truth is, he's winning."

Heads nodded all around in understanding, but I was still on a roll.

"Y'all heard of a show called *Man Enough*?"

"Are you kidding?" Sebastian looked offended. "It's on upstairs in the fire-house every Thursday night."

"You wanna know who Violet favors to win?" His name in my mouth gave me a nasty taste. "Eric."

"*That* guy?" someone said while others shook their heads.

"That guy," I confirmed. "Guys like Eric and Rod are my competition. And, yes, she's dating a guy named Rod."

Grizz looked at me disgustedly, shaking his head in a way that proved he finally appreciated my dilemma. Then he turned to the other guys.

"We've got to help out our brother." He slapped down his deck of cards. "And there's only one thing we can do." He turned back to me then. "We're gonna get you out of that friendzone."

Chapter Sixteen

VIOLET

I *need to buy more detergent.*

I added a mental note to the to-do list that was as bottomless as my laundry, all while holding the overturned bottle over the receptacle long enough for the dregs of the thick liquid to slide out.

I also need more hand cream, I noted, as I took in the slight ashiness of my skin. Late October in Tennessee was dry and I was starting to see the evidence. The percussion of small feet across the kitchen floor foreshadowed the arrival of one of my children. I was in the garage. It was wide enough for two cars, but home to only one. Living in a small house meant I needed the space, not only for the washing machine but for everything else I didn't want to cram inside.

"Mommy!" An excited-looking Bri appeared. "Uncle Chase is here!"

"Uncle Chase comes here every Saturday." I downplayed her enthusiasm despite my own excitement to see him.

"But he didn't come in his truck."

"You've been in Chase's other car."

"But, Mom!" She shortened "Mommy" to "Mom" only when I was being particularly obtuse. "He didn't drive any of his cars. He drove his motorcycle."

"That can't be right." I said it mostly to myself. I hadn't seen him on his bike in years. Plus, if he came up on a motorcycle, I should have heard it. On second thought, I wasn't too sure. The dryer was running and the washer was already dispensing water. It could be that my appliances had drowned out the sound.

"I didn't hear a motorcycle," I said cautiously to Bri. "Are you sure?"

In lieu of answering, she stood on her toes to press the button that would open the door to the garage.

The heavy door rose slowly, revealing my driveway inch by inch. I watched in rapt attention, not sure what might come into view. When I got an eyeful of Chase, my jaw went slack. He really had arrived on a motorcycle—the Harley his grandpa had given him—which I'd practically forgotten he owned.

When I'd first met him, he'd ridden it exclusively. He hadn't even owned a car back then. Seeing him on it now brought memories flooding back. Suddenly, I was twenty-two again with my arms around his solid body, the wind whipping around me as he took me on my first ride.

When I'd first climbed on, I'd expected him to take me on a short trip around the block, a literal interpretation of his offer to take me for a spin. But he'd quickly abandoned the stop-and-go traffic of downtown and taken us on a beautiful mountain road. For a second, I could smell his leather jacket, and feel the vibration of the engine beneath me, along with the heady mix of exhilaration and safety I'd felt on the back of his bike.

Today, he wore heavy black boots and a dark gray helmet, but I could barely focus on those. I was too busy appreciating his motorcycle suit. I didn't know if that's what you called the pants and jacket with the soft shell designed to protect you from the road. All I knew was, the jacket was sexy as all get-out, and the pants fit him like a glove.

Bri started running up to him as he peeled off his helmet. Once it was off, he ran a hand through his hair and—I swear to God—it went in slow motion. Trey was already outside, checking out the bike. Seeing no way not to approach now that the garage door was wide open, I put down my detergent and walked outside.

"I remember this old thing."

Chase's green gaze finally found mine. His eyes sparkled in the sun. "You've been on the back of her a few times."

His smile gave me shivers.

"That was a million years ago."

"Not so long as that."

He held my gaze in a way that I didn't expect. In a way that I wasn't sure he ever had.

"I want to go for a ride!" Trey made active attempts to climb onto Chase's bike.

"Sorry, buddy. You're a few years away from that." Chase was talking to Trey but it took seconds for him to peel his eyes off of me. "But c'mon. I'll help you sit on it."

No sooner did he concede to a lesser request than he plucked Trey right off his feet and set him astride the motorcycle. Bri was soon to follow. Chase removed his key and let them play. Their bodies were so light, the bike didn't budge as they leaned to the right, and the left, pretending to zip through the streets.

"You still got plans tonight?" Chase said to me. I appreciated that he asked discreetly. I was scheduled to go out with Rod, which meant that Chase would take the kids for the afternoon and evening. My class today was halfway between Green Valley and Knoxville, and Knoxville was where Rod wanted to take me. The plan was for me to meet him there. It meant I would leave in a little while for class and not see Chase and my kids until tonight.

"Yeah," I confirmed. "I've still got plans. What are y'all going to do?"

"We've got rodeo tickets." Chase grinned.

I smiled for appearances' sake, but, in truth, I was sad to be missing out.

"The kids will love that," I praised. Going to the rodeo was one of our favorite family outings.

Chase gave a beckoning smile. "It's not too late to cancel your plans and come with. Tatum just texted me. Said she wants to come."

The hurt that came from the idea of the two of them alone together was swift. For a second, I actually thought about going. Petty Violet was itching to cock-block one of her best and sweetest friends. Also, I didn't know what Rodney had planned after we met up for drinks. All he'd said was that we'd "take it from there" but I doubted anything he could serve up would be more fun than going with my kids and Chase.

"I'll join you all another time." I reminded myself to be resolute, to give this dating thing a real shot, to climb out of my comfort zone and resist the urge to climb Chase. Easier said than done when he turned his sexy biker energy on.

* * *

RODNEY PICKING me up for our second date was less anxiety producing. We met in Knoxville in broad daylight. I'd driven there after my classes ended to join him for an early drink. It turned out when he said he'd wanted to "grab a beer," his plan had been to drive us to a brewery to take a class that taught us how to make the beer ourselves.

First off, what was with this guy and working for his own sustenance? Second, making our own beer had no bearing on what we actually drank. We left with the bottles we'd made and nothing more. That was how I'd already spent two hours on this date and hadn't even been served a drink.

At least the place had valet parking.

I thought about it as we waited for his SUV. I couldn't decide whether Rodney was classy for taking me to an upscale home-brewing workshop or smart for suckering someone else into parking his big yellow tank.

I legitimately wondered whether he went to the post office or the grocery store in that thing, but opted not to ask. There was no such thing as asking Rodney a simple question. Even the most straightforward inquiries were met with lengthy commentary.

Not that he needed me to prompt him to talk about his Hummer, or his snow-mobile, or his ATV. It was already clear that he had a penchant for impractical vehicles.

Not any less practical than a motorcycle.

I really wished my inner voice would shut up. Errant thoughts had infiltrated a peaceful afternoon, every last one of them about Chase.

I'd thought about him in the shower, and in the car, and when I should have been paying attention to my lecture. Five hours had passed since I'd seen him on a motorcycle and I was still *right back there*, even halfway through my date with another man. Now that they'd come back, I couldn't let go of memories that gave me feels I hadn't felt in a long while, memories of a version of Chase I had somehow forgotten.

How did you not see him back then?

The question came to me, unbidden. Mid-thirties Chase was a mature kind of sexy, the kind who didn't just look good, but had all the qualities of a self-actualized human being. He was responsible and hard-working, noble and self-less, and possessing of countless practical talents. But Chase had always been an amazing guy, and seeing the bike reminded me: mid-twenties Chase had also been smoking hot.

Why didn't twentysomething Violet date twentysomething Chase?

I'd known him months before I'd met Todd. We'd always talked easily and kept each other laughing. If he'd asked me out, I would have said yes. But he hadn't asked me out. And I'd been young and stupid enough to buy into the idea of waiting for a man to initiate, and to be flattered when he did.

Pull yourself together, Vi. Remember, you're on a date.

Rodney was at the wheel and we were driving now and, God help me, I was tuning him out. Last I remembered, he was talking about the time he went to Keith Urban's house to buy a banjo. I should've been rapt with attention as he described the decor.

Interior design was one of my favorite things to talk about. Rodney was trying to engage me in his own way. And it wasn't like he and I didn't have anything in common. We both geeked out on *Shark Tank* and entrepreneurship. We both appreciated handcrafted wares. He just happened to have ten times more to say on every matter than I did.

But I did find my attention when I saw where we seemed to be headed. We had just passed the billboard on the side of the road. It showed a man with a lasso on a horse.

"Where did you say we were going again?" I asked with alarm.

"Cowtime Rodeo," he answered, unfazed that I had interrupted him to ask. Then, he went right back into whatever he'd been talking about before.

"We can't go to the rodeo." I interrupted him again. Again, he seemed nonplussed.

"I thought you like the rodeo." He looked genuinely surprised. "You said you did, the last time we went out."

That was all it took to make me feel like a jerk. Rodney talked a lot, but he also listened. I had, indeed, told him I liked the rodeo on our first date. I also told him how much I loved interior design shows that took you through fabulous mansions, which was possibly why he was so busy talking about Keith Urban's house.

"It's just, my kids are there. And they don't know I'm dating again. And they don't know I'm out with you right now."

The lightbulb over his head seemed to turn on, an indicator that he appreciated my situation.

"If we run into them—and that's a big if—we'll just tell them I'm your friend from work, and that you came to the rodeo to see my band."

"Your band?" Where had he come up with something so random?

"The one I told you about last week? My buddy's band that I play banjo in? Last time, I told you, you ought to come see us some time, and you said that sounded nice."

"Oh, that band!" I pretended to remember, cringing inwardly for having tuned him out to such a degree.

With nothing else to say that wouldn't make me sound like a flaky weirdo, I crossed my fingers and shut my mouth, hopeful that Rodney's prediction would hold.

If we were there to see a band, we would be at the honky-tonk, which wasn't a place where you saw a lot of kids. The rodeo covered a large area and, on a Saturday evening, would be mobbed with hundreds of people. If we were there for what Rodney said we were, what were the chances my kids would find their way into the bar to listen to live music? I was hoping the answer was slim to none.

Chapter Seventeen
CHASE

"Do you think they'll have puppies this time?" Trey asked the question, his hand in mine as we approached the rodeo gates. After happening upon an adoption van from a local shelter on National Adopt-a-Pet Day, he'd started asking every time we came. It had only happened once, but recollection never seemed far from his mind.

"I don't think so, bud."

"If it's here, can we meet the puppies?" Trey was undeterred.

"Sure, but you know we can't take one home."

Tatum, who walked next to me on the other side, chimed in. "Chase is right. Your momma would have his hide."

Trey seemed disappointed, even though there was no adoption van in sight and this question was purely hypothetical. "But can you take a picture of the doggie and send it to Mommy?"

Trey knew I was on Team Canine. He'd never missed a chance to make me a co-conspirator in his schemes to get a dog.

"Sometimes with your momma, the best idea is to play the long game. You try too hard and she's got a chance to say no. But if you can be just a little bit patient, and work on her in small ways, you might be able to turn a no into a yes."

I sounded wise and confident for someone who had only recently cried into his beer and been so desperate as to wind up at secret poker. By the end of that night, no more poker had been played. For two solid hours, we'd come up with a plan. Confronting Violet directly was getting me nowhere. The best path forward was to subtly lead Violet to the same conclusions I'd drawn all along, while letting her think it was her idea.

The first conclusion was simple. Violet didn't need to leave the farm, not if it was like Jules said and she was bent on proving something. Her rightful place was with me, adding on to the house she built. The second conclusion would reveal itself in time. I had no plans to return to the fire service. And the temporary nature of my current project would soon be revealed.

The third conclusion was one I'd striven for every woman I'd ever had a crush on to come to: that I wasn't a platonic friend. Goddamnit, I was dateable.

Trey might have been a bit too young to appreciate my appeal for subtlety, so when he fell silent, I let it lie, content to spend quality time with him and Bri. The fourth conclusion that I needed Violet to reach was that I would never, ever leave her and the kids. When Tatum had called to see what we were up to tonight, I'd thought to invite her. Getting Violet's friends on my side couldn't be a bad idea. Maybe Tatum would put in a good word.

Along those lines, I leaned in to what would promise to be a fun and relaxed outing. Evenings at the rodeo were always the same. We'd start with cotton candy while watching the riders from the stands. More than they loved the skill of the riders, the kids loved the bevy of other players. Bri was old enough to study the movements of the bullfighters; Trey was just young enough to delight in the gags of the rodeo clowns; I'd gone to the rodeo with my dad and remembered loving all of it at their age. Cowtime Rodeo hadn't changed in all the years I'd ever been going. Being there with Bri and Trey took me back.

"It's nice how much you do with them." Tatum paid me the compliment as she sat next to me in the bleachers. All four kids sat together at my left. Tatum's and Violet's kids got along like gangbusters. Tatum's twins were full of mischief and the older Bri lived to thwart their attempts. Trey just liked to be included in the high jinks of older kids.

"I'm telling you—they're easy. People don't believe me when I tell 'em that, but they are. They are seriously two of my favorite people." I beamed over at Bri and Trey while I was talking about them.

"Every kid deserves that." Her voice was somewhat wistful. "Someone who thinks the world of them."

I turned back toward her. "I couldn't agree more."

"You ever think of having a family of your own?" Tatum wondered aloud. "Or will you forever be the cool uncle?"

I shrugged. "I wouldn't mind being promoted from cool uncle to cool dad."

"You mean you wouldn't mind being both," Tatum lightly corrected. I realized what I'd said. Thankfully, she didn't dwell on it.

Given their young ages, the kids lacked the stamina to sit calmly for an entire show. We usually made it forty minutes before someone got antsy. When they did, it was my cue to move them on to the next attraction. It was smart to do rides second and to save them for during the show. The lines were shorter then, and a kid with an empty stomach was less likely to get motion sick on a ride. Bri had a stomach made of jelly. The rodeo had ended badly once or twice.

"Y'all ready for the bucking bronco?" I asked when I heard Bri's stomach growl. An hour earlier, we'd all left the ring. By now, I'd won Trey a floppy elephant at the ring toss and taken all four kids on most of the smaller rides. Trey liked the giant turkey legs, but there was always a line and they took him about forever to eat. And I still had to get them home and in bed at a decent hour.

The final stop the kids were hell-bent on making before we ate was to ride the mechanical bull. Ten minutes later, I was lifting Bri onto the child-sized bronco that moved comically slowly in its bucking. That didn't stop the kids from dissolving into giggles whenever they rode. Trey liked to fall off dramatically on the ample padding beneath. In addition to actually riding the bull, they loved for me to take video so they could go back and laugh at themselves.

After each of the four kids took a go-round, we stood in line for them to go again, watching their videos to kill the time. All of us laughed good-naturedly at the replay of Bri's technique. Her black sparkly leggings, ornate black-and-blue cowboy boots, and a tasseled black jacket made her look like a miniature version of the Lone Ranger. She held on to the padded rope with one hand while the other held on to her hat. Waving it in the air for balance caused her to really look the part.

"Show it to Mommy!" Bri held my bicep and jumped up and down with the exuberance only a seven-year-old could display.

"All right, all right," I appeased. "I'll send it."

"But you can show it to her right now."

"I know, shortcake. I'll text it *right now*."

"No, you don't need to text it." Bri pointed her small finger. "Mommy's standing right there."

My gaze tracked where she was pointing and I prepared to see a look-alike. When it landed, I couldn't believe my eyes. Violet stood not thirty feet away. She looked amazing in a far more sophisticated variation of the outfit Bri wore —leggings and boots, and a very soft-looking sweater.

Before I could stop what happened next, Bri was running toward her mother with my phone in her hand. Before I could call after her, Trey was on her heels. I couldn't fathom what had possessed Violet to come to the exact place where we would be. Seeing her on another man's arm—not physically touching him, but looking at him attentively—gave me a familiar punch in the gut.

I'm losing her again.

I hated myself for thinking it, but this was how it had felt when she'd gotten together with Todd. Except this time, I hadn't just caught feelings. This time, I was deeply in love.

"Mommy!" Bri launched herself into Violet's arms. An astonished Violet reared back until she realized who had just pounced on her. Bri and Trey were not supposed to know that Violet was dating. The look of horror on Violet's face foreshadowed the total shit-show that was soon to come.

"Baby, I didn't expect to see you here." I was walking toward them at a normal pace, but within earshot when Violet spoke in a panicked voice.

Bri, being seven, called her on it immediately. "But Uncle Chase told you we were coming here. He even tried to get you to come."

Violet's expression turned swiftly to one of chagrin.

"Go easy on your momma, now." My interjection was soft and firm at once. "She already had plans with our friend Rod. You might've seen him around the farm. He's one of our suppliers."

I didn't like the guy, but I didn't want to out Violet. She'd made it clear that her kids didn't need to know she was on a date, which—no thanks to *Man Enough*—they had the capacity to understand. Also, Rodney needed no help discrediting himself. He was dressed not like a spectator but like a rider who had just exited the ring. The man had on assless chaps.

Bri and Trey slid their gazes over to Violet's companion. Trey asked, "Who are you?" At the same time Bri wanted to know, "Your real name is Rod?"

Good girl.

I threw Bri an approving look even as I tried to smooth things over.

"Well, hello, young lady." Rod crouched down and spoke to her in the manner of somebody who, literally, never spent time with kids. "Can you show me with your fingers how old you are?"

Bri frowned and threw Violet a *Who is this guy?* kind of look.

"I'm seven." Refusing to suffer the indignity of showing fingers, she used her voice.

"And I'm four." Trey seemed to want to get ahead of things.

"And we're five." The twins, who spoke in unison, had caught up now.

"You're very pretty," he said to Bri in a still-too-slow and saccharine voice.

"And smart." My arms were crossed as I glared at Rodney.

"Of course. That, too," he stammered.

"Y'all having fun at the rodeo?" I asked Violet. I wanted to move the small talk along. That meant skipping some of the introductions. Violet could politely say that all was well. I could politely wish them a good night and make our excuses about needing to eat. The kids would try to get me to show her their bronco videos. I'd tell them they could do it tomorrow, at home. Then, all of us could be on our merry way.

"We're just killing a little time," Rodney answered for Violet. I didn't like it, even a little bit. "Making rounds before the main event. My main event, that is. I'm playing with the Chubby Dingus band. I've got too much going on to commit to every show, but I catch up with them when they're in town. Me and Chub grew up together. We've known one another for years."

"Oh, that's nice!" Tatum stepped forward until she was next to me. "What instrument do you play?"

I'd never thought of Tatum's extreme friendliness as anything but endearing. But I wished she would cool it right now. Hearing Rod talk about himself wasn't my idea of a good time.

"A mean banjo," Rodney boasted. "Or so I'm told."

"You and Chase ought to jam some time," Tatum continued. "I'm sure Violet's told you, Chase plays. He's too modest to ever tell you so, but he's real good."

"Is he, now?" Rodney gave me a sly look, then smiled like the cat who ate the canary.

I made sure to look bored. "So I'm told."

"You ought to come up on stage tonight, and jam with the band," Rodney challenged.

I knew what Friendzone Chase would say. He'd tell Rodney to take a rain check—then he'd tell Violet to get back to her date. He'd mention that he had to tend to the kids and say they could jam another night. But Friendzone Chase was sick as hell of losing. So sick, it turned out, that Man Enough Chase had already emerged to make an unscheduled appearance.

"Alright, man, I'll jam with you." Man Enough Chase accepted the challenge. "Long as you think you can keep up."

"It's been ages since I've heard you play," Tatum chimed in again, helpfully. "I'd love to hear you," she gushed.

"I don't know if that's a good i—" Violet began, but her children cut her off with twin versions of, "Mommy, please, we want to see Uncle Chase play!"

"The band won't go on for another half an hour," Rodney cut in before Violet could fully decide. "The kids can grab a table. We'll order them a few Rob Roys and Shirley Temples. We can head over right after I ride this here bull."

Rodney jutted his chin in the direction of the adult-sized bucking bronco. It was down the way from the one they had for the kids. Naturally, a guy like him would show off for Violet.

"Come on, Chase," Tatum prodded. "You ought to go on, too!"

Friendzone Chase looked over at Tatum wide-eyed. Seriously. What was up with her tonight? Predictably, the kids came in with things like, "Pleeeease, Uncle Chase?" and "We're not even hungry right now."

"Yes, Chase. Why don't you do it, too?" Violet had crossed her arms in front of herself. Her voice was sweet, but I could tell for certain: she was pissed.

Small talk was even more awkward for the next few minutes it took us to get to the front of the line—awkward for everyone but Tatum and the mostly oblivious kids. Though, I was secretly proud of Bri for her active side-eye of Rodney. She, too, seemed to sense that something with him was off.

"After you, part'ner."

When we got to the front of the line, Rodney feigned chivalry. Both of us knew what this was—him wanting me to go first so he knew what time to beat. This wasn't us riding for fun or to compete for the night's $500 prize. This was purely between me and him.

Not that I was great at this, but I had a secret weapon. I'd spent my early twenties doing a lifetime of stupid things, most of them in honky-tonks just like this. I'd picked up a bevy of nontransferable skills—from bull riding, to holding my own at chug-offs, to swallowing flaming shots without ending up in the ER.

Rule number one of bull riding was grip with your nondominant hand. All the better to have your stronger hand free to break your fall. Rule number two was to scoot forward and grip the thing with your thighs. Rule number three was the see-saw—when the bull went forward, you went back and vice versa. All of this, of course, while keeping my eyes on the bull.

That's exactly what I did as it jostled me to and fro, reminding me with every nanosecond what a bad idea this was—what a bad idea it had always been. It wasn't until I was on my back, staring at the ceiling that I realized I'd been thrown. It was more déjà vu from years before—having the spins for a minute so I could orient myself. I pulled myself up to walk out of the ring and tried not to weave.

When my brain came back to fuller focus, Rod was mounting the bull. His assless chaps reminded me that I'd already won. Even if he blew me out of the water on time, I wasn't wearing those. Plus, a glance at the tournament clock on the wall told me I'd stayed on for a respectable fourteen seconds—well above average and only three seconds shorter than my freewheeling days.

I was met by the children and Tatum with laughs and pats on my back. Violet looked at me—arms still crossed—with an expression I couldn't read. She didn't look pissed off anymore but she also didn't look like herself. She broke her gaze from mine in order to look back toward the mechanical bull in the ring.

I followed suit and caught a glimpse of Rod long enough to see him waving at Violet. But a flat-hand wave was what you used to signal the operator to start. What happened next happened very quickly: the operator started the bull, which caught him unaware. It took just a second for him to flail, just one good buck to send him airborne, one good fall to cause him to land with a sickening crunch.

Chapter Eighteen
VIOLET

"Mommy, can we read a story?"

"Baby, it's ten o'clock." At least two hours after Bri should have been in bed.

"But I'm not tired." She whined in the way she only did with me.

"It is *way* past your bedtime," I pointed out.

"I know. But I really want to read a story. Can we go back to the rodeo next week?"

"The season's almost over," I said reasonably. "Plus, I think we got a little more rodeo than we needed tonight. Don't worry, this won't be our last time."

"I want to watch Uncle Chase ride the bull again."

"Baby, the grown-up bull is dangerous. You saw what happened to Rod."

"Uncle Chase was amazing. Is that what Daddy was like?"

I couldn't deny it. Chase had been damn sexy. Not on the bull, of course, but when he had worked on Rodney. He had jumped right into gear, stabilizing Rodney in the minute it took for the on-site EMTs to arrive. He'd performed field tests to rule out a spinal injury and a concussion. He'd remained calm while a loudly screaming Rodney had insisted he'd broken his leg. Once the guys on duty did finally come, Chase had identified himself and his former rank and given his medical assessment so far. The EMTs were clearly impressed, bordering on reverent. Chase gave them back the scene, but they asked him to stay on.

Given all that was happening, I asked Tatum to take the kids while I went with Rodney, and Chase, and the gurney. As Rodney moaned and whined, Chase was all but teaching a master class to the younger EMTs, explaining advanced topics in field response that sounded Greek to me.

After Rodney was in the ambulance, Tatum and I had taken the kids. Chase had taken Rodney's keys and driven his car to Green Valley, promising to park it outside of his warehouse for one of Rodney's guys to pick up.

"Yes, baby. That's what Daddy was like. But Uncle Chase has specialized training. That's why those other EMTs were listening to him."

Bri finally yawned. "I'm gonna ask him to teach me tomorrow."

"Alright, baby. Go to sleep. We'll talk about it all in the morning."

I was grateful when she finally relented.

Not five minutes after I'd closed her door, I was in my kitchen with an enormous glass full of the rum punch Chase had made me. After a long afternoon, I still hadn't had a drink. Given the company I kept—with Chase—I was culinarily spoiled. There were always delicious things to eat and drink whenever he was around. He'd even cooked earlier and left a large Tupperware full of barbecue chicken in the fridge, chicken I was about to avail myself of.

Seeing him with Tatum hurt.

It had been ten times worse than I'd imagined. I'd anticipated the straight-up jealousy I'd feel at the idea of seeing him with another woman. I hadn't known what it would be to see Chase and Tatum as a family unit. Watching the two of them with our four kids made me feel like the ex who had been replaced by a new wife—a spurned woman who had been left for a second family.

But that's ridiculous.

Because Chase and I had never been together, and never having been together meant we couldn't break up. And not having broken up meant that I couldn't have been replaced. I knew it was irrational. And that I had absolutely no right to take it out on either of them. But how would I pretend to be so unaffected when my feelings were so real?

My phone buzzed on the counter next to me. Chase was texting to make sure I'd gotten home. I tried to sound like I always did when I responded with confirmation. But I couldn't kill the unsettling feeling that we were coming to the end of an era. And that the days of how it used to be were gone.

* * *

BY MONDAY MORNING, I had dusted myself off, picked myself up, and pep-talked myself into getting ready for a new day. I'd spent most of the day on Sunday resting and planning. The "resting" part had involved snuggling with my kids in bed and snoozing while all of us watched the *Trolls* movie. The "planning" part had involved modeling out my design business's first year.

I wanted a luxury-for-less type of focus, where folks could call me and let me help them make easy, inexpensive upgrades based on what they already had. Part of my business would be consultation: viewing my clients' space and assessing their needs. I wanted a showroom in order to put some sample motifs on display. I also wanted a storage space for great pieces that I'd secured on discount. Versatile pieces that could work in a lot of homes.

The truth was, I would miss the wedding planning business. But it felt too close to what I'd been doing for Chase. And to become a competitor, after everything he'd done for me, was unconscionable. However bittersweet it would be, my highest hope for Noble Farms was for the events business to remain successful. That was why my first order of business today was to bring in candidates who might replace me to interview in the second round.

I'd already done a fair bit of screening. Only about half of the applicants who seemed qualified on paper had made it to the second round. These would be folks who I liked enough to put them in front of Chase. Once I saw how he took to each of them, I would think through who to put in a third-and-final-round interview, which would involve standing in as the planner for an actual event.

Chase had initially seemed reluctant to be involved. But lately, he'd seemed on board, or at least more respectful of my decision to leave his employ. He didn't pretend to like it, but he'd gotten over reminding me how much he hated the idea. I should have felt gratified by his willingness to help smooth the transition. The truth was, I did not.

"Reagan?" After hearing a knock on the door of the events barn, I headed down to let our guest in. She nodded affirmatively when I asked her name.

"Welcome. I'm Violet." I held out my hand and she shook it a bit limply. Not that I was the finger-breaking type, but still. A handshake said a lot about a person.

"I'm Reagan. Spelled like the president, pronounced like it has a double-e!"

Her voice was chipper. She'd given me the same pronunciation key when we'd had our initial video conference call. I waved her inside and took in her presentation. Her long, blond hair was loose and cascaded past her shoulder in soft waves. Her eyes were bright and alert, almost like she'd widened them in astonishment when struck by a good idea.

"Chase should be here any minute," I explained as I ushered her in. "In the meantime, I can tell you what you're seeing. This is what we call the events barn. My office is upstairs but, as you can tell, we're standing in our showroom. We usually start event tours right here to give clients a sense of the possibilities in terms of decorative style."

"This is beautiful!" Reagan complimented. "Who designed it?"

"I did."

Reagan's eyes widened, impossibly, more. "But where'd you see it?" she asked.

"In my mind's eye."

She still seemed amazed by this. So much so that I had to ask: "How do you find inspiration for the spaces you create?"

"I tend to work on trend with the bridal magazines."

When it came to copying trends, I definitely had opinions. I tried to think of a delicate way to say that Noble Farms was a cut above—that we liked to go beyond what was ordinary and create unique experiences.

"You know, we've been featured in magazines," I pointed out instead, hoping she would get the message that we weren't trend followers—we were trend-setters.

"Oh, which ones?" she asked, just as the door to the barn began to slide open.

I took more satisfaction than I should have in the slow and stilted way that Chase was walking in. The man was clearly sore on his bottom half, no doubt from all the showboating he'd done on Saturday night on that mechanical bull. I hadn't heard from him yesterday other than him texting me to let me know that Rodney was fine. Rodney himself had called me to say the same and ask me for a rain check on our date.

"Sorry I'm late," he said, cringing a little through his smile. It might not be noticeable to Reagan but it was noticeable to me. Speaking of which...

"Chase, this is—" I began, getting only two words in before she cut me off.

"Reagan." She rushed to Chase and extended her hand. "Spelled like the president, pronounced like it has a double-e! And you are?"

I rolled my eyes, partially because it sounded a lot like cheesy flirtation, but also because I knew she knew his name. I'd made it clear in the email that she would be meeting both of us, but I had also literally just said it.

"Chase Greenleaf," he said, greeting her with a handshake and smile I'd seen before. Chase was nothing if not charming. I'd given him a set of interview questions we needed to ask and we'd talked about the hiring criteria and deal breakers, but I had a secret list of my own. Not flirting shamelessly with Chase was right at the top.

True, I didn't like the idea of someone sliding in to take my event director position while also sliding into his bed. But my "no shameless flirting" rule was about more than jealousy. I wanted my successor to keep growing the house I'd built. I didn't want their ability to do the job well or to stay in the job to hinge on their romantic relationship status. For the sake of Noble Farms, I wanted someone who would focus on the business, and the work.

Much to my chagrin, she interviewed well once we got past our introductions. She was poised, spoke convincingly about her project- and budget-management skills, and had a solid background in wedding planning that was easily transferable to other events. There was no doubt in my mind that she had the ability to keep up with the demands of the job. It was also clear that she brought a few things to the table that I didn't. For starters, she was a lot more available than I was to personally oversee evening and weekend events.

Forty-five minutes after she arrived, we had shaken hands and parted. Reagan had left the barn and was starting her car. We'd held the interview at the small table we used to confer with clients downstairs. Instead of suggesting we walk up to the loft—to sit in our far-more-comfortable meeting space—and to grab snacks from out of the kitchen, I took mercy on Chase and his clearly sore legs.

He winced a little as he eased himself back into the chair. He noticed me noticing and I arched my eyebrow. He shrugged and shook his head a little, as if to say, "yeah, that was pretty stupid."

"I've got Advil in my purse," I offered.

"I'm already taking the maximum dose," he admitted sheepishly.

I could have said a lot of things right then—about how asinine it had been for him to get on a mechanical bull just to show off for Tatum—but I didn't think I needed to. It seemed the aftermath was punishment enough.

"So. What did you think of Reagan?" I asked instead, bracing myself for what I was sure would be a favorable response, and a well-deserved one at that.

"Do you trust me to give you my objective opinion and not stack the deck against anyone who isn't you?"

His blunt question surprised me. Even as I was taken aback by what he was insinuating, the truth was, I did. I let him know as much and waited for him to say what he wanted to say.

"I don't think she's right for the job." This comment was even blunter. "I have no doubt that she can manage the logistics—the scheduling, the vendor management, and all those things. But none of that is at the heart of the business. Folks love having their events here because of the unique experience they encounter at Noble Farms. She seemed a little like a one-trick pony. Like there was one single right way to run a wedding—one single right way to think about space, and flow, and decor. But the events you run…they aren't cookie-cutter. They're customized to clients, and they're original. She seemed competent, but she lacked imagination."

I was gobsmacked. "You picked up on all of that?" Now it was my turn to be blunt.

He gave a little eye roll and a slight shake of his head. "Come on, Vi. I pay attention. I get compliments, and thank-you notes, and I read the reviews. I can't go anywhere in this town—hell, in the whole damn state—without someone making the connection to who I am and telling me how much they loved an event they went to at Noble Farms."

"But she can come to actual events. She can—" I halted myself, sputtering a little. "She can provide a level of personal service that I can't. I've created a job that works for me and my kids, but most event directors don't work this way. Most event directors give a lot more than I do to their events. As event directors go, I'm part-time."

"Do I grow mediocre peaches?" Chase gave me a pointed look.

"No." I answered his leading question honestly.

"Do I run a mediocre supper club? A supper club that was a hundred percent your idea?"

Now, I rolled my eyes. "You mean the award-winning supper club that earned one hundred percent of its status based on your cooking?"

"Noble Farms isn't a mediocre operation, Violet. You're a big part of how it's become what it's become. Every week, at our meetings, those reports you present show me just how high the bar is. If I expect complete excellence from your successor, it's only in response to the standard you've set. I'll say yes when you bring me someone who can actually fill your shoes."

Chapter Nineteen

CHASE

It turned out if you wanted to know how to leave an anonymous tip with an attorney, the one to talk to was Loretta Boggs, the same Loretta Boggs who was married to Buck Rogers. Forrest had mentioned her name to me after we'd run into Buck at secret poker night. It turns out she used to be a PI. Now, she was the lead investigator with the county sheriff. She'd invited me to meet up with her at their house seeing as how she was currently on maternity leave.

Hey, Loretta. It's Chase. I'm right outside.

I sent her a text, knowing she was home alone with the babies. Not a minute after I sent my message, she swung open the front door. She and Buck had been to The Noble Pig once or twice this past summer. She had skin the color of chestnuts and a crown of thick coils that brightened to a golden blond and corkscrewed at the end.

"Chase! It's good to see you. You could've rung the doorbell, you know."

"I wasn't sure whether the babies were sleeping. I remember those days of not wanting to wake them up."

"Oh, I'm sorry. I didn't realize you had kids. How old are they?"

"No, not my kids—Violet's. Even when they were babies, she used to bring them to work at the farm. Her youngest is a light sleeper, but her oldest could hear a pin drop."

She smiled a knowing smile and waved me into her house, then ushered me into the kitchen. Something was mulling on the stove—the source of the smell that had been strengthening since I came in.

"What smells so good?" I wanted to know.

"I'm playing with a recipe for a hot cranberry punch. I figured, you being a foodie, you wouldn't mind. I was also hoping you would give your honest opinion."

I could already tell from the aroma how sumptuous the flavor would be. The acidity of the cranberries would be balanced by some caramelized element I smelled—it would be spices, and flavors, and sweetness. It was rare for me to be a guest. So much of my time had been spent hosting. Already, I felt welcome, and at ease.

"I've never tasted anything like this," I complimented when I took my first sip.

"In a good way?" she chuckled.

We spent the next three minutes geeking out over the many underrated uses of burnt sugar.

"But I know my cranberry punch isn't why you came."

"I have some questions. Hypothetical ones, of course."

Buck had already told Loretta the basics. "I found information in classified documents that could serve justice in a civil trial. I want to help the attorney on the right side of things win the case."

"But you can't give it to her 'cause it's classified?"

I wasn't about to admit to an officer of the law that, legal or illegal, I planned to share that information. So I focused on the other part.

"Let's say that some of what I know could be discovered independently if they knew what rabbit holes to go down. Could I leak something that would lead them to the classified information without sharing the classified information itself?"

"Maybe," Loretta hedged. "What are you worried about here? Breaking your NDA?"

"Maybe," I hedged right back. I was willing to take whatever measures I had to, to make sure Violet would win. But did I also want to not test the anger of the Secretary of the Interior? Hell, yes.

"I mainly want to know what obligation I'll have to explain how I got the information on the off chance that someone follows that path. For instance, would there ever be pressure for an attorney to reveal their sources?"

Loretta nodded in a way that told me she finally understood. She took a thoughtful sip of her drink before responding.

"Attorneys are in the business of uncovering information. Most good ones keep a private investigator in their employ. Anything that could be found out as a matter of legal surveillance or a matter of public record would be considered fair game. It's unlikely that a judge would drill down on sources that fit that description. But you're right—any information that seemed extraordinary in origin would fully be investigated."

"So what's my play here? To leave breadcrumbs that could lead to the discovery of publicly available information and to leave the rest alone?"

"If you want to work within the law, yes. If you've got a good attorney on the case, they should be resourced to follow leads."

"What if I'm running out of time?"

Once again, Loretta seemed to think about this a little. "Then make sure your breadcrumbs are huge. Say as much as you can say without it being a riddle."

"Is there any chance I would ever be called to the stand if someone found out my identity?"

"If your attempts to leak the information backfire, it's a small risk but—yeah —it's there."

A long minute passed with us sipping our drinks, both of us deep in thought.

"Why wouldn't you want to take the stand?" she finally asked. "If you want justice to be served and you're already active in a related investigation, why not appeal to the higher-ups to declassify?"

I hadn't thought of that, but I couldn't say whether it was even possible.

"The higher-ups are very high." It was the best way I could explain it for now.

Loretta nodded again.

"Well, apart from that, just be careful. As a former federal employee, your fingerprints are in the system. There are cameras everywhere. And digital footprints are very easy to follow. Leaving something that would be difficult to trace is doable if you take precautions and treat the drop like everyone is watching."

* * *

"YOU BROUGHT the car with the spaceship doors!" Bri began running toward my car the second she spotted me on the curb in front of her school. I'd arrived early to pick her up, so I was one of the first cars in line. The spaceship doors she referred to were the ones on my blue Tesla, the kind that pull upward like wings, rather than outward like…well, doors. She launched herself into my arms for a brief hug, then I handed her the fob, the one I had procured specifically for her enjoyment. They didn't come standard with this model, but Bri liked to be the one to open just about anything using a remote.

I crossed my arms, stood back, and enjoyed the wonder on her face as she watched the doors slowly open.

"Awesome!" she exclaimed, before slipping off her backpack and tossing it to the far side of the car. I'd attached her booster in a way that sat her behind the passenger seat. That way, I could see her in my peripheral vision while I drove.

"What'd they teach you today in school?" I asked as I merged into traffic. Bri could always be trusted to give me the full account. It took her ten minutes to tell me all about her day. She'd remembered how to spell "believe" on her spelling test; she'd taken out two books from the library; they could wear their costumes to school—but had to take them off before lunch—on Halloween; she wanted to enter the pumpkin decorating contest.

I listened attentively, as I always did, asking questions at all the right times. Animated Bri was a good thing. She was a kid who wore her heart on her sleeve, and these were the best spirits I'd seen her in for days.

Instead of keeping on the road that would take us to Violet's, I turned right and parked downtown, right across the street from Daisy's Nut House. When I turned off the engine and glanced toward the backseat, Bri's eyes were lit up with hope.

"Are we stopping for a treat on the way home?"

I stepped out of the car, closed my own door, and went around to retrieve her.

"Sorry, shortcake. No treats."

Her face fell a little. "Then what are we doing at Daisy's?"

"I thought we might go shopping. I heard you need a dress. Didn't you tell me your school was having a dance?"

Something complicated came over her expression, but she nodded to answer my question.

"You didn't mention it was a father-daughter dance," I pointed out gently, crouching down to her level. She'd unbuckled her seat belt, but still sat in the car.

"If you don't have a daddy, I don't think you're allowed to go." Her head bowed low, and her gaze studied her hands.

"You do have a daddy." I gave her an affirming look. "One who loved you very much. He'd have given anything to be able to go to that dance with you. "

"I know," Bri whispered, still looking at her hands. "But he can't."

Bri looked close to crying. If she started, I wouldn't be far behind. I steeled myself, to ask what I'd come to ask.

"After your momma told me about the dance, I was waiting and hoping that maybe you'd ask me. Since you didn't, I figured I'd have to gather up the courage to ask you myself."

"You would go to the dance with me?" It broke my heart to hear her voice so small.

"I'll go anywhere with you, shortcake. Any day. And I know going with me wouldn't be the same as going with your dad. But, if you'll have me, taking you to the dance would be my honor."

She nodded excitedly and smiled more widely than I'd seen her do in a long time. I suspected my grin matched hers.

"So what do you say we see what they've got at The Honey Child?"

Two doors down from Daisy's Nut House was a children's boutique.

"Last time Mommy took me there, they had a dress that was all strawberries."

I rose to my feet and held out a hand to usher her out of the car. "Well, let's just hope they still have it."

I handed her the remote, so she could use it to close the car door. But she held off. With the hand that didn't hold the clicker, she reached out and took mine. She looked up at me in earnest and squeezed as she said, "Thanks."

Chapter Twenty

VIOLET

"Trick or treat!" Bri and Trey shouted in unison the second my down-the-street neighbor opened the door. As predicted, they were gratified by the presentation of a huge bowl of candy. Bri was always polite and thoughtful, carefully choosing one. Trey, on the other hand, had to be reminded at every house not to take a handful.

Our neighborhood didn't have a ton of kids, which meant the neighbors were too happy to oblige and often encouraged that each of the kids take more. As a result, we had only been trick-or-treating for half an hour and, already, the kids were on track to take home a nice haul.

Trick-or-treating was one of Chase's favorite family traditions. The man loved Halloween. And I loved not having to do Halloween alone. I was secretly relieved that Chase had not invited Tatum. I would have welcomed her if she had wanted to come; and, I knew that group trick-or-treating made sense. Tons of families did it. But I was still conscious of my growing dread that the day was soon to come when I would be a third wheel.

Chase had insisted on a group costume. We'd decided to go as the cast of *Cobra Kai*. I was Mr. Miyagi, as indicated by my white karate gi with the Miyagi-Do logo on the back—a red circle inside of which was a bonsai tree. Trey was dressed as Miguel, on *Cobra Kai*, and Bri was for Miyagi-Do, dressed as Sam. Chase had agreed to be Johnny Lawrence, mainly because the kids loved his impression. They collapsed into giggles every time he used his growly voice to say, "Fear does not exist in this dojo."

The kids mostly ran up to doors by themselves. Chase and I mostly hung back, waving at my neighbors and thanking them unless they were people I knew well enough to stop and have a chat. Chase had made us travel mugs full of Baileys-spiked hot cocoa to keep the two of us warm as we strolled. It was a clear night—pleasant and crisp and fragrant with the aroma of crushed leaves.

I was glad for the rest and respite. It had been a bit of a week. The day before, I'd gotten a call from Katrina. There had been another curveball in the case. Just when she'd been about to let me know her investigator hadn't turned up anything new, she'd received an anonymous tip. She didn't know what any of it meant yet—it had come in the form of a specific list of procedural details to look into. Someone on our side had given us clues they thought could help us win this.

But who?

The question had plagued my mind. Katrina hadn't given me much insight. She'd only told me that what had been sent had been postmarked from California. From there she gave me a broader list of who it could be. We'd talked about who might have a motive to give us tips.

It could have been someone in the chain of command—someone who had worked the fire that day who could no longer allow hidden information to weigh on their conscience. It could have been some underling at the insurance company who knew what the defense knew and who felt I had been wronged. It could have been anyone else who had been privy to the investigation or who was taking a fresh look now that both sides were rebuilding our case—another widow or another mother who had come across new evidence, who sympathized with my situation and wanted to see me get justice for my kids.

Regardless of who had sent it, everything about it rattled me. It confirmed with certainty that there was new evidence in the case, which—until this week— had been strong logic but speculation nonetheless. That, plus the sheer fact that the clock was ticking and the retrial was nearing was making me anxious. I was not looking forward to spending days in a courtroom again.

"You feeling alright? About all that's happening with the case?" Chase asked me in a quiet moment. The kids were ahead of us as they turned the corner and began walking onto a different street.

When I'd heard about the tip, Chase had been one of the first people I'd told. He'd been curious and sympathetic, and commiserating, as always. I wasn't surprised that he was asking about it now, to check in with me again.

"Honestly? No. All of this…it's just a lot."

"It's almost over," he pointed out. He said it with a certainty I didn't understand.

"It doesn't feel like that," I admitted. "It feels like we're at the beginning of going through it again."

"I know, darlin'. But I think you ought to have faith."

He said it so calmly, so comfortingly, so steadily that I couldn't help but lean into him.

"Do we have to go to this house?"

Bri had stopped in the middle of the sidewalk and waited for us to catch up, suddenly comprehending what street we were on and pointing to the unassuming ranch style. We had officially reached the most disappointing house in the neighborhood. The homeowner—apparently a dentist—had completely eschewed handing out candy. Instead he handed out toothbrushes inscribed with the name of his practice, and spools of floss.

"There's nothing wrong with a free toothbrush," I pointed out.

"Mo-om…" Bri whined out my name until it had lengthened to two syllables.

"You get your toothbrushes and I'll take you up to the scary house," Chase promised.

The legendary "scary house" was also on this block. It was a foursquare with a covered porch and a lower roof upon which the homeowners always put an enormous, hairy spider. Michael Jackson's "Thriller" blared from speakers hidden on the porch. And you didn't just trick-or-treat there— they'd converted the entire bottom floor into a haunted house. The rooms connected to one another and, when you walked inside, you took a circle around the bottom floor. Trey loved to be scared but Bri was a bit more timid.

Chase would have taken them inside the scary house anyway, but, when presented with what seemed like a bargain, the kids wisely took it, proceeding to the dentist's house to receive their dreaded hygiene products.

Fifteen minutes later, Chase and the kids were walking up the front walkway of the scary house. As usual, I hung back. The house was popular and there was always a line and I didn't love the scary house so much that I had to go in every year. Instead, I stood next to the fence, appreciating the effort. Fake headstones were erected on the lawn and skeletons had been half-buried to look like they were trying to crawl out of their graves.

My phone rang.

Who would call me at prime trick-or-treating hours on Halloween night?

Rodney, apparently, according to the caller ID. He'd left a voicemail earlier that week. I'd called him back and missed him. After that, we'd only texted. I didn't want to be broken out of my enjoyment of the moment, but I also didn't want to keep playing phone tag. Letting the latter sentiment win, I picked up.

"Hey there, Rodney."

"Hey, Violet." Increasingly, he spoke my name with affection. I didn't know what to make of that. Rodney seemed to like me but he hadn't made a real move. I wasn't strictly complaining about that fact. But I did find it curious. When I'd dated in my twenties, or even just went out places with my friends, sex was all men seemed to think about.

"Our date last week was cut short," Rodney continued. "I'm sorry about that."

"I'm just glad that you're okay."

I didn't call Rodney out or tell him my real feelings about his stupid display of masculinity, just like I hadn't called Chase out for showing off to Tatum.

"So? Do I get a rain check? Will you let me take you out again? Nothing dangerous this time. We'll just grab some food."

"Sure. Grabbing some food sounds nice."

If I wanted to get good at dating, I had to continue to practice. The truth was, I did want a family life. This thing I was doing with Chase tonight? I wanted it locked in. That meant having a confidant and a companion, with whom I had mutually committed. One day, my children would leave home.

"Great. How about Saturday?"

"I think I could get away for a couple of hours."

"Perfect. I'll make reservations. I know you've got to call your babysitter. Why don't you look at your schedule and send me some good times?"

I didn't miss the sarcastic way he emphasized the word "babysitter" when talking about Chase. We were going to have to talk about that.

* * *

WHEN RODNEY HAD SAID we would go to dinner, I'd thought this was finally it —that he would take me to a restaurant. That we would order off an actual menu, and have a relaxed time. Especially after how things had ended at the rodeo, I'd figured he would want to notch things down. I was beginning to learn my lesson: Rodney only operated in active mode.

Tonight's "dinner date" had turned out to be a class in backwoods foraging. We'd started with a group at a teaching cabin in the woods. After an hourlong course on edible plant identification, the instructors had turned us out on our own. The next two hours had involved me wearing a crosswise satchel and traipsing through the forest in not-sensible shoes to collect mushrooms and onions and berries, only to return to the cabin to cook the least satisfying meal I had ever eaten.

Historically, I'd always been a happy recipient of homegrown goods. The enormous bag of sylvan items I was returning home with this evening left me underwhelmed. For one, they were covered in dirt, so much that I would need real time to wash them thoroughly. Also, what the hell was I going to do with more than five pounds of mushrooms?

In the Hummer all the way back to civilization, Rodney was talking about a time when he'd survived in the woods for days after what he only described as "a compass mishap" when my phone began to buzz with numerous texts. They were coming through in rapid succession. It reminded me that I was somewhere I didn't have to be. Rodney's foraging date had taken me out of cell phone range. The unusual number of texts from the people who were watching my children had me on guard. I had one text from Jules and three texts from Chase. Thinking the worst, I scrambled to unlock my phone and see what was the matter. Intellectually, I knew there was no safer place in the world for Bri to be than with a Fire EMT. Trey was a different story.

Earlier that afternoon, Chase had picked up Bri for their dance. The plan was for him to start by taking her to dinner. After I'd helped her dress and seen her off, Jules had come in to watch Trey. At this point, I'd been offline for a good three hours and I was eager to see what had been urgent enough to text me. I waited impatiently for the messages to load.

Jules had texted to confirm Trey's claim that I always let him have two desserts. I replied with two messages in rapid succession. The first was the eye-roll emoji. The second simply said, Absolutely not. Chase's three messages turned out not to be texts at all, but pictures of him and Bri having a good time.

I couldn't help it. When I saw them, tears sprang to my eyes. The first was a photo in the restaurant that the server must have taken. An untouched ice cream sundae in a tall glass sat between them; in front of them were two long spoons; both of them beamed at the camera. The tabletop appeared with an artistic design that looked like Van Gogh's Starry Night. Chase had connections in the culinary world and had taken her to an impossible-to-get-into restaurant in Knoxville that delighted its guests with 3D tabletop art.

The second was a group photo of kids and their dates, Bri lined up next to all her friends as corresponding father figures stood behind them. The other kids were looking at the camera, but Bri gazed admiringly up at Chase.

"Is everything okay?" Rodney halted mid-sentence on his survival story to ask the question.

"Sorry," I said in a watery voice. "I'm not usually the person who's on my phone like this. It's just, tonight is the daddy-daughter dance and he's texting me pictures of him and Bri."

"He?" Rodney looked like he knew the answer, but asked the question anyway.

"Chase. She wanted Chase to take her."

It was true. After Chase had actually asked and Bri had actually accepted, she'd confessed that she had hoped for this outcome all along—that Chase was the only person, apart from Todd, who she would have wanted to take her. The day he'd brought her home, him carrying her tiny backpack while she carried the enormous white shopping bag...her proudly opening the dress box and showing off her strawberry-dotted dress...that day had touched me deeply. So much so that after Chase had left and Bri had gone to show Trey, I'd stepped out into the garage, sobbing in relief about the way things were turning out.

Every day of my life, I mourned for my kids—mourned for the hole left in their lives after Todd's passing. But Chase…he filled us up. Moments like this one, and last week on the farm, were the ones I thought about the most. Every kid needed steady adults in their life. More than one person who reminded them how special they were, who bonded with them and loved them more than anything. Chase was a better father figure than most actual dads.

"How are things going? Are they having a good time?" Rodney asked politely.

I couldn't stop my smile. "The best time, from the looks of it. I don't love the theme of the dance, but the school did a nice job with the decor."

We had just halted at a traffic light, so I held out my phone to show Rodney the third photo—Chase sitting in a large throne and wearing a bejeweled crown with ermine trim; Bri sitting in the smaller throne next to him wearing a tiara she hadn't had on when she left the house. The two of them gazed at each other, laughing at the moment the photo had been snapped.

As usual, Rodney asked whether I wanted to go to town for a nightcap. As usual, I thanked him but told him I needed to get home. This time, it was truer than ever. I wanted to be home when Chase got back with Bri. There was a window of time that I needed to get home if I wanted to be there to meet her and if I also wanted to avoid questions from Trey. Not wanting to explain what I was doing with Rodney on yet another Saturday night, I texted Jules to make sure that Trey was already in bed.

This time, Rodney insisted on coming inside to help me with our take. He briefly met Jules. I was successful in shooing her out before she could give him the third degree. I was less successful in shooing him out. I made the mistake of starting to rinse the dirt off of the onions. I'd hoped he would take the hint that I was taking steps to wrap up the night—that I was switching back into home and domestic mode. But he didn't take the hint. Instead, he fell in next to me and started to help me. It would have been sweet if I hadn't been so tense about Chase's return.

Thankfully, we made quick work. I had him help me bag them up. I went to the garage for a cooler to preserve some of them for Chase. I was back and forth between the freezer and the cooler on the counter, scooping ice when Rodney boldly stepped in. He did it in a way that halted my motions. He pulled the ice scoop gently out of my hands and set it on the counter, looking at me with what might have felt like softness if his blue eyes hadn't been so intense.

"I like you, Violet," he said humbly. In that moment, I believed that he did. My heart started racing in a way that was confusing. Was it racing because some part of me liked him too? Who saw that, beneath his showiness and excessive chatter, was a man who listened in his own way and who was genuine in his odd sense of adventure? Was I attracted to how much he seemed to support my endeavors to strike out on my own? Or was my heart simply racing because I knew the moment had come—the moment when I was about to be kissed?

I was immobilized—unable to echo his sentiment because, even after weeks of dipping my toes back into the dating pool—I wasn't sure what liking a guy again meant. Rodney seemed to pick up on this.

"I know I'm the first guy you've been out with since your husband. I know you might not be ready to say it back. But still, I wanted you to know."

I nodded, still feeling unable to fully react. I had known this moment would come. Rodney had taken things so blissfully slow. And still, I was unprepared for it.

"Can I kiss you?" he asked.

I didn't say yes. But I also didn't say no. And when he lowered his face to mine, muscle memory kicked in and I tipped my chin upward.

Inside, I knew what I ought to be thinking at that moment. That I truly wanted him. But I didn't want him so much as I wanted this. I needed to get over my fear of dating again for all the practical reasons. I'd developed a new level of comfort when it came to being taken out—to be able to say that I was dating. Now I needed to build my level of comfort at being kissed.

Just get it over with, I thought to myself. Not the most romantic notion, but legitimate all the same. From there, I tipped my chin up even more and I even leaned into him a little. To his total credit, Rodney was gentle and slow. He brushed his lips to mine softly at first, then pressed them firmly, with no intrusion of his tongue. My stomach churned, not with butterflies, but with a sort of panic.

It wasn't until he pulled away that I broke from my odd, intellectualized detachment and slapped with the first raw emotion I'd felt yet—guilt and shame over what I'd just done. But it wasn't the guilt I expected. Kissing Rodney didn't make me feel like I was cheating on Todd. It made me feel like I was cheating on Chase.

Chapter Twenty-One
CHASE

"My lady."

I made a huge show of bowing deeply as I helped Bri get out of the backseat. I'd just opened up the back door of my Tesla, the doors that Bri happened to love. She had already unbuckled herself from her car seat and smoothed down her dress.

"My lord," she said as she took my hand, allowing herself to be escorted from the car. After I let her close the door with the key remote, I offered my elbow and walked her to her front stoop.

"I had a lovely time with you tonight," I said to her sincerely. "Thank you for letting me come with you. Now, what do you say we go inside and tell your momma all about how it was?"

Bri nodded and I used one of the other keys on my ring to open Violet's front door. I knew I wouldn't find her alone. Jules had watched Trey that night and her car was already gone. But a big, yellow Hummer sat in the drive.

The second we got inside, Bri ran through the foyer and toward the kitchen, the natural place she might find her mom. It occurred to me for the first time that both Bri and I might encounter something that would be detrimental for both of us to see. What was Rodney doing inside? Worse than that, what were the two of them doing together? Maybe walking right in hadn't been such a good idea.

I was relieved to find that Violet and Rodney were fully clothed, and in the kitchen rather than on the couch or—even worse—the one place I didn't want to think about at all—the bedroom. I knew in my rational mind that Violet was cautious of her kids knowing she was dating. Logically, knew she would never jeopardize that. But the way I felt having to see her with Rodney was anything but logical.

Violet appeared to be putting something away. A lot of somethings, from the looks of it. She was loading something in the drawer of her freezer and had a cooler out. It was an odd thing to be doing upon one's return from a date.

"Hey, Vi. Hey there, Rodney."

I hugged Vi and gave her a kiss on the cheek even as Bri was glued to one of her sides, then moved on to shake hands with Rodney. I still didn't like him, but I still had to be civil to the guy.

"Looks like you're feeling better since last week. Glad to see it," I remarked.

"Well, I got lucky," Rodney said. "Though I did have to go back down there on Monday, and have a talk with the manager of that rodeo. That mechanical bull —there was something wrong with it. The way it threw me off, it wasn't safe. They're lucky I'm not a litigious man. I might have sued."

"That's funny." I made sure to sound more curious than sarcastic. "Seemed safe when I rode it a minute before you did."

Rodney glared openly at me. Violet threw me a look.

"I'm glad for the rodeo's sake that you showed mercy. I've always found that to be a good quality in a man."

Neither of them looked convinced by my recovery compliment. Violet changed the subject, clearly wanting the pissing contest to end. Instead, she turned her attention to Bri.

"Did you have fun, baby?"

"Everything was amazing! You'll never guess what kind of cake they had! It was strawberry shortcake and they gave us punch. They had big thrones for us to sit on and they gave me my own tiara and all my friends saw me in my dress and did you know that Chase can really dance?"

Violet laughed richly—in a way that she rarely did. I loved to see her like this. "He sent me a picture of you sitting in your thrones and, yes, I did know Chase can dance."

She looked over at me then, her eyes still warm and alight with joy. It made me remember earlier days when we'd been a lot younger, parties we'd been to where we had fun dancing as friends.

I hadn't only barraged her with photos so she'd be able to join in on the fun. I couldn't let her have too much fun on her date, though it searched me what she was still doing going out with Rodney. After the way he'd bitched and moaned on that gurney over a non-injury that had been born of true stupidity, I'd figured Violet would just say no. I'd casually mentioned to her that I'd called up my buddy at the Marysville Hospital—an ER doc I knew back from my days in the fire service—to tell him I'd been at the scene and wanted to follow up on Rodney's status. It turned out that nothing was wrong with the guy. He'd been examined and X-rayed—surveyed and scanned—and they hadn't found a scratch.

"I want to wear this dress again, Mommy. Can we go out tomorrow morning, maybe to a fancy brunch and you can put on a fancy dress and Trey can wear his church clothes and Chase can wear his suit?" Bri turned her attention to me. "Chase looks good."

Violet chuckled at the way that Bri drew out the word. A bit embarrassed, I scratched the back of my neck, at a loss for a graceful way to take the compliment.

"Yeah," Violet agreed, her voice quieting some. "Chase does clean up nice."

She and I looked at each other a little too long before she appeared to remember herself and answer Bri's question directly. She turned her attention back to her daughter. "You can wear your dress again, sugar. But brunch tomorrow isn't in the cards. I'll bet Chase is tired from all that dancing. It seems like you really wore him out."

"I think we wore each other out," I said good-naturedly. "We'll both sleep well tonight."

"On that note…" Violet used her mom voice. "It's time for you to go to bed."

But Bri didn't walk in the direction of her bedroom. Instead, she ran from Violet to me and hurtled into my arms for a final hug. She was small, but she was a nice, tight hugger. I hugged back, a little choked up, filled up with the knowledge that this was a night I would never forget. Then, she killed me when she said in her sweet voice, "I love you, Uncle Chase."

It took me a second to reply. "I love you, too, shortcake."

* * *

THE DAYS after the dance found me busy again. Cody had to go out of town, which left me to myself with all my standard duties at the farm. On top of all of that, my investigation into what had really happened that day with the Cranston Fire was relentless. I farmed by day and drove to Bandit Lake, to meet with Forrest, by night.

All of it added up to me not seeing a lot of Violet. A typical day on the farm with a normal workload gave me time to drop in. I missed our normal rhythms —me bringing her lunch and having time to stay and eat with her, me dropping by to see Jameson, but really just wanting an excuse to spend time with her.

Not seeing enough of Violet that week was half of the reason why I now stood on her front stoop. I rang the bell this time, since I was unannounced. I had it on good authority that she would be home given the situation.

"Chase! What are you doing here?"

Violet swung open the door, looking surprised to see me. I held two insulated bags, one full of hot food I'd brought from home, and another reserved for items that needed chilling.

"Hey, Vi."

She stepped aside so that I could come in.

"You didn't hear? Girls' night in is canceled. Bri and Trey are sick."

"No, I heard." I proceeded inside anyway and she followed me to the kitchen, where I set down my bag and started pulling out Tupperwares full of food.

"Jules did call me. Told me not to pick her up. Told me the kids had a stomach bug. I figured I'd come over and help."

Violet looked at me like I'd lost my marbles. "Do you mean, help get yourself sick? If you stay here, you're just gonna get what they have. And, it was sweet of you to cook, but they can't eat."

"I didn't cook for them." I gave her a look that said, "have you met me?" "I'm going to make chilaquiles for you."

I chuckled when her eyes widened with excitement. She loved her children, but their tastes could be a bit bland. Family meals were flavorful, but not spicy. But Violet was like me. She liked her food with a little kick. With the kids not eating, I could make her one of her favorite dishes. And I knew how to make it just right.

"But it's not even breakfast," she gushed with the delight of a person who absolutely wouldn't let that stop her.

"Chilaquiles are delicious any time of day."

Something was happening to me lately. I was losing my grip on the pretense that I only had friendly feelings toward Violet. I steered clear of the answer Man Enough Chase wanted to give—that I'd be happy to serve it to her for breakfast if I got to stay the night.

"Now, let me pour you a drink," I insisted. "It'll only take me a few minutes to put it all together. And I'm guessing you could use a rest. It's still Thursday night, even if the kids are sick. But there's no reason me and you can't watch *Man Enough*."

I felt only slightly dastardly when I reached into the chilled bag for the cocktail I'd already prepared—a vodka-spiked ginger limeade that I'd whipped up at home. When Jules had called with the cancellation, I'd immediately seen my chance for some adult time.

Telling the other guys I was in love with Violet had lifted a weight. Making the conscious decision to fight for her had done more than make me feel hopeful and determined—it had made me feel like a man in love. And the desire was getting stronger to spend time with her, and just her.

I poured our drinks over ice in a mason jar and garnished it with candied ginger. She sat on a stool at her kitchen island and took an indulgent sip, making what I thought of as her "I needed this" face. Being part of her everyday—doing small things to make it better—now that was my idea of domestic bliss. So was coming home to each other and talking about our days, or just shooting the shit while we did everyday things. Her companionship was worth a lot to me.

As I plated the thick tortilla chips, interspersed them with pan-fresh flat-scrambled eggs, I began to pour on two different hot sauces. We got to talking about food, and where the best Mexican restaurant in Knoxville could be found. I said something about a hole-in-the wall gem on an obscure back street I described in detail. She said something about a taco truck I'd heard of, but never managed to catch.

"You know, we ought to go out sometime. Check out that taco truck." I had practiced saying that first part casually, in front of the mirror and in the car. But just now, I had said it on impulse. The natural course of conversation had given me the perfect in. But good timing didn't diminish the enormity of what I was suggesting. My heart thundered so strongly, I was sure that Violet could hear.

"The kids are older now," I pointed out. "And easier to leave with Jules. You left Trey with her just last week."

I hoped the smile I threw her achieved my goal of looking playful, especially given my nerves. And I hoped my quip would lighten things up. It was an open secret that Jules wasn't the best babysitter. But, the older kids got, the easier it was to watch them. Suggesting a casual outing was a good first step to something more.

"I'll go with you to the taco truck." It was a simple enough thing for her to say —but the way she said it was kind of shy, almost like it meant the same thing to her as it did to me. Wanting neither to overplay my hand, nor to break out into a stupid grin, I took the victory and turned our talk to Bri and Trey.

"I take it the kids are sleeping?"

"For now." Violet looked skeptical that she thought it would last.

"Who got it first?"

"I'll give you one guess." She gave me a look to tell me I already knew the answer.

Trey was a generally clean kid, but he would lick anything that had food on it. His dinner plate. A bowl with the dregs of baking batter. His fingers and hands. Trey was the reason why Violet was never more than ten feet away from a bottle of hand sanitizer.

"Trey was sick in the car on the way home," she recounted. "We came in and I put him to bed, but it took me an hour to clean the car. Not ten minutes after I sat down to rest, Bri was in the bathroom. It was literally—and figuratively—a mess."

I gave her a pitying look. "If they're sick again, I can see to them," I offered gently.

"Chase." There was always so much in the way she said my name, and to how different she made it sound depending on what she meant. This particular uttering of my name conveyed the familiar sentiment: "Chase. You do too much." But I was used to standing up to that.

"Come on, now, Vi," I protested. "You know I've seen it all. Nothing that happens today could be worse than Diapergate."

The laughter she broke into at the recollection was immediate and pure. One day, when Trey was a toddler, he'd gotten hold of a bag of sugar—he'd pilfered it from the kitchen table while I was baking with Bri. By the time we'd discovered him, the mess of granules that surrounded him plus a thick trail of sugary drool sliding down his shirt told us he'd been eating it a fistful at a time. The fact that he was actively eating a handful when we spotted him was a clue. At the time, we'd had a good laugh. Then, we'd seen the aftermath and learned the truth the hard way—that eating straight up sugar had consequences. Specifically, explosive diarrhea.

"I still have the pictures." Violet chuckled.

"Pictures? Plural?" I laughed.

"That picture I sent you with him on the floor, with the poop coming out of his diaper? That was the day after the sugar."

Now I was really laughing. I hadn't thought of that picture in a while but it was a total classic. Trey sat on the floor in nothing but a diaper, smiling the biggest, broadest grin up at Violet, unaware that he had a whole mess flooding out the back.

"Man, you've been through a lot with those kids."

"We've been through a lot, Chase." Violet got a little serious. "You've been here every step of the way."

"Well..." I didn't know how to take the compliment. She'd been giving more of those herself, lately—a fact I didn't want to read too far into. "Raising kids isn't easy. And it isn't meant to be done alone."

"You know…" Violet looked pensive now. "Losing Todd made me feel a lot of things. But alone was never one of them. I owe a lot of that to you."

Sitting down to watch *Man Enough* in her living room a few minutes later, things felt uncommonly quiet. Watching the show alone was something we hadn't ever done. Despite the couch that was frontal to the TV being wide open, we still gravitated toward the love seat off to the side, eating our dinner over the ottoman before stacking the plates on the coffee table and putting up our feet.

Tonight was a big night on the show. We'd reached the semifinals. Only four suitors remained in the game, Marcus and Eric among them. The weekly challenges had gone from showy and extravagant to far more pragmatic. It was less about whether the suitors were man enough to chop wood, do dirty jobs, or catch a fish with their bare hands, and more about whether they were emotionally prepared for an adult relationship—whether they had the emotional intelligence and maturity to talk about their feelings and admit when they were wrong.

Tonight's challenge was straightforward: were the suitors man enough to cry? Marcus, of course, had passed with flying colors. Only Chelsea knew what the challenge was. It was to ask them to tell her about their most painful memory. Marcus had spoken so passionately and sorrowfully about losing his childhood beagle, named Daisy, the man even had me crying. Marcus was still my hands-down favorite. He was so genuine and heartfelt, it was hard not to fall in love with the guy.

He even carried a handkerchief. Now, that was a boss move, one that I might have to adopt myself. Granted, it was usually Marcus himself who had a need for his hankie. But when Chelsea cried at his sad story, he gallantly gave it to her.

Now it was Eric's turn. Unsurprisingly, he was having trouble. Not that there was a single right way to show sadness and grief—not that crying was the only true litmus test for emotional range and vulnerability. But Eric…he didn't even seem capable of connecting with something sad. The conversation between him and Chelsea went around and around, with Chelsea trying to get him to talk about his life and the kinds of sadnesses and disappointments that had shaped him. But Eric was clearly struggling. It was more than a little fascinating to watch.

Violet and I had been relatively quiet given the somber nature of the show. She also seemed a little sleepy. Who could blame her after the way things had been? It hadn't been the easiest past twelve hours, not with all that had happened with the kids.

"Can I ask you something?" I finally said when I could contain the question no more. Her hummed reply leaned affirmative.

"What's special about Eric? I mean, what does he have that the other guys don't?"

When she didn't answer right away, I thought maybe she had nodded off. When I tore my gaze away from the television to confirm my suspicions, I found her to be awake. She spoke softly, but in earnest.

"Eric isn't the best and he may not be the brightest, but he's also just…" She paused. "Safe. I mean, with him, Chelsea doesn't have to try too hard."

"I'm sorry. You're gonna have to explain to me how a guy who's obsessed with chasing after wild boar in the woods constitutes safe. It's like he's never heard of a supermarket. Why would you want to be with a guy who's always got something to prove rather than the guy who proves himself every day by just showing up? By just being there and being steady. What makes Eric so special? I just don't understand."

Violet was gracious enough not to mention that I had just switched from "she" to "you."

Now that I'd asked the question, I wasn't sure I wanted the answer. I didn't want to ruin what I desperately hoped we were moving toward.

"It's not about that kind of safety," she finally said. "Sure, Eric's stupid. But he's also pretty harmless. Beating his chest and showing off…that's just who he is. He's safe because he's the kind of guy who it's easy to not fall too deeply in love with. If she fell in love with Marcus, well…"

Violet paused but I hung on her every word.

"Loving someone who really sees you? And has the power to break your heart? Loving a person like that—it's scary."

For a long second, I debated whether to speak or to let it lie. Ultimately, I settled on the latter, but I held her more tightly to me. Whereas my arm had originally been draped across the back of the love seat, at some point, it had closed in around her shoulder. Now I pulled her into me. She laid her head on my chest.

The show continued as we looked on silently. Soon, Violet did fall asleep, leaving me awake to think on all she'd said. But even that didn't last for long. Between the alcohol in the limeade and pulling double duty this week and the emotional turmoil that came from fixating on her impending departure, I was exhausted.

It also felt a little too good to be lounging next to her like this. Her head had moved from my shoulder to my chest. To feel the weight of her body against my side, and the softness of her skin where my hand rested against her arm was intoxicating. Put together with the rhythm of her breathing and the smell of her hair, it was sensory bliss. But this was more than the sublime intimacy of holding her in my arms. Being with Violet always gave me a sense of peace.

I drifted into the kind of sleep that could only be called delicious—I was asleep, but not—drifting somewhere in between awareness and surrender. I was relieved of conscious thought; at points, I might even have been dreaming. But through it all, I never lost consciousness of Violet—never stopped feeling her ensconced within my arms.

Somehow, in the night, our bodies grew closer. Between the love seat and the width of the ottoman, slanting sideways, we could both sort of lie. When all was said and done, I was all the way in the left corner with my legs stretched out in front of me. Violet had pulled her legs onto the love seat and curled her body into me.

At some point, my consciousness rose. I emerged somewhat from my deep half-sleep to find that Violet herself was awake, or at least wakeful enough to be gazing up at me. I tipped my chin downward, to better see her face. For a moment, we just studied each other, breathing together in synchronicity. The TV had long since turned itself off, leaving the room dark.

"Chase."

I saw in her eyes what she wanted before the rest of her extended an invitation. Seconds after she said my name, she pulled herself farther up my chest and tipped up her chin. She lifted her face toward mine until our noses touched and tangled, but it was me who made the final move to capture her lips.

I'd never been one to believe in fireworks. For me, kissing was an art that was best done slowly—something that needed to be savored and enjoyed. I delighted in the practice immensely, but it had always felt comfortable and enticing, a pleasant teaser for what might be to come.

But this…it was all-consuming. It wasn't lazy. It wasn't nice. It wasn't just a better version of every other kiss I'd ever had because this time, I got to share it with Violet. This was a head-to-toe experience I felt down to my bones. Kissing Violet was a revelation. It was shocking proof that, after more than three decades living on this earth—I could feel something completely new.

No. Not just new. This new feeling was essential—something I honestly didn't think I could live without. Something that was at once perfect but not enough. Violet's soft lips against mine…the luxurious sliding of our tongues. The fusing of our bodies, as if we were trying to climb inside one another. We were urgent, but not frantic as we drank each other in. It ended with her breaking the kiss—her hand on my chest and my name on her lips again.

But I didn't want her to say anything—I didn't want her to break the magic of what had happened. I didn't want the real world, or any of the real implications of this to encroach. The only thing I wanted in that moment was for her to feel.

At some point during our kiss, my hand had found its way into her hair. Hoping to calm her, I smoothed it now. Her eyes softened and we shared a long gaze before she rested her head back upon my chest. That time, I fell into a deep and dreamless sleep.

Chapter Twenty-Two
VIOLET

"Focus, Violet," I scolded myself as I pored over the checklist that needed my attention for tonight's event. I'd been at work for a solid two hours and I was still stuck on the same simple task. I could make excuses and blame the fact that my kids were with me today for how inefficiently I was working. The truth was, I was fixated on having kissed Chase.

I could still feel the pressure of his lips on mine—could still feel the tingling awareness his touch created everywhere. Could still feel the knowing in my body that everything about it was right. Kissing Chase reminded me how much I loved kissing. It made me wonder how I'd gone without it so long. Chase kissed me so good, I wondered whether I'd ever really been kissed.

Thoughts like that were half of what had me reeling. Some part of me couldn't comprehend how I could feel so strongly for Chase when I had felt so strongly for Todd. It forced me to face where I'd really set my expectations. In my heart of hearts, I'd never believed I could ever love another man as much as I'd loved Todd. But I'd still held out hope that I'd find contentment. I'd believed I would date or remarry, but hadn't pinned my hopes on anything better than some romantic half-life.

But that hadn't been a half kiss.

Chase had me feeling it all, which forced me to admit that this wasn't some foolish crush, or an infatuation with my protector, and the father figure who loved my kids. This was so much more. I could barely even talk to Tatum and she was one of my best friends. It all added up to an undeniable truth. I was stupid in love with Chase, and he'd figured it out.

A call from Katrina broke me out of thoughts I really needed to stop dwelling on if I wanted to be productive. There were three events this weekend and I needed to be on top of things. Not to mention, I was still juggling work with tending to Bri and Trey. They were feeling better, but not 100%, so I'd brought them with me to the farm. They were watching a movie on their tablet on the daybed while I worked.

"Hey, Katrina," I said. Our court date was less than two weeks away. We had time on the calendar next week to prepare for the trial. We'd done the same thing the first time around. She'd walked me through how to present myself well in the courtroom, how to be a credible witness on the stand, and generally prepared me for what to expect.

"Morning, Violet. I have some news."

My body went into high alert. "News" didn't sound good. I hated the way that anything having to do with the case had the power to send me into a panic. Plus, it was a lot to deal with on top of everything else. Katrina never put too much suspense into what she had to say, a fact I was grateful for. She didn't make me wait to hear what was going on.

"The insurance company reached out—they're deadlining the offer. If you don't accept by end of day, they'll take it off the table."

My sense of dread erupted into full-blown panic.

"There are two possibilities here," Katrina continued. "Either their case just got a lot better and they think they can win at trial, in which case they might be giving you one last chance to take the settlement as a courtesy—"

I was already on my feet and walking down the stairs. This was not a conversation I wanted to have in front of my kids. I also didn't want them to see me upset and I was well on my way, probably not to anger, but to tears.

"What's the other explanation?"

"They want you to take it. And they think applying pressure will move you along. Telling you it's take it or leave it on a Friday morning and giving you only a matter of hours to decide is designed to intimidate you, and back you into a corner."

"Mission accomplished." I felt dazed as I slid open the barn door and stepped outside, the cool fall air a welcome respite to the maelstrom of emotions that had erupted inside my body. I had no idea what to do. Five hundred thousand dollars was a lot of money. There was so much I could do with it for Bri and Trey. Was winning the case even important if the money came through and I could use it on what it had always been meant for?

"I'll say what I've said to you before, Violet. That this has to be your choice. And the way to make that choice is to know what's important to you. But I would be remiss not to tell you—I think the intel we got through the tip is getting us somewhere. My investigator is on top of it and there are clearly some irregularities to the way things were managed on the day in question. But, at this point in time, we don't fully know what it means."

I quieted for a long time. The hand that wasn't holding my phone crossed in front of my body and I stared out at the sprawling orchards beyond the clearing where I stood. I didn't realize I was crying until I shut my eyes tightly, as if to ward all of what Katrina had just told me away, and felt the warm slide of a tear down my cheek.

"What time do we have until?" My eyes were still closed as I asked.

"Five p.m.," she said. "Close of business and then it's off the table."

When I opened my eyes again, I felt the wetness of my lashes as they brushed my face. "I might need until four fifty-nine."

A minute later, we'd hung up and the hand that held my phone rested listlessly at my side. I was really crying now and I knew why this hit me so hard. Knowing we might actually crack this case had given me something I hadn't held in a long time—it had given me hope. It had made me want more than justice for myself and my family against an insurance company that was doing all it could to avoid paying out on a policy. It had given me hope that there could be justice for Todd.

"Violet."

I turned toward the sound of my name being spoken quickly enough to see Chase jogging toward me in utter alarm. He let the canvas bag he was holding slip to the ground, and whatever was in there landed with a clink, as if glass bottles were sliding together. Before I could explain what I was doing standing in front of the events barn, sobbing, he had swallowed me up into his strong arms, engulfing me tightly and completely.

"What happened?" he asked in a voice compassionate enough to show sympathy but firm enough to convey that I'd better go ahead and tell him what was going on. It wasn't every day that he came upon me like this. But him asking only set me off again. Another wave of overwhelm crashed over me. Next thing I knew, I was crying harder.

"Violet." His voice was desperate now. "You've gotta tell me what happened. I need to know how I can help."

"You can't help," I finally said through deep gasps and sniffles. "There's nothing you can do."

From there, it took me a minute; and, when I say a minute, I mean five, to collect myself to explain everything to him—about the deadline for the offer and the fact that Katrina was making progress on the tip.

"What do you think I should do, Chase?"

He had held me close throughout the recounting of my dilemma and he held me close right now, as I gazed up at him, searching his face for guidance.

"I mean, look at me. I'm a hot mess. It's got me on the worst kind of emotional roller coaster. I don't even know how I'm going to step into that courtroom again. You remember what it was like—how hard it was for me last time. Now, I need to walk in there, knowing how last time we lost; knowing they think we have something that—as of the day I need to take the offer—hasn't materialized."

"Hey." Chase stopped me gently because I was rambling now. "Come on, now. It's okay. Just breathe through this, alright?"

He started taking deep breaths himself, silently prodding me to join him. It gave me déjà vu—to remember the grief-stricken panics I had spun myself into early on. How, even then—when Chase had been grief-stricken himself—he had helped me through.

"First of all," he began once I was a little calmer. "You're stronger than you think. Even when you don't feel like it, you are. And you know you won't have to walk into that courtroom alone. I'll be there, and so will Forrest. Tatum and Nikki will be there. We're all standing right behind you, Violet. And not just in the courtroom itself—we'll be there when you get home. Before, during, and after, you've got people. And that's not going to change."

Even though I had mostly stopped crying, I let out a loud, involuntary sniffle. It only prompted him to hold on to me more tightly.

"Second of all…" He brought his hand up to cup my cheek. "You're never a hot mess, Violet LaRue. Even in this moment, you're beautiful. Going through it like you are—feeling it deeply—doesn't make you a mess, it makes you human."

Chase had just called me beautiful. I don't think he ever had. It was enough to send my mind back to last night—to what it had felt like to sleep in his arms, and breathe in his scent, and press my lips to his. The balance of what I was dealing with should have felt bigger—so much bigger—than a kiss. But it didn't feel that way in this moment. And soon we were going to have to reckon with that fact. That something big—no, monumental—had happened between us last night.

"What's the third thing?" Knowing Chase, there would be a third.

"Faith, darlin'. I want you to have faith. I want you to believe that this will all work out. And I don't want you to feel like you have to decide based on the money."

I shook my head, not quite believing what I was hearing. "Why wouldn't me and the kids needing the money factor in?"

The half-repentant expression Chase sported when he was about to tell you something he should have told you before washed over his face. "You and the kids have more money than you think."

I closed my eyes and took a breath before reopening them and pinning him with a look that told him I meant business. "Chase Greenleaf, don't play with my emotions today. Now tell me what the hell that means."

"If you'll remember…" he began somewhat defensively. "You went absolutely ballistic when I gave you that first bit of money."

"Fifty thousand dollars is not a 'bit.'"

"That's neither here nor there," he defended. "Point is, you didn't take it well. It was obvious you weren't in a place to fully accept and appreciate the generosity around you. But, Vi…so many people love you, and Bri and Trey. So many people loved Todd."

"Dammit, Chase." I cursed him because now I was crying again and it had taken me a lot to stop.

"The rest of the money went to trust funds for the kids. Technically they're meant as college funds but the terms of a 529 plan felt too restrictive. I'm the trustee and I've been managing the investment portfolio. But they're the beneficiaries."

"Chase," I whispered. I couldn't stop saying his name.

His gaze softened as he looked down at me.

"Now might be a good time to let you know there's also money for you. We only gave you their fifty thousand dollars initially because that was the maximum gift that it made sense for you to receive for tax purposes. Your portfolio is doing well." Chase seemed to blush a little. "Maybe at our next meeting, I'll work up a report."

I'd managed to stop my crying but I had a giant lump in my throat. "Chase," I choked out again. Because the feels I was feeling right now weren't about the case or the money. They were about the man standing in front of me—the man who so obviously cared about me and who had given me so much. The man who I'd pined over and who, I was coming to the astonishing realization, had also pined for me.

"Last night—" I began, then cut myself off.

He leaned forward until our foreheads touched.

"What happened last night…it'll keep. Given all that's happening, today's not the day to take it on."

Neither of us made a move away from each other. We just stood there, eyes closed and bodies intertwined.

"I brought lunch for us and a homemade ginger drink for the kids," he finally said. "It's cold out here. Let's get you inside."

* * *

RUSHING around the barn to close things up was not how I liked to end my day. I'd been rushing since my kids recovered from the flu, working until the very last minute every day this week to make up for lost time. Planning my departure had taken its toll on my productivity. It had been a scramble to do final checks on the weekend's bookings. And I'd had to cram a study session for my midterms into lunch.

It wasn't a good time for my phone to ring. But "not a good time" was when it always did. Such were the laws of the universe when you were in a hurry. I was so much in danger of being late to pick up my kids from school, I didn't stop to look. In place of fishing my phone out of my purse to screen the call, I kept on jogging down the stairs. My Bluetooth was still in my ear, so I tapped to pick it up.

"Hello? This is Violet." I answered in my professional voice just in case it was someone affiliated with the events space at the farm.

"Hey, gorgeous."

I regretted not having looked at my caller ID. It would have set me back time-wise but that might have been worth avoiding this call.

"Oh, hey, Rodney."

This was a conversation I wasn't prepared to have—one I had known was coming. When we'd parted the other night, he was already talking about what we would do the next time we saw each other. Not only did I not want to meet him for a 5 a.m. hunting start, followed by a trip to the butcher and us grilling our lunch, I didn't want to see him again.

"Had a nice time with you the other night."

I knew I should have been able to muster some grace. But, increasingly, Rodney's flattery and our relationship felt tone deaf and odd. Our kiss had been passionless. Pedestrian. Middling at best. It was the least exciting kiss that two people had ever kissed. Yet, here he was, insisting that we do all of this again.

On the bottom floor of the loft now, I stalked toward the sliding door, where I would turn off lights before I left. Rodney's penchant for talking gave me time to grasp for what I wanted to say. After praising our date, he'd launched into a story about his past foraging mishaps, including some psychedelic mushrooms he'd once unwittingly picked in Great Smoky Mountains National Park. I had fully locked up, climbed into the minivan, and tossed my bag into the passenger seat, and Rodney was still talking. He showed no signs of letting up. I ripped out my earpiece as the Bluetooth in my car took over. Now, I was driving down the labyrinthine roads of Chase's farm en route to the main gate, listening to Rodney through my car speakers, in stereo.

"Rodney," I finally said, interrupting him before he could go too far off on a tangent about fungi. "I don't think this is going to work out. I mean, I don't think we should see each other anymore."

He quieted—went completely silent for seconds. It was the longest silence we had ever sustained. Instead of feeling awkward, it felt…refreshing. Like stopping the chatter had finally, *finally*, taken us someplace real.

"Things between us…for me, they're not right. Things don't feel the way they're supposed to feel."

"I thought you wanted to take things slow."

"I did want that. And I can't tell you how much I needed you to go at my pace—how much it's meant to me that you gave me time."

"Then, why?"

It was the most succinct question he'd ever asked, and the longest he'd ever given me to answer.

"I think I'm in love with someone else."

PART III

Chapter Twenty-Three
CHASE

I walked into my kitchen to choruses of "Hey, Chef" and pats on the back from my summer crew, who had returned to cater a VIP event. I was pulling out all the stops for Forrest and Sierra's engagement party. Though I had a catering staff and a commercial kitchen for the parties Violet booked through the events business, the kitchen I ran myself was separate from that.

For starters, everything for The Noble Pig was cooked in my home kitchen which had also been zoned for commercial use. And I worked with a different team, a set of chefs who—like me—didn't run a restaurant full-time. Most guests didn't know that the crew who helped me were retired chefs from the most iconic restaurants and private chef services in Tennessee. A combination of lust for being back in the kitchen and pure joy for the craft was why all of it tasted so good.

The guests of honor had given me carte blanche on how we'd choose to have it catered. I'd gone back and dug up the menu I'd served on their first date. Reaching back in my texts to see the first night they'd attended together had taken more than an hour. All of it would be a surprise.

"It's so good to see y'all." I took a good, long minute giving hugs all around. It had only been three months since we'd all cooked together. Since then, every-thing in my life had changed. I was not the Chase who had been bored and restless at the end of the summer. Forrest had shown up on my doorstep with an offer; I'd discovered foul play in my best friend's death; and Violet had told me she was leaving Noble Farms.

But now, at this moment, I loved being back to cooking a fine dinner in my kitchen. In my kitchen, I had control. I could engineer operations so that everything turned out right. I was in the flow when I started to direct my team; excited about the smells that were already emanating from the fresh ingredients crowding my table; grateful for the honor of preparing something special for my friends.

True to its name, The Noble Pig was heavy on things like short ribs, pork belly, and bacon. Tonight's short ribs would be served with a creamy horseradish sauce. A sticky Chinese pork belly would be cooked with ginger and chili glaze. We would oven-bake candied bacon to serve in a warm sweet potato salad. This, and there would be an addition to what we had served at their first dinner—an homage to something that had brought them together—Sierra's legendary bacon bites.

And we wouldn't stop with the dinner menu. We would make the same dessert and we would even be pairing the menu with the same drinks. Violet had gone back in her own files to hire the same bluegrass band that had played for them before. Violet had added other surprise touches beyond what the couple had requested: lanterns like the ones we had hung that night strung outside to welcome guests in, and accents around the room that looked like firefly jars.

Unlike most events that took place on my farm, I would also be a guest. It meant I could only be in the kitchen in the afternoon. After prepping the pork belly, I left things to my second-in-command. From there, I went up to my bedroom, showered the smell of the kitchen off of me, and put on a suit that I'd had tailored expressly for this event. All week, I'd been sentimental thinking about how the supper club Violet had prompted me to start had created so much magic, and brought so many people together.

When I walked into the dessert barn—the name of the venue where the party was being held—I couldn't help but search the room for Violet. It was so long since I had attended an event myself that walking inside gave me pause. I was mostly in here when the barn was empty, dealing with periodic inspections and doing repairs. I couldn't remember the last time I'd seen it all decked out.

Round tables circled a dance floor. Tiny strings of lights in a style I couldn't name created what looked like a bunting made of lights. Enormous flower arrangements hung above the wooden dance floor—crowns of flowers on top of disco balls. Guests who were already seated at tables appeared to be having a lively time. A large bar was off to one side, but guests needn't go to it if they didn't want to. Floating servers passed hors d'oeuvres and took orders for drinks.

But not all guests were at their tables. Two photo booth areas had been set up on opposite corners of the room. An extravagant arch had an artful vine of different-sized balloons rising upward in soft whites, sage greens, and muted golds.

The other photo station featured another planked-wood backdrop. A neon sign that said *It Was Always You* in a pale fuchsia was lit up on top. In front of the sign was a tufted French sofa in dusty rose on top of an elegant rug. Professionals had been brought in to take photos of the guests.

And those were just the adult spaces. The party was a family-friendly event. Violet had coordinated an entire corner for kids. It was covered over in green astroturf and she'd set up a five-foot-tall Jenga set, giant Legos that were bigger than any Legos I had ever seen, and a Connect Four that was taller than Bri. The kids' corner had its own photo booth. A rack full of dress-up clothes sported outfits that appeared to be split between two themes: mini turnout gear to transform kids into firefighters, and beige uniforms and park hats to turn kids into rangers. The backdrop was an eight-foot-tall forest made of felt. Nannies from a local service wearing khaki pants and uniform shirts had been hired to give respite to weary parents.

"This is fucking unbelievable," Grizz Grady wasted no time informing me. "I didn't know Violet could do all this."

He motioned around the room with the hand that held a signature drink. It had ginseng to represent Sierra and the park and mezcal to represent Forrest and his firefighting. It even had wildflower honey to represent a meadow that was special to them. It was complex, with notes of citrus and something herbaceous. Violet had formulated the drink based on the story of their relationship. I couldn't have done it better myself.

"Told you she was fucking amazing," I pointed out to Grizz.

Firefighter Dan Means found the both of us soon after Grizz found me. But I had yet to put my eyes on Violet. She was who I really wanted to see.

Dan wasn't one of the firefighters I'd worked with when I'd been with Green Valley. At secret poker night, we'd formed a bond. Dan was a family man, just like me. He'd come to it later in life, having been in his thirties before he married and started a family. He'd proven himself to be circumspect and wise.

"She's just like you described her." Dan had only been with Green Valley Fire for about a year. He hadn't known Todd and had no previous occasion to know Violet. He was sharp in a suit, and wore an infant in a carrier on his chest. "I knew her the second I saw her. It was obvious. You can see how much she loves what she does."

He jutted his chin into the crowd and I followed his gaze. Suddenly, there was Violet. She sat at the head table near the front. I recognized the people she sat with as Sierra's elderly grandparents. For long seconds, I just watched her— her warm smile, the animation on her face as she spoke, the attention and happiness on Sierra's grandparents' faces. Violet herself was a guest at the party. But this—it was in her nature. She cared so much about making sure people felt welcome, that everyone could be comfortable and have a good time.

By the time I broke from gazing at her, more members of the Secret Poker Society had materialized at my side. Jed Lawson, Sebastian Kirkwood, and Buck Rogers all fell into form. The guys were literally at my back as I gathered the courage to approach her and say what I wanted to. So much had happened these past two weeks, between Violet turning down the insurance company's final offer and preparing to go to court. But I hadn't forgotten about that kiss.

Not that I liked to kiss and tell, but I'd been to another meeting of the Secret Poker Society. Or, rather, another special meeting had been held for me. The guys had implored me to recount the kiss in painstaking detail. The consensus had been unanimous based on my retelling—that *she* had initiated the kiss.

"It's on now, brother." Buck gave me a hard clap on the back. "Remember what we talked about Wednesday. Tonight's your night."

"Daggone right it is," Grizz encouraged. "You look good in your suit. You're all clean and fresh-smelling. Now go on and ask that woman to dance."

I gave a curt nod. Even though the dance music hadn't started yet and the blue-grass was ambient for the time being, I appreciated the pep in his talk.

"It's like I told you that first night." Jed was next to offer his two cents. "What she needs most is permission. She put herself out there. Now it's time for you to make a move."

I had to admit—the guys were really pumping me up.

Sebastian was the last to lend his support. He came right in front of me, put both hands on my shoulders and looked me in the eye. "Go get her, tiger," he said.

* * *

TWO HOURS INTO THE PARTY, I hadn't seen nearly enough of Violet, though I had greeted her after the guys gave me their talk. I walked right up to where she was sitting with Sierra's grandparents and sat down to join in with them in their talking. Only when the food came out and the room had been called to order did we have a moment alone. As folks were finding their own tables and we should have been relocating to ours, I insisted that she walk with me to take a picture. I told her I wanted to remember everything about this night.

As we'd waited to take the photo, I told her what an amazing job she'd done for Sierra and Forrest. As we sat underneath the neon sign, I told her how ravishing she looked. It was true—she'd never looked so beautiful. She was iridescent in a silk evening gown that started on top as a flattering olive before descending into a deeper green. It somehow hugged her in delicious places but it also flowed as she moved, giving the illusion that she was floating. As the evening progressed, it did seem that way. Moving among the tables to make sure the guests were happy and tended to, she was ethereal in her glow.

I need to get her alone.

It was easier said than done for the both of us. Most people in the room knew we were the hosts, that Violet had been in charge of the party and that I had been in charge of the food. It was an embarrassment of riches—both of us subsumed for most of the night in a barrage of gratitude and compliments, seated together, but thoroughly chatted up.

"I'm gonna take the kids up."

I placed my hand on the small of her back and said it discreetly, as she was in conversation. Trey was practically falling asleep. Bri was getting restless in that way that told me a combination of the late hour and too much sugar foreshadowed a meltdown.

I fully expected a protest. Violet only gave me a soft look and did something she rarely did—she just nodded, acquiescing to my plan.

"Come on, shortcake," I said to Bri, rising from the table and scooping Trey up into one arm. "You want me to carry you, too?" Bri nodded and I scooped her up. Carrying both of them like this reminded me of firefighter training.

The barn was warm, and walking outside into the cool night air felt refreshing. It would only take a few minutes for me to get them to my house.

I talked to keep them awake. If I put Trey down asleep, he would stay that way. But if I let Bri nod off now, then woke her up to get her to bed, she would stay wide awake.

"What did you like most about the party?" I focused more on Bri than Trey.

"I've never been to an engagement party." Her voice was soft.

"I'd imagine it's a bit early for any of your friends to be engaged. Any kids at your school said anything about getting married? Not in second grade, but maybe in third?"

I expected her to appreciate my joke, but she didn't giggle.

"I want Mommy to get married again."

Maybe the pouty look she'd sported back at the party hadn't been fatigue at all. Her voice was still soft and it seemed clear: this whole affair had gotten her thinking. It broke my heart a little—the earnestness of her wish and the kinds of worries she had at only seven years old.

"Do you think your momma's not happy?"

I wondered whether Trey was awake. I couldn't tell whether his eyes were open from the way his head was turned.

"Not happy like Miss Sierra and Uncle Forrest are."

I made a sound of acknowledgment, but quieted for a spell, not knowing what to say in this situation. Wanting her mother to experience the same joy as Sierra and Forrest was definitely a beautiful thing. But feeling the weight of Violet's happiness? That was a lot for a kid. It was a burden I didn't want for her.

"Is there any other reason why you want your momma to get married?"

Asking more questions seemed like the safest bet. I'd leave it to Violet to give her advice. Plus, as I'd come to learn from watching *Man Enough*, sometimes a listening ear was all a woman needed when she wanted to get something off her chest.

"I think it would be nice to have a dad." Now, Bri's voice was a whisper, almost like she was choked up. I got the sense that what I'd just stumbled upon was what this was really about. I knew better than to recite my standard response—that Bri *did* have a dad. And that Todd had loved her very much.

"How do you think your life would be different if you did have a dad?" My own voice softened when I asked the question.

Bri sniffled and it broke my heart. "I don't know."

By now, my house was coming up in the short distance. There were still cars outside from the kitchen crew, who would still be there cleaning up now that dessert had been served. The lights in the upstairs were on. We had briefly discussed the possibility of taking the kids to the loft in the events barn to sleep and giving them a walkie-talkie. When we'd realized we wouldn't be able to hear it over the noise of the party, we'd asked Jules to come and stay.

"You know one of the things I love about you?" I finally said to Bri. "I love that you have the courage to say what you think and to ask what you really want to know. And I feel honored that I'm one of the people you trust. You know I'll never tell your momma anything you say to me in private unless you ask me to."

Her little head nodded against my shoulder.

"Is this something you want me to tell your momma or is it something you've already said to her?"

Bri yawned as I maneuvered carefully to enter the door of the house.

"If I told Mommy, it would make her sad."

"Well, your momma's happy tonight," I said. "Even if it's not the same as Sierra and Forrest. Just remember, even if your momma seems sad sometimes, she has a lot of blessings in her life, and a lot of joy."

"I know," Bri murmured.

The reflection in the front mirror showed me that Trey was dead asleep. Jules sat in my living room and rose upon seeing me enter. I jutted my chin toward the stairs, to let her know that I was going to put them down.

I'd gotten one of my guest rooms ready for the both of them. Standing at the foot of the queen-sized bed, I was careful in setting them down.

From there, it was repositioning both of them, carefully removing shoes and socks, sending Bri to the bathroom to change into her nightgown and stripping down Trey, who was still asleep. Once Trey was in bed, Bri was out of the bathroom and I tucked her in. It was too late for a story, but I offered to sing her a song. By the end of it, she had drifted off.

Shutting the door to my guest room, I closed my eyes and took a few breaths, doing what I could to reconcile what Bri had hit me with on our walk home. When I opened my eyes again, Jules stood a few feet away. The woman moved with catlike stealth.

"Jesus Christ," I muttered in surprise.

As usual, Jules was pinning me with a hard glance.

"Violet'll like you in that suit."

My confused expression was only half put on.

"Julia Watson…did you just pay me a compliment?"

She rolled her eyes. "I didn't say *I* thought you looked good in your suit. I said Violet will. Seems like as good a time as any to hit her with some woo."

"I'm sorry—" I cut myself off, truly unable to believe my ears. "You think it's time I *hit Violet with some woo*? You mean, you're actually in favor of me and her? There is literally nothing about me you like."

I said that last part in a hushed whisper and steered us away from the room where the kids were sleeping and back toward the stairs.

"It wasn't you I didn't like," Jules admitted. "It was the way you never took your shot when you first met her. You'd sit there watching her with that pining look in your eyes, but you never made a move. Then, when Todd came along, you didn't fight for her, even though you would've been good for her. Even though she was worth fighting for."

Her take knocked the wind out of me. It also weakened my filter. "When Todd came along, I didn't stand a chance."

Jules's expression became thoughtful. "Maybe not. They were right for each other in a different way."

I quieted, unsure whether to feel vindicated or affronted. The questions that arose from this revelation burned. After a long minute, I could no longer contain them.

"If you knew how I felt about Violet—how I *still* feel about Violet—why didn't you just help me?"

Jules's stern look returned. "Why do you think I spend so much time pointing out Marcus's flaws? He is you. You are Marcus. He's perfect for Chelsea but he's got one fatal flaw: he won't be bold and claim her. You and him both need to piss or get off the pot."

Wow.

I held my tongue on mentioning that Violet wasn't a jacket at the coat check. In no way was it my thinking that she could be claimed. But I did think both Marcus and I could stand to be more direct. Jules's advice bore striking resemblance to that of the secret poker night crew. Before Violet changed everything about us, I had to let her know I was an option.

"Point taken," I finally said, then cast my gaze down the stairs. If I wanted to woo Violet, I needed to make it back to the party.

"And thanks." For the second time in weeks, I was grateful for Jules's advice.

She was glaring at me again. "Don't fuck it up."

Chapter Twenty-Four
VIOLET

"Come on. I'm buying you a drink."

I was mid-conversation with one of Todd's old friends, Grizz Grady, when Sierra hooked me by the elbow and started to whisk me away.

"You don't mind if I steal her, do you, Grizz?" she asked quasi-politely. Not that she needed to. She was the honored guest.

"I can catch her later," Grizz said in a way that proved he knew the score. One did not mess with Sierra Betts.

"Thank you!" Sierra said sweetly, then moved us along.

She kept our arms linked as we walked in the direction of the bar.

"Is everything alright?" I asked in alarm, the event manager in me wondering whether something had happened.

"Everything is literally perfect," she said, somewhat dreamily, to my great relief. "And you," she said with emphasis, "are a guest who is not supposed to be working tonight. And I want to toast a drink in your honor. This is absolutely amazing and I have you to thank for it."

"Technically, you have Chase to thank."

When Forrest and Sierra had arrived early to see the room for the party, Chase had asked me to deliver them the bill. On the line where it said "Amount Due," Chase had simply had me write, "Congratulations!" He'd thrown the entire party on his dime.

"I'm telling you. All of this…" Sierra motioned around herself. "Is making me rethink our plan to have the wedding at our house on Bandit Lake. We've talked about having it there since the beginning, but being here now—seeing what you can do—I don't know."

I chuckled at the compliment. "Chase'll host y'all any time. Just say the word and I'll find you a date. There's a couple I'm betting is gonna break up. Right now, they've got the best spot in June…"

Both of us had a giggle at my offer.

"Sierra. I'll plan your wedding no matter where you have it. I'll do it as a wedding gift. Actually, you could be one of my company's first clients."

Sierra's eyes widened. "Your company? For real? You're starting your own thing?"

I nodded. Apart from my Thursday night crew, Sierra was the first person I told.

"Why?" As ever, she said what she had to say bluntly.

"Because all of this." Now it was me who motioned up and around us. "Was supposed to be a temporary thing."

"Who cares what it was *supposed* to be? Forrest was *supposed* to be my nemesis. I wasn't *supposed* to fall for his wily charms. We weren't strictly *supposed* to have a workplace romance, but things happen."

"It's different," I protested.

"What's different?" she wanted to know.

"Chase upended everything for me and my kids. He has literally put the rest of his life on hold to fulfill an obligation. But you and Forrest…you met each other at the right time in your lives, and you fell in love. I've known that man ten years," I told her. "But I've never seen so many sides of him as I've seen since he's been with you. It's a beautiful thing."

I expected her to fire back another rapid protest because that's how Sierra was —quick on her feet and smart as a whip. But she looked at me with sentimental eyes.

"Forrest says the same thing about you and Chase, you know."

Her comment validated how confused I was. "That's the other reason why I think I need to leave. I don't know if there is a me and Chase."

"Maybe there should be."

I grasped for how to explain.

"Being all tied up the way we are…with me having feelings for him when he's my work husband and he's half-raising my kids…it's getting kind of messy."

Sierra gave me a sympathetic look. I picked up my drink and took a long swallow.

"Sometimes I think there's a me and Chase," I admitted. "But then I don't know. Like if there is, why do I think he might be dating my friend? And if he's interested in her, why did he kiss me last week? And oh my God, this is your engagement party and I'm venting to you by asking you unanswerable questions." I put my face in my hands, then sighed into them, in embarrassment.

"Those questions aren't unanswerable, you know." Her voice was all compassion. "I know someone who could tell you the truth. He's looking sexy in his suit and he's coming right this way."

* * *

"PARTY'S ALMOST OVER," Chase commented lightly once we were alone. Sierra had made a rather flimsy excuse for her retreat. She abandoned the bar mere seconds after Chase's arrival.

"Seems like it was a success." I handed him my drink so he could have a sip. "Forrest and Sierra are over the moon."

"It's not over yet," he said casually. "And I was hoping to get a dance with the prettiest woman in the room." He gazed at me with eyes he'd been giving me all night, the ones that took on a different look. It was dangerously close to the look he'd given me that night we'd fallen asleep on my love seat. The night that had proven how much between us stood to change.

I looked in the direction Sierra had taken when she walked away. "I think you just missed her."

God, I was bad at this. I wanted Chase so badly. But it was still hard for me to lean in.

"I'm not talking about the guest of honor, Vi." Chase set down the drink and stepped even closer. "The prettiest woman in the room…that's you."

All those times I'd been out with Rodney, I'd feared the dreaded kiss. But as Chase led me to the dance floor, my insides were trembling. It dawned on me how much more intimate than a kiss dancing could be. I'd been close to Chase before. We'd exchanged endless measures of comfort. But things between us had never been like this—so laden with intention—so far up against the line we were clearly about to cross.

Do all the reasons not to even matter?

We began to sway and I took in the friends around us. They seemed to be cheering us on. Courtesy of the Green Valley Fire Department, there were a couple of wolf whistles and even some shouts of "About time!" It gave me déjà vu for an era of my life when all the guys from the firehouse had been around a lot and in my business. The peanut gallery had its own charm.

I buried my face in Chase's shoulder, tuning the other guys out, wanting the rest of this moment to belong to us. I plugged into the feeling of his solid body holding me, and the romance of the song. It was an old one by Ed Sheeran that I loved.

"So how does this stack up?" Chase murmured the question close to my ear as we danced.

"Stack up to what?"

"Your dream wedding. The one you never got to have."

I remembered Sierra's question from her tour of the farm. Chase had clearly been listening. The truth was, I *had* thought through my dream wedding. All the way through, in fact, in a way I hadn't admitted to anybody. Having planned so many, I'd taken my inspiration. I could tell you down to the detail every feature, finish, and flower bloom I would want in the room should I ever decide to marry again.

"I want the same thing lots of girls want…a Saturday in June; all my family and friends; Bri and Trey happy; the right guy standing up front. And I'd want to do it right here."

"Here on the farm?" he asked.

"Here in my favorite space."

"You never told me this was your favorite space."

"It is now," I murmured into his neck. "It's the place where me and the guy I have a crush on had our first dance."

I tried to sound light when I said it, but I didn't pull it off, not that I was fooling anyone.

"How long have you liked this guy?" Chase's voice went lower.

"I think some part of me always did. But before…it wasn't our time."

Chase seemed to squeeze me tighter then, even though we felt so close.

"This is my favorite place, too. It's the place where I gave my crush her first real kiss."

"What's a real kiss?" I tipped my chin up, whispering in his ear.

"The kind where no one's halfway sleeping. The kind where you're wide awake and no one in the world exists but you."

The music went on, but we stopped dancing.

"Not here," he said. "I want you all to myself."

The dessert barn had a small annex out back, a place where horses had lived when Chase had been a boy. A wide center aisle bisected two short rows of stalls. The place had been empty for years until Chase literally stumbled upon a better use for it. One morning, he'd walked in to find a wayward partygoer who had gone in to sleep it off after hitting the whiskey too hard. After that, he'd set the stalls up for sleeping.

He'd filled them with meadow hay, which was softer than real straw. Heavy base blankets and warm shearlings had been folded over the cover of each and he kept a water cooler with paper cups at the far end. He'd offered the space up quite a few times. The event folks enforced it, holding on to the keys of guests who'd had too much to drink. We called it having a roll in the hay.

Chase took off his jacket and put it around my shoulders before he took me outside, keeping his arm around me to warm me as he walked us to the annex and closed the door behind. He made no move to turn the lights on, but he did fire up the heat. The barn was cold enough that warming it up would take time. He kept his jacket around my shoulders, but grabbed a shearling for good measure, throwing it over his own shoulders and making it into sort of a cape until he had both of us held in the warmth of the blanket and me held in his arms.

"Jules said we could take our time," Chase reported. My eyes were adjusting to the darkness. I'd started to make out his face. "All night if we needed to. I'll tell you, Violet—I wouldn't mind just holding you."

I wouldn't mind doing more than holding him. He made me want to throw my "go slow" mantra away. Every second I touched him stoked the embers of my yearning. I'd neglected that part of myself for so long, but Chase turned up the heat, and my body longed to be set aflame.

"I wouldn't mind that kiss you promised me," I said instead.

He squeezed me even closer, then swooped down to capture my lips with an urgency and a confidence that buckled my knees. The cinch of his arms kept me upright. He kissed me deeply, drinking me in with unbridled thirst. It made the luscious kisses we'd shared on the couch feel like pecks on the cheek. It was redemption and revelation all rolled into one. Redemption because we had freed ourselves. Revelation because, hallelujah, Chase Greenleaf wanted me as fiercely as I wanted him.

I could feel it in his body, through every inch of us that touched; from the way he leaned further in, as if trying to get even closer; from the way he whispered my name when we came up for air. His hardness growing against me was a thrill. How long had it been since I'd held a man in the palm of my hand? But we were mutually possessed—him by me and me by him.

Chase was the first to pull away, but he kept his head bent and closed his eyes as he touched his forehead to mine.

"I've been waiting for you, girl."

I let my eyes fall shut. "I'm sorry I took so long."

But he shooshed me. "No apologies. No guilt. No regrets."

The contrast between his warm breath fanning my face and the cool air on my neck made me shiver.

"I don't want to mess this up," I finally whispered. Maybe that was what I'd been afraid of all along.

He must have felt me shiver because he pulled the blanket tighter around us. "I'm not going anywhere, darlin'."

Chapter Twenty-Five

CHASE

This time, when I woke up with Violet in my arms, the morning sun streamed through thin spaces between the wooden slats of the old barn. The heavy woolen blanket underneath us formed a snug base. The luxury of the shearling blanket around us added extra comfort. Cozier than both was the sublime joy of holding her.

Her cheek was against my bare chest. Her mop of ginger hair was a mess of soft curls that obscured her face, but her shoulder peeked out from beneath the blanket. My impulse to run my fingers over it, to revel in its smoothness again, sent me back to the night before—back to my hands touching her in places I'd always wanted to, and my lips taking their time.

Being with Violet, even without *being* with her, had surpassed my wildest fantasies. She had awakened sensations I hadn't known were dormant—things I didn't even know I could feel—not just in my body but in my very being. Her touch and every sound she made, every movement of her body against mine, swelled powerful forces inside of me, like hot magma beginning to stir. Even now, they were still swirling, in some ways more powerful than they'd been the night before.

Thoughts of how good it had been made me want to wake her up, to take in her lovely face by the light of dawn, to pick up where we had left off last night. It was morning, and every part of me was awake. But there was perfection in how we fit together, in how well her body molded to mine, in the peace of her warm breath.

Something started buzzing from somewhere beneath the hay. It could only be my phone. Last night, Violet hadn't worn anything but her dress. I reached out with the arm she wasn't tucked under and held to my side and pawed around for the device.

Seconds before I located it, the incessant buzzing stopped. I'd taken it for a phone call, probably Cody, given the early hour. If something was up on the farm, he would try to reach me like this.

But the screen of my phone soon told me otherwise. It was not a missed call from him. It wasn't a call at all, but a series of texts from Forrest.

I got a call from Washington.

Monica applied pressure to the bosses of one of our POIs and we've got a meeting this morning.

We've got to get on a plane.

My attention shot to the top right corner of my phone and I searched for the time. It was 5:43 a.m. The fact that I wasn't left-handed slowed down my ability to return the obvious question.

Can't it wait a day?

Forrest's responses were rapid.

The guy we need to interview is about to be deployed.

If we wait a day, he'll be on a submarine.

"Shit," I whispered aloud.

I tossed the phone down on the hay pile next to me and let out a frustrated sigh, squeezing my eyes shut as if doing so would allow me to tune out what I had just read. I wished for the peace of five minutes ago. The last thing I wanted right now was to leave this woman.

My phone buzzed again and I read the text. Forrest had sent flight numbers for an itinerary that was leaving in less than three hours. Knoxville to Dallas Fort Worth; DFW to San Francisco. He would pick me up in twenty.

I put down my phone a final time, bargaining with myself over how much longer I could hold her. But me fussing with my phone must have caused her to stir. She shifted her head and did a cute little stretchy thing before looking up at my face. A stab of panic pierced my chest as we neared the moment of truth. Did Violet have regrets? It would take only a moment for me to see. If she did, I wouldn't know what to do.

All these weeks, I'd thought that her leaving was the biggest tragedy I could suffer. I knew now, that wasn't true. The biggest tragedy would be ruining everything that was good about us and never bouncing back.

"Good morning." She was lovely as she gazed up at me, her voice even shier than her eyes. I took it as a positive sign. Shy was better than awkward.

"Morning, darlin'." My voice was gentle but sure. "Did you sleep okay?"

It was a good sign when her answer was a contented smile. "For my first time sleeping in a hayloft, it was actually kind of great."

Great?

"Hayloft sleeping is underestimated, I've found."

"It depends on who you're with." She looked a little bolder now. "I wouldn't have rolled around in this hayloft with just anybody. I wanted a roll in the hay with you."

In some ways, the past eight hours had felt like a protracted confession. I wanted to tell her I loved her, but it was way too early for that.

"You're my favorite person, Violet LaRue."

"You're my third favorite person, Chase Greenleaf." She smiled.

I chuckled, unoffended. "I don't blame you. They're great kids."

"Speaking of them…"

Hesitation came over her expression, but I quickly shook my head. "They don't need to know anything about this. Not yet."

A short vibration emanated from next to me yet again. Forrest needed to quit blowing up my phone.

"Who's texting you this early?"

I glared in the direction of the offending device. "Forrest."

"Shouldn't he and Sierra be off in their own hayloft somewhere?"

As she looked mildly tickled, I was sure I looked grim. "Forrest already left the house."

"Left the house? To go where?"

I sighed, resenting that I had to destroy this moment.

"He's on his way over. They called us in. We have to get on a plane."

Now, her face really changed, the sublime contentment that had been in her expression moments before was replaced by something closed off.

"I'll only be gone a couple days."

She didn't look appeased.

"You know I don't wanna leave you, right?"

She was looking right at me, but something in her had withdrawn.

"I know." Her voice didn't sound itself.

She laid her head back on my chest and nodded, as if to underscore that she *did* know. I wished I could see her face.

Chapter Twenty-Six
VIOLET

Due to the abrupt nature of his departure, Chase hadn't had the time to arrange a sitter for Jameson. So I'd done him a favor and agreed. If I didn't know better, I'd have thought he and Trey were in cahoots to wear me down. My son was in his happy place spending every minute in the backyard with the lovable Irish setter while I sat inside and seethed.

Damn you, Chase Greenleaf.

I had let this man infiltrate every part of my life. He was tied to my work, my home, and my kids. Last night, I'd given him some of the last parts of me he didn't already possess. But my biggest mistake had been letting myself fall. I was incurably in love with Chase Noble Greenleaf. I loved him and he was gone.

He'll only be gone a few days.

I repeated the words he'd said to me, words my intellect believed. But memory was a bitch. Todd had said the same thing to me scores of times. In fact he'd said the exact same thing the last time he had gone to California. Him being "gone a few days" had turned into him not coming back alive.

I can't do this again.

It was obvious from this "project" he and Forrest were working on—Chase was back in the fray. He was turning into a firefighter again. He'd sworn to me that he wasn't doing anything dangerous, but it was only a matter of time. Fire-fighters didn't work desk jobs. There was no such thing as a trivial pursuit. Firefighting was in Chase's blood. Seeing him at the engagement party surrounded by his friends proved what I'd tried to ignore. Chase hadn't hung up his uniform for good.

You've got to move forward, I told myself.

It meant I had to press "unpause." For weeks, I'd dragged my feet on my plan to strike out on my own. I'd told myself it was because of the trial—and how busy I was from needing to get ahead of my work. But some part of it had been about what I hoped was happening between me and Chase.

So I finally did it. I opened the contact I'd had since Rodney texted it to me after that first date. The real estate agent's phone number had sat, unused, in my phone. So, while Bri played at a friend's house and Trey rolled with Jameson around in the backyard, I made the overdue phone call—the one that stood to change our lives.

* * *

DICK WIENER WAS AN AVERAGE-HEIGHT, clean-shaven white man who kind of reminded me of Rodney. He was on the early side of middle-aged with intense, light eyes. He drove an impractical car—as I discovered when he pulled up to the curb in front of the building and had to make a twenty-point turn to squeeze his enormous truck into a parking space—and he looked like he spent a lot of time in the gym.

From the way Dick greeted me—asking me how long I'd known "Rod"—I could tell he didn't know much about our status. That part was a relief. I hadn't talked to Rodney in the weeks since I'd let him down. One of the things I'd liked most about him was how much he'd gotten behind the idea of me starting my business. Out of all the things he'd loved talking about, he'd loved talking about that.

True, at times, Rodney's business brainstorming had felt like one long mono-logue, but some of it had given me ideas. And the parts that hadn't expanded my thinking had taken on a pep talk kind of feel. Standing inside the space I'd passed by a hundred times—on the other side of the window I'd practi-cally pressed my nose up against to see inside—I needed that encouragement now.

"Can I ask how you plan to use the space?" Dick wanted to know. "Rodney said something about an interior design business. I'll admit, I don't know much about those."

My eyes continued scanning the empty room, even as I answered the question.

"The downstairs would be the inspiration room." I repeated the name I'd given it in my business plan, seeing it come alive in my mind. "It's where I would put pieces on display, like a showroom for my clients to peruse different looks and styles. I'd put the consultation desk right there, in the back…" I motioned left. "And I'd have a play lounge on the other side, so that clients could bring their kids."

I could see it—could truly see all of it in my mind's eye. It unfolded in front of me as I described it. Standing inside the space made it so real.

"Upstairs in the loft," I went on, "is where I would have my private offices and also my sample gallery."

Dick looked at me like he had no idea what a sample gallery was. I listened with half an ear as he listed off features I could mostly see myself. But most of my attention was fixated on my own vision.

I'd come into the meeting knowing the listing price. I couldn't afford it just yet, even if I took out a second mortgage on my house. And I'd done enough research to know that I was a risky prospect to receive a personal loan. A lack of earning history would hurt me and quitting my job with Chase would mean I was losing my stable income stream. It meant I had to come up with a lot of it in cash.

"Is the owner willing to come down on price?" I asked Dick directly. "I know this building's been on the market for quite some time."

Two hundred seventy-six days exactly according to the commercial real estate website I'd been using.

"Two weeks ago, I'd have said yes. But there's another interested party. It's a good thing you called me when you did."

The bubble of happiness I'd inhabited for the ten minutes since we'd arrived burst abruptly.

Another interested party?

"How interested?" I asked bluntly.

"Very. It's a restaurant group from Nashville. They've already filed for a liquor license. If all goes in their favor, they'll be making a cash offer at the asking price."

No.

The sting of tears came upon me quickly, though I didn't let them fall. The past few days had been a lot. For the first elation I'd felt since Chase had gone to be crushed so quickly…it devastated me.

"How long do I have to put in a competing offer?"

"The sooner the better," he said. "And don't be surprised if it turns into a bidding war."

* * *

It wasn't often that I "just dropped by" Katrina's office. It was where I found myself after leaving my meeting with Dick. I'd taken the sort of long, aimless drive I used to take when my kids wouldn't sleep. This time, it was me who needed the scenery around me, the hum of the engine, and the rocking of the car to shift into a better space.

The drive didn't quite calm me, but it gave me the privacy to shed a few tears. The plain truth was, I didn't have the money. I had banked on my ability to negotiate the price and I didn't have a plan B. It left me with one choice, and that was only if I still had the option. I had to try to settle the case. It was the only way I could guarantee the money, and be in a position to pay it in cash.

Chase told me to stay the course.

And he wasn't the only one. I'd heard encouragement from all sides—friends who had told me to keep the faith about the trial. I appreciated the support but it felt irresponsible to keep ignoring the facts. I'd lost the case once already. Katrina's new investigation was turning up clues, but nothing that would clinch the case. Legally speaking, I had nothing. Was I really willing to stake my whole life—my whole future—on winning against an insurance company? It was Gambling 101: the house always wins.

"A callback would have sufficed," Katrina remarked when I walked into her office. It was the surprise on her face at seeing me that alerted me to the unprecedented nature of coming here unannounced.

"A callback?" I momentarily forgot the speech I'd been set to give her.

"It's only been five minutes since I called. Were you in the neighborhood or something?"

"No…" I said it slowly and unpocketed my phone. Indeed, I had a missed call from Katrina. It showed me how off-kilter I was. The stress from all of this was compromising my basic ability to perform mundane tasks like hearing my phone ring and picking up.

"Well, it's lucky you're here now." For some reason, Katrina was smiling. "We got a break in the case. Precedent that another policy in an accidental death sustained out of state was paid out. It wasn't in relation to the fire that killed Todd—it wasn't even in the same year—but it's something. It will let us challenge their questioning of your claim."

"How tight is your case?" I didn't sound excited, even to my own ears. I only sounded tired. And I really was. We were going on year four of legal proceedings.

"It's the most promising lead we've gotten so far." Katrina was still smiling. "My job now is to understand whether there are any issues within state law that would impede us from making that case."

I sat down in one of the chairs in front of Katrina's desk, defeated. Only then did she begin to look concerned.

"I need to win this case." A lump had risen in my throat. "I need the money," I finally said. "I came here to tell you I wanted to settle—to ask whether the offer is still open on their end."

Katrina's look was sorrowful. "As your attorney, if you direct me to do so, I'm obliged to ask."

"But?"

"But asking to settle now would be a strong signal that we don't think we have a case. I would be shocked if they gave you the 500,000 dollars. They might offer you a token amount to free up their attorneys to avoid time spent at trial. But—legally speaking—for them to offer you anything more at this point would be a bad move."

A deep wave of dread and disappointment crashed over me—even larger than the wave from an hour and a half ago when Dick had told me about the other bidder.

"I can ask opposing counsel if a settlement is still on the table if you would like me to, but I don't think it's in your best interests."

"I guess I'm stuck, then." Now, I might actually cry. Katrina had seen it before. My grief had been so recent—so sharp—that the last trial had taken a serious toll.

"I'm sorry for whatever has changed in your financial situation." Her eyes were full of compassion. "I hear that you have a need for the money. Just remember—a settlement isn't the only way. It's still a new trial. A new judge, new jury, new evidence. All of this could still go your way."

Chapter Twenty-Seven
CHASE

Damn. I missed her again.

I stepped out of the building where I'd taken my last statement and into the Uber car that awaited me. It was 8:30 according to the dashboard clock on the car. That is, 8:30 p.m. California time, which made it 11:30 at night in Tennessee. And 11:30 was around two hours later than Violet typically went to bed. We'd texted a couple of times—I'd even done FaceTime over the computer with her and the kids—but it wasn't nearly enough.

For one, there was the distance. Not being with her wasn't the same. I couldn't touch her or hug her through a text. But on video calls, I could see her face and hear her voice. It should have gratified me—should have found me reveling in being able to see her and knowing she was okay. But I could tell in her face and in her voice, she was not.

Not wanting to prod her into telling me what she was struggling with in front of the kids gave me even fewer chances to dig in. She'd been somewhat tight-lipped and at a distance despite my reassurances, though she did confess that things had gone sideways with the building she wanted to buy. At the same time it made me feel for her, it reinforced the sense that she was drifting away.

I did what I could from where I was. I was relying heavily on Cody to hold together the farm and I had a small army of other friends helping look out for Violet. I had an agent friend looking into her real-estate situation and chef friends from The Noble Pig dropping off food. But I'd still left her at the worst possible moment. The trial was coming up and she was getting nervous about the case. If there was any way for me to do what I needed to do and still be there for her in person, I would.

But there wasn't any way. The meeting Forrest and I had jumped on a plane to get to had opened a can of worms. Our interviewee had been on duty the day of the incident—a dispatcher who had reported irregularities that had been swept under the rug. Since his dispatching days, he'd joined the military—the navy to be exact. By the time we found him, he'd been on the brink of deployment. Hours after we took his statement, he'd shipped out.

But not before giving us the keys to the case. His recollections had been precise. He'd even kept a little black book, a personal log from his shifts. He'd been glad to hear from us—said that fire had always haunted him—and that it was high time someone told the truth about that day.

Beyond his own opinions, he'd given details and named names. It had left us with so many leads, we'd been in California a full ten days. Now, I was on my way to the airport, to catch the red-eye to Washington, DC. Forrest was already there.

The good news was, we'd cracked the case. But what had really happened that day was an awful truth. Reckoning with all of it was putting me through my own hell. The only thing keeping me going was Violet—knowing we were that much closer to delivering justice, not just for her, but for Todd.

Night, darlin'

I'll be there as soon as I can

You got this, girl.

I had to let her know I was thinking of her. My hope was that she was already asleep. She was good about turning on her Do Not Disturb when she wanted to rest. She would need all she could get tonight because tomorrow was a big day. It was the first day of her retrial.

After I sent the texts, I pocketed my phone and laid my head down on the seat rest. It would be a long drive to SFO and I needed my own rest to get ready for the flight. Despite the fact that it was the red-eye, I would not be sleeping en route. I would be finalizing the evidence file.

Forrest had started working on it. He'd worked on it all day. He'd flown ahead in order to guarantee that at least one of us would be there to beg. Our findings hadn't even been turned in yet, let alone reviewed or vetted. We needed far more than that in order for them to be admissible in court—we needed them to be declassified.

Declassifying documents was every bit as complicated as it sounded. It was a process that typically took months—time that we absolutely did not have. Based on our findings, there could be reasons not to ever let the truth come to light.

Not only had Todd's death been wrongful. The lawbreakers at the center of it were powerful people. People who could make things political for the Secretary. We had no way of knowing where her allegiances were. It meant that, despite all she had tasked us with and regardless of the hard evidence we'd uncovered, our findings might never see the light of day.

Violet might never know the truth.

The thought alone gave rise to pain in my chest. Because, if this didn't work, I could never tell Violet. Without justice to serve along with it, it would only pain her to know that Todd didn't have to die.

My phone buzzed in my pocket minutes after I drifted off. I was incredibly exhausted, having burned the midnight oil for days. When I woke up, I was crossing the Golden Gate Bridge, the dark city sprawling before me. It was Violet, answering my text on a delay.

Where are you?

I responded immediately, elated to hear from her even though I didn't like her being up at this hour. It meant she couldn't sleep because of the trial.

On my way back to SFO.

She responded just as quickly.

Thank God. You'll be here tomorrow morning for the trial.

My heart sank at the impression that I'd given her.

Sorry, Vi. I'm on a plane to Washington tonight. I'll be there as soon as I can.

I looked at my phone expectantly, hoping vainly for more dancing dots to foreshadow a response. But no further message came. And there was no way to give her an explanation. For now, I was relegated to the status of the asshole who was abandoning her in her darkest hour.

I prayed then—prayed all the way to the airport, all the way through the security line and as the plane taxied down the runway—that the Secretary would do the right thing, and that Violet would forgive me for all of this.

Chapter Twenty-Eight
VIOLET

Where the hell is my attorney?

I had just sat down at my seat in the courtroom. It was 8:58 a.m., two minutes before the start of day four of the trial. Katrina and I usually met in the lobby and walked into the courtroom together. But I hadn't heard a peep, neither had I seen hide nor hair of her that morning.

She was a beacon of professionalism, which made it hard to imagine where she might be. When the judge entered the courtroom from her chambers a minute after I arrived, I felt on the verge of panic. If she didn't show, what was I supposed to do? Would we get in trouble with the judge? Would I be called on to speak on my own behalf? I checked my phone—no messages—then craned my neck to look behind me. Things would go to hell unless Katrina walked into the courtroom this minute. I closed my eyes in relief as she did.

"In the case of LaRue vs. DCH Mutual, I call this court to order." This time, the judge was at least a woman. She was senior in her career—gray-haired and every bit as cranky as judges were rumored to be. I supposed you had a right to be when you'd seen enough bullshit. There was enough coming from the defense to fill a truck.

"We will continue with the testimony of DCH Mutual," Judge Lassiter proclaimed.

"Defense, you may call your next witness."

It had taken Katrina two days to present my entire case; she'd covered the original elements more quickly than she had the first time. Now, she'd dug into the new evidence. Not only had DCH been ordered to pay out on the claim by two other courts in two separate states, they had been litigated against in fourteen other cases over the same issue. To boot, they'd failed to clarify their policy language since my original trial.

After Katrina rested, the insurance company had begun to make its case. The way they looked at me and talked about me—the poor widow—made me sick. It was patronizing and false. The way they tried to convince the jury in their opening remarks that they empathized with our plight; the way they pretended their hands were tied—that they owed it to their shareholders to adhere to the letter of each policy; the way they tried to shunt the responsibility off to the State of Tennessee, who they said "should have taken out special policies" for firefighters put on out-of-state relief crews.

The one thing I had going for me was that all my friends had shown up. Jules, Tatum, and Nikki literally had my back. So did Sierra and Loretta, the latter of who had called in Buck's mother to watch her twins all week. Every member of the Green Valley Fire Department who wasn't sleeping or on duty had shown up for the trial. Firefighters who had known Todd but now worked at other houses had shown up to the trial, too. The first day I'd seen all of them, I hadn't been able to contain my emotions. I couldn't help it. I'd burst into tears.

Almost all of them.

That was the other hard thing about the trial. So many people were with me, but not the two people who had loved Todd the most. Forrest and Chase were suspiciously absent, off working on their mysterious project Chase wouldn't tell me anything about.

Not that I hadn't asked him. I most certainly had. He'd been infuriatingly vague, which only underscored the conclusion I'd come to. Chase was back in the fire service—truly back inside.

Sure, he would return to Tennessee, but it would only be a matter of time before we had to have the talk. The one where I admitted to him the feelings I'd struggled with for longer than he would ever imagine; the one where I'd tell him I loved him, but that I had to let him go.

One of the DCH attorneys stood. "Your Honor, the defense rests."

I looked over at Katrina, whose abrupt arrival had her a bit out of breath. She was too busy unpacking her briefcase to regard me back. She had told me after yesterday's proceedings that this was the best possible scenario. The defense was second to present their case and their last scheduled witness had spoken yesterday afternoon. It meant we'd be likely to have a decision today.

Judge Lassiter turned to the jury, who I also hoped would be better than the first. This one had better representation. There were two more parents than we had last time, which boded well for my side of things. At the beginning of the trial, the judge had given them a brief speech about their duty to consider only the evidence and nothing more. At this moment, she simply said, "Now, you may begin your deliberations."

"Excuse me, Your Honor." Katrina stood. "I received word just minutes ago that new evidence has come to light. I would like to enter it into the record. I would also like to call an expert witness to the stand."

"Objection, Your Honor." Opposing counsel stood back up not a second after he'd sat down. "The defense requests rediscovery. We haven't had time to review the evidence or prepare our defense."

"Your Honor," Katrina cut in before the judge could respond. "Neither me nor my client has conferred with this witness or received information about their testimony. We would also be coming in without knowledge of what they might present."

For the first time since the proceedings had started, the judge's eyes brightened.

"And may I ask, Miss Stephens, why you would call a witness without first gaining an understanding of whether their testimony will help your case?"

Katrina lifted her chin. "Because this witness is highly qualified, and has presented recently declassified information. And because my client's goal is to get to the truth."

The judge leaned back in her chair and thought about it for a minute. It explained where Katrina had been. Her investigator had obviously turned something up. I kept my eyes on the judge, whose gaze shifted from me, to the defense attorneys, then back to me. She steepled her fingers in front of her face and thought it through for a long moment before finally saying, "I'll allow it."

Katrina smiled. "Thank you, Your Honor. The defense calls Chase Noble Greenleaf to the stand."

* * *

Faster than a speeding bullet, my head whipped back around. Every ounce of composure I had mustered to make it through the trial flew out the window. Sure enough, there was Chase, striding down the middle aisle in a sleek blue suit. His hair was combed back and his beard was trimmed. He was nothing like the man who made cinnamon rolls and held tissues up to my children's snotty noses. He was nothing like the Chase who visited the barn to cuddle his dog. This Chase carried an unmistakable air of gravitas and looked like an expert witness with the federal government.

I was still wide-eyed with shock when he stepped onto the stand—still agog as the bailiff swore him in. The next thing I knew, he had taken a seat and was looking at Katrina.

"Please state your name and occupation for the record," she began.

"Chase Noble Greenleaf. My primary occupation is as a peach farmer, and a chef. I'm the owner of Noble Farms and proprietor of a seasonal supper club."

"And have you always been a farmer, Mr. Greenleaf?"

"Yes, in the sense that I grew up in the orchards helping my momma. But farming wasn't my initial profession."

"And what was your initial profession?"

"I was a firefighter with the Green Valley Fire Department in Tennessee and later with the National Forestry Service."

"How long were you a firefighter, Mr. Greenleaf?"

"I worked in the fire service for nine years. I graduated with honors from the fire academy, started as a probationary firefighter, and worked my way up to battalion chief."

I was captivated despite my intimate knowledge of the answers to all his questions. Chase was utterly poised—calm-spoken and credible, well-mannered and polite. I shifted my gaze to the jury, who, just minutes earlier, had seemed worn out from days of testimony. Now, with Chase on the stand, they were notably altered. Suddenly, they seemed interested, and engaged.

"Was it common for a man of your age and experience to become a battalion chief?"

"No, ma'am," he answered. "I was one of the youngest in the National Forestry Service."

"You must have been good at your job."

It wasn't a question, but Chase spoke to it. "The federal government entrusted me with protecting some of the most treasured lands in this country. I took that very seriously."

"Thank you, Mr. Greenleaf." Katrina turned to me briefly, then back to Chase.

"I also want to establish your personal connection to this case. Isn't it true that you were present for previous court proceedings?"

"Yes, ma'am. It is." Chase nodded, his expression becoming somewhat grave.

"Can you describe the nature of your connection to the case?"

"I was on the scene on the day of the fire. Todd LaRue and I were sent from Tennessee as part of the same relief crew. That was the day I lost my best friend."

It pained me to see the anguish on his face. Talking about that day was something he usually avoided. It begged the question, what was he doing here? How had he been identified as an expert witness? Why was he being called at the last minute? And why the hell hadn't I known about any of this?

"Can you please tell the court about your relationship with the plaintiff, Violet LaRue?"

Chase looked at me for the first time, his gaze going from anguished to soft.

"After the fire, I suffered badly with post-traumatic stress disorder. Violet and her kids gave me a reason to wake up in the morning. When I quit the department, she came to work with me at Noble Farms. My parents had recently left me the business, but the truth is, I didn't quite know how to run it. She helped me sort myself out and built a thriving wedding and events business. The supper club I mentioned earlier—it's called The Noble Pig—that was all Violet's idea."

Judge Lassiter shifted her enthralled gaze from Chase to me.

"Impressive," she murmured with the familiarity of someone who had been to The Noble Pig before. Only when she spoke her praise did I shift to look up at her face. Chase's gaze had been locked on mine, and mine on his, ever since he'd made his astonishing claims.

"Objection, Your Honor." The head attorney for opposing counsel was on his feet again. "The witness obviously has a personal relationship with the plaintiff. I move to dismiss him. Mr. Greenleaf can't be considered both a character witness and an unbiased expert in the case given Ms. LaRue's standing as a friend and a critical employee."

The judge looked at Katrina. "Counsel?"

"Your Honor, Ms. LaRue's character is not on trial here. She needs no character witness given her role as the plaintiff in this case. Additionally, I can establish that Mr. Greenleaf is here in an official capacity."

"Establish it quickly," the judge warned before returning her attention to opposing counsel. "Overruled."

Katrina didn't miss a single beat. "Mr. Greenleaf, can you please tell this court what additional authority you have to comment on this case?"

Chase nodded. "Five weeks ago, I was personally asked to investigate this case by the United States Secretary of the Interior."

I audibly gasped, then slapped my hand over my mouth.

"Who else knew about the investigation?" Katrina continued.

"Federal Fire Marshal Forrest Winters, the appointed head of the Special Counsel on Wildlife Prevention. He worked with me directly in investigating the Cranston Fire."

"The Cranston Fire?"

"The name of the fire that killed Todd LaRue, Chuck Oakley, and Stewart Upshaw."

"So you didn't tell my client about the investigation?"

"No, I did not." He looked at me again. "I told her I was working on a project with Federal Fire Marshal Forrest Winters, but I didn't tell her it was an investigation. Even if she'd known that much, it wouldn't have made a difference. The entire project was classified."

Oh, Chase.

It explained so much. Working so many late nights. All those strange visits to Bandit Lake. Him telling me that even though he was firefighting again, I didn't have to worry. Now, I knew why he'd kept things from me, and why he'd seemed tired and stressed. He'd had to relive it all.

"Your Honor," Katrina continued. "I would like to introduce Plaintiff's Exhibit J, the official findings from the Department of the Interior."

Katrina approached the bench and handed Judge Lassiter a thick report.

"Your Honor, this report is quite extensive. We agree that opposing counsel should have an opportunity to fully review the report. However, my client views it as critical that certain new evidence come immediately to light. Requesting permission to continue in my questioning of Mr. Greenleaf."

The judge didn't look up from the report—which she had already started to page through—when she answered, "Permission granted."

"Thank you, Your Honor." Katrina didn't return to her questioning until she had handed opposing counsel the same report.

"Mr. Greenleaf, given your knowledge of the case and your involvement in the previous proceedings, can you tell the court what is important about the findings of this exhibit?"

Chase nodded, his face grim again. "The findings contained in this report challenge the originally reported cause of death."

A soft murmur went up in the courtroom, but I went deadly quiet.

"Mr. Greenleaf, what were the conclusions of earlier findings?" Katrina's voice softened.

"That the deaths that day were accidental." Chase said it with some difficulty.

"And the new findings?"

His voice broke on his answer. "Wrongful death."

The murmur that rose in the courtroom this time was so much louder that the judge banged her gavel and called for order. The part of me that picked up on this felt removed from the rest of me. I had the sensation that I couldn't move. My gaze was on Chase and his was on mine until I squeezed my eyes shut and the tears began to fall.

"Was a specific party found to be at fault, Mr. Greenleaf?"

All I heard was Chase's voice. All I felt were the hands of my friends behind me, holding my shoulders.

"Our battalion was deliberately deployed to the wrong fire, a fire that wasn't a priority because it couldn't be fought."

"Couldn't be fought in what sense?"

"Fires are typically prioritized by the likelihood that they can be contained and the threat they pose to life, limb, and property. The blaze we were fighting the day Todd died was on extremely remote, mostly undeveloped, unincorporated land."

"You said you were 'deliberately deployed' there," Katrina continued. "Who would want to send you into a fire you couldn't fight?"

"A corrupt senator who wanted the land on the fire we should have been fighting to burn. He made some calls, pulled some strings with a few people he had in his pocket, and made sure they switched the prioritization. Anyone who questioned it was either lied to or forced into lying down. Thanks to that senator, ten civilians died in the fire that should have been fought and three men from Tennessee died."

Why didn't you tell me?

It was the one question that kept running through my mind. Because I'd stopped needing the answer to why. I'd long since learned there would never be a good-enough answer for why Todd was gone. I didn't care if whatever he was working on was government classified. Chase had gone back and forced himself to relive the most traumatizing day of his life. He should have come to me for support.

"I couldn't tell you, darlin'." Chase answered the question I hadn't thought I'd asked out loud. "I couldn't talk to you about it at all, not just because I wasn't supposed to, because I was ashamed. When we reinvestigated, I didn't know what I might find. The truth is, I was in charge that day. Todd died on my watch. Until me and Forrest found what we found, I always felt like Todd's dying was my fault."

Now, I was sobbing. "Is that why you've been helping me all these years? Was it all because you felt guilty?"

If so, that would answer a lot—why he was so hell-bent on being everywhere all the time with his charity and not letting me refuse it.

"Objection, Your Honor." Opposing counsel stood up. "Now the plaintiff herself is questioning the witness?"

"Withdrawn," Katrina said quickly. "My client will refrain from speaking."

But when she turned back toward me, she didn't throw me the expected look of reproach. She gave me a little wink and a sly smile.

"Mr. Greenleaf," she continued, facing Chase and speaking in an authoritative voice. "Is that why you helped Ms. LaRue all those years? Was it because you felt guilty about Todd LaRue's death?"

"No, ma'am," Chase answered in earnest.

"If it wasn't guilt over feeling you were responsible for her late husband's death, can you explain your motivation?"

Chase shifted his gaze to look at me, his face full of emotion. He looked like a man about to jump off of a cliff.

"Please answer the question, Mr. Greenleaf." Katrina's voice was gentle.

"And please remember—you *are* under oath." The judge's voice was stern, but her face registered interest.

Chase looked back at the judge, then the jury, then at his friends, then finally at me.

"I couldn't help it. I was in love with her."

Chapter Twenty-Nine
CHASE

Silence settled over the courtroom after Jules muttered "It's about damn time" and a whistle came from someone—probably Grizz. The judge looked entertained. Opposing counsel looked predictably exasperated. Katrina smiled in a way that proved she had set me up. Violet still didn't say anything, though tears streamed down her face.

I didn't know what they meant, but the only person whose reaction I cared about was hers. I'd said a lot already, but it wasn't the full story. And I'd just sworn on a bible to tell the whole truth. So I decided to go on.

"I'm sorry, Vi," I began again, finally breaking the silence. "I know the first time I say it to you shouldn't be in a court of law, in front of God, and all our friends, and the whole state of Tennessee. I know how wrong it's been for me to have feelings for you all these years. But there's something you ought to know. I fell in love with you a long time before you and Todd even met. And I've spent every day since y'all two got together trying to shut my feelings down."

Now, her tears ran faster. It occurred to me how badly I'd put her on the spot. That everyone was looking at her and that she probably didn't want them to be. I was the one who had put it all on display, so it was me who ought to do something to take the heat off of her.

"Do you have any further questions?" I asked Katrina.

Katrina looked to Violet, who began scribbling things on the legal pad. Katrina looked down to read it, giving a little nod before she asked her next question.

"Do you plan on staying in the fire service, Mr. Greenleaf?"

"No, ma'am." I looked at Violet. "Though it's been my honor to serve my country again, on my farm is where I belong now."

Violet scribbled another question on the pad. Katrina smiled before she asked it.

"Do you promise to quit doing stupid things, like driving a motorcycle and riding mechanical bulls?"

"Objection. Relevance." Opposing counsel didn't bother to stand up, he was so out of sorts.

"Sustained." The judge finally shot Katrina a warning look. Katrina only looked mildly chagrined. "Withdrawn, Your Honor. The plaintiff rests."

The judge looked at the DCH attorneys. "Counsel, do you wish to cross-examine?"

Opposing counsel stood. "Yes, Your Honor. We request a three-day recess to review new evidence."

"Permission granted." The judge turned to me. "Mr. Greenleaf, you may step down. Please be available to return in three days' time."

I nodded and made the short walk toward the back of the courtroom. Now wasn't the time and this wasn't the place to talk to Violet, but I could do at least one small thing. I reached into my pocket and gave her my handkerchief as I walked by.

Her friends shifted down the bench they were on to make room for me to sit. Nikki gave me an affirming nod. I tried to return it with a smile, but didn't succeed. I had finally told the truth about how I felt, only some of which Violet ever suspected. All of this was a lot for a single day.

The judge picked up her gavel, looking ready to adjourn. It was midway to striking its sound block when Violet called out.

"Wait!" And she didn't just call out—she stood up. "I'd like to take the stand."

She looked over her shoulder at me, then with pleading eyes toward Katrina. "I'd like to testify about Chase."

Katrina exchanged a long look with Violet, until the subtle confusion on her face melted into a smile.

"Your Honor, the plaintiff calls Violet LaRue to the stand."

"Objection, Your Honor." The opposition sounded even more put out than before. "Counsel cannot call a witness in the middle of a different witness's testimony."

The judge gave him a sharp look. "This is my courtroom, Mr. Morone. Counsel may do whatever I allow her to do." She turned to Violet. "Ms. LaRue, you may take the stand."

Violet hastened to the witness box, wiping her eyes with the handkerchief I'd given her as she walked. The bailiff swore her in and Katrina went through the same thing she had with me—establishing Violet's full name and identifying her relationship to the case—then she started in on the real questions.

"Ms. LaRue, can you please explain why you wanted to testify today?"

"I'd like to serve as a character witness to Chase Greenleaf," she began. "The other side called his character into question, but I've known this man going on ten years. I can honestly say, Chase Greenleaf is one of the most upstanding people I've ever known. He promised Todd he'd be there if he ever died in the line of duty. Chase has been there for us every single day."

"Who do you mean by 'us'?"

"Me and my two children, Brielle and Trey."

"Can you give some examples?" Katrina prodded gently.

"Chase was at the hospital the day my son, Trey, was born. Todd was already gone by then. I was struggling a lot, between the hormones and the grief, and later postpartum depression. There were days when I wanted to give up, but Chase was there every day. He was the one who convinced me to get help. And he didn't just tell me to go to therapy or walk on eggshells around me like everybody else did. He made the appointments when I couldn't, and he put me in his car and gave me a ride."

Violet was testifying to the court, but her gaze locked on mine again. Emotion from the times we never talked about shone clearly in her eyes.

"He walked the floor with both of my babies," Violet waxed on. "He woke up with them at night. Made sure they were clean and fed and clothed, and happy and loved. Made sure they never wanted for anything, especially when we didn't have any money. This man made my children baby food from scratch. All of this was while he was going through his own grief. All of this after he'd lost his own best friend. After he had inherited a farm he had no idea how to run."

Nikki handed me a tissue and strong hands grabbed my shoulder from behind. Knowing my friends had my back did nothing to staunch the flow of my emotion.

Katrina nodded. "What would you say to the opposing counsel's claim that Mr. Greenleaf might be biased?"

Violet broke her gaze with me long enough to send a glare toward the other side and lifted her chin.

"I would tell them that Chase is a man of duty. That I've just demonstrated how he fulfilled the duty he had to his best friend. That he fulfilled his duty to the Secretary of the Interior by not disclosing his investigation to me and going through the proper channels to ensure he could testify in court. That he fulfilled his duty to the people of Tennessee through his work with the Green Valley Fire Department and to the people of the United States of America through his work with the National Forestry Service, protecting the people and the land. I would tell opposing counsel that Chase Greenleaf is a goddamned hero."

A hoot went up from the back of the room—the firefighters, of course—but they weren't the only ones who were getting behind Violet. Members of the jury were nodding their heads and one even applauded. But it turned out Violet wasn't finished.

"If Chase's character is being called into question, then I'd ask Mr. Morone how many burning buildings he's ever run into, and how many burning forests, and how many lives he's saved. I'd ask him how many terrible things he's had to see and how many friends he's lost to the job and how—if all that happened to him—he finds a way to wake up in the morning. And if he's never had to go through any of that, I'd tell him to thank Chase for his service."

God, I love this woman.

I thought it at the same moment the courtroom erupted into cheers. The judge tried to call order in the court but it took her a solid minute. The jury had begun to talk amongst itself and firefighters were a rowdy bunch. The second-string player on opposing counsel was busy objecting, which seemed like pretty much all they knew how to do. Head counsel, Mr. Morone, had finally shut up and was looking rather salty.

I shook my head as I looked back at Violet, my lips melting into a smile at the same time as hers did the same. We stayed that way until the judge managed to quiet the courtroom, urging Katrina to finish with her line of questioning and get Violet off of the stand.

"Ms. LaRue, I just have one final question: is there anything you can say on your own behalf about whether you might be biased in favor of Mr. Greenleaf? You've just indicated to this court that you may feel indebted to him. Don't you have incentives—personal incentives—to portray him in the best possible light?"

"You're right—I am indebted to him. But what I owe him is something that no court testimony could ever repay. And I *am* biased in his favor. I'm head over heels in love with this man."

Now, Violet was grinning and I was pretty sure I was, too. And the next thing I knew, I was on my feet. And, suddenly, she was out of the witness box and we were walking toward each other. And then, all hell was breaking loose again but I couldn't have cared less, because Violet and I were kissing in the middle of the courtroom floor.

The judge demanded order, but we made no move to stop. For starters we were among the least disruptive. Plus, I hadn't seen this woman in ten days. I had needed her through all of this and I had craved holding her. The truth was, we had needed each other—not just this past week but for all the times when we'd had to downplay our feelings. Our need for connection could no longer be denied.

We took our cue sometime later only when the judge admonished us directly.

"Mr. Greenleaf, Ms. LaRue, please be seated at once."

Violet sat back next to Katrina and I sat back next to Nikki. Once again, there were hands on my shoulder—not squeezes of support but pats on the back.

"Your Honor, permission to speak about a mitigating factor?" Katrina was still on her feet.

The judge actually rolled her eyes. "If this has to do with anybody in this courtroom being in love with anybody else, the answer is no."

"No, Your Honor. Rather, I would like to inform this court that DCH is not only the insurer for the fire service of the state of Tennessee but also the insurer of record for Cal Fire. If the court agrees that this is no longer a case of accidental death, but a case of wrongful death, my client will revise her claim.

"My client also wishes for the court to know that DCH made a settlement offer of 500,000 dollars, which is 100,000 dollars greater than the value of the policy in question. Due to the unusual nature of the settlement offer, we request permission to call additional witnesses to understand what additional evidence DCH may have had about the case and to determine whether an obstruction of justice has occurred."

Damn. Katrina's good.

Titterings of surprise went up in the courtroom. When the judge spoke again, she was overtly hostile.

"Defending counsel, you'll have your three days. However, if the revised cause of death is irrefutable according to this report, you will act swiftly to offer this woman justice."

She leaned forward and narrowed her eyes.

"And, furthermore, Mr. Morone, Ms. LaRue is not the only party who may be inclined to look into obstruction. If I catch a whiff of wrongdoing, I'll file federal obstruction charges myself."

"Yes, Your Honor."

I took great pleasure in watching him squirm.

"Good. This court is adjourned."

Chapter Thirty
VIOLET

"I found you something to wear."

Chase opened the door to the bathroom a crack and reached an arm inside —an arm that held a T-shirt of his that would fit me more like a dress. I knew the shirt—it fit him snugly, a likely reason why he had chosen it for me. Dark blue in color, it was made of a fine cotton.

"Thanks," I said shyly and took it out of his hand. I had just gotten out of his shower—a luxurious waterfall affair in his en suite bath, which I'd designed myself. I met my own gaze in the mirror as I slowly dried off my body. Today had been an incredible day, one that had to be experienced to be believed. It was amazing to think how—just twelve hours earlier—I'd been in the doldrums: nervous about my attorney being a no-show, devastated by Chase's mysterious absence, and anxious over the outcome of the trial.

The court had adjourned at 10:30 a.m. We'd received a settlement offer from DCH before noon. The payout amount for wrongful death in California according to the Cal Fire's policy was $2.5 million. When Katrina had told me the amount, I'd nearly fallen over. Chase had caught me when I'd swooned on my feet and taken the phone from my hand.

There was more I hadn't been ready to deal with just then. The criminal charges against the senator. The civil suit I was entitled to file. The obstruction of justice charges against DCH. Most of that could wait for another day, though I did call the widows of the other women whose husbands had been killed and told them about the proceedings. For the first time in a long time, we'd cried together.

But that wasn't where it ended. Our friends had done more than rally around us in the courtroom that day. They'd rallied around us after, insisting all of us come back to the Green Valley Fire Department given the unexpected turns. Not just for me and Chase, it had been a roller coaster of emotion for everyone —a secret investigation had been revealed; new information had been presented about a fire that some guys in the room had fought.

The best way to describe what happened that afternoon at the firehouse was a kind of a second mourning. It took on the feeling of a wake, complete with the newness and disbelief that came on the heels of a shocking death. Chief Carter McClure stood up to speak about Forrest and Chase, about the service their investigation had done in bringing justice not only to Todd but to the others who had died that day. Grizz Grady stood up to speak about Todd, about the man he was and about what he would have thought of this moment, about the gratitude he would have felt at his death being avenged.

Then, Forrest had spoken. Not about Todd, but about me and Chase and all the *other* information that had come to light that day. He spoke earnestly about his genuine belief that our union would have Todd's blessing if it were something he could give. He talked about the man Chase was apart from Todd, and the woman and mother I'd become. He said that everyone in the room had known for years that we were perfect for each other—and had just been waiting for the two of us to figure it out.

By the time we got back to Chase's house, we were both exhausted. Our friends' final act of kindness was taking the kids. For the next two nights, they would spend the weekend at Tatum's house with her twins. It was further proof that Tatum was just about the nicest person in the world. I'd apologized to her at the firehouse—told her I hadn't meant for her to be collateral damage—told her that when I'd given her the green light for dating Chase, I hadn't been actively deceiving her. I'd just been lying to myself.

When I emerged into his bedroom, Chase was already on the bed, looking like all of it had just caught up to him. He held out his hand to beckon me forward, and I sat.

"Sleep?" he asked.

"Sleep," I agreed.

Then he pulled me next to him and tucked me under his arm.

* * *

THE NEXT MORNING was a different story. I woke up to bright, streaming light in the room, clear evidence that we'd slept for many hours. Chase felt so good, I'd drifted into a deep sleep—one so heavy, I swore I hadn't changed positions since last night. I was a short woman and he was a tall man, but I fit perfectly in his arms. More than that, I reveled in everything that was him.

Coming to my senses meant coming into his smell. I'd very much liked using his soap in the shower. Just like I very much liked sleeping between his soft sheets, a high thread count set I'd furnished myself. They smelled like him in a different way, their silkiness an indulgent contrast to the hardness of his body.

He must have felt me rousing, because he chose that moment to pull me closer. Damn if I didn't love the squeeze. Whatever time I hadn't spent cursing him for being away, I'd thought of him like this. Of what we'd almost done that night in the hayloft. Of what I didn't regret not doing then, but knew in my bones I was ready for now.

But is he?

Right now, my head was on his chest and the arm that wasn't pinned under me was draped across. He'd worn a T-shirt of his own and loose boxers to bed. I slid the hand that sat on him toward his waistline. My face was attuned to the rise and fall of his chest—to the rhythm of the beat of his heart. The latter sped as he held his breath.

In the interests of taking things slow, I slid my hand beneath his shirt, and put my hand where it had been seconds before. We were in the same position—I'd just opted to get closer. I wanted to be skin to skin. I snuggled in a bit more and settled there for a while. Chase kissed the top of my hair. I let out a contented sigh. A minute later, I slid my hand farther up on his chest, fanning my fingers out, letting one of them graze over his nipple.

I smiled a little at the light gasp of his breath. "You trying to kill me, darlin'?" His voice was deep and rough from disuse. "I thought you were a kind woman. Thought you'd let me be content for at least a day. You keep doing that, you might send me to the great beyond."

"At least you'll die happy." I finally looked up at him.

He gazed down at me softly. "That, I will."

It was all so familiar, and yet so new. We'd just declared ourselves, but it felt like we'd been together forever.

"I haven't done this in a long, long time," he confessed.

"Me neither." I stated the obvious. "If you're not ready..."

Instead of answering, he lifted his own hand to mine. He went slowly, guiding it south of his waistline, proving to me just how ready he was. Whatever seduction game I thought I'd had a minute ago flew out the window at his touch. Chase let out a held breath the second my fingers closed around him. Feeling his hardness and his girth sent a jarring pulse through my nether regions. The playfulness I'd felt just moments ago drained from my consciousness at the same speed lust filled his eyes.

"Fuck, Vi." He raised his hips to meet more fully with my hand. But both of us needed friction. Every part of me longed to be touched—a replay of that night in the barn, but even more. I removed my hand from him long enough to rise to my knees and remove my only scrap of clothing—the T-shirt he had lent me last night. Seeing what I was doing, he did the same, rising to his knees and shimmying off his shorts before pulling off his shirt with one hand. Though we'd been together in the dark hayloft, this was our first time seeing each other in the light of day.

He's perfect.

I'd known he would be. It was hard to hide a body like that. He was all ripped shoulders and chiseled abs—all strong legs and a tapered waist that could have been molded from clay. Less than I'd anticipated his own perfection, I had pondered my lack thereof—my childbearing hips, the breasts that had fed my babies and seen better days. But the way he was looking at me now...I wished I could see myself through his eyes. Chase took me in with unabashed reverence and hunger.

There were things I'd thought I'd feel. Trepidation at being touched. Guilt from doing this with anyone other than Todd. But the only ones in the room were me and Chase and our incredible bond. We'd made an art of not saying how we felt, but showing each other our caring every day. This was our most sacred gesture.

He lowered his hand to cup my behind as he lowered his mouth to suck at the juncture between my shoulder and my neck—we were on our knees and his erection brushed my stomach. I felt my nipples harden as they brushed his chest. When he'd had his fill of suckling my neck, he arched me backward and let one strong arm support my weight. From there, he made his way downward doing more sucking than kissing until he had me on the mattress, laid all the way out.

During his slow descent, I'd taken my own license, reaching between us to cup his heavy sac, though I steered clear of his shaft, cautious not to go too far. It was clear in the air between us—in the vibrating hum of our bodies—it wouldn't take much to set either one of us off.

This theory was solidly proven when he asked if he could keep going down. And then his tongue was on me and he slipped a finger inside. When he began to suck my clit with meticulous precision, it catapulted me to another place. Though I was away in my own bliss, I felt closer to him than I'd ever been. He was right there with me as he coaxed me forth.

I panted his name, and his answering hum only enhanced my pleasure. I was too far gone to try to make it last. He hummed more deeply when I bucked beneath him and grabbed a fist full of his hair. That, plus a clever stroke of his finger sent me to an ecstasy that blew my fantasies away.

I should have been boneless—exhausted—as he extricated himself from between my legs. But I didn't want to rest.

"Can I get on top?" I whispered the first words we'd spoken in minutes. A glance at Chase's midsection proved just what a gentleman he was. His erection stood proud, but heavy, bobbing a little as it wavered over his belly button, its tip slick.

"Fuck, yes," he ground out in a way that spoke to his restraint. He wasted no time finding a condom and I wasted no time straddling the man and rolling it on. And then I was over him, sliding down to glory.

He had more than enough to fill me up, to create the best kind of friction inside —to touch me places I hadn't been touched in too long.

"Chase."

I whimpered his name, because where he had me now was ten times more sacred than the place he'd just taken me, and he was coiling me up again, making everything tighten inside me once more, as if my body was bent on holding him in her grip.

At first, he lay flat beneath me, let me set the pace. But it was good, so good, too good for me to keep up the rhythm. That's when he sat up and changed our position—with me still on top, but him doing the work from below.

Then, he hit a different angle, one so good it hoarsened my voice. Chase stopped his movements immediately, asking me directly if I was okay. I practically begged the man to keep going, then slung an arm around his neck so he wouldn't buck me off. It was hard and wet and all-consuming and so, so satisfying to feel him lose control and to know that I was the cause.

I could have stayed suspended there for much longer, but he ripped my second orgasm from me. His own climax was hot on its heels. For a glorious minute, we rode it out. I remained astride him as we came down, melting into kisses that became lazy, taking our sweet, sweet time before settling down.

Epilogue
CHASE

One Year Later

Where the hell is Forrest?

My watch told me it was only 12:02. Still, it wasn't like him to be late. That was even less so when he was scheduled for a meeting of the utmost importance. He was set to meet me at Kimballs, the most elegant jewelry store in Knoxville. What could be more important than helping your best friend pick out a ring?

I certainly wasn't qualified to choose one myself. Women could be particular. Google had already taught me about color and clarity and more than I ever thought there was to know about cut. I'd learned enough to know that this wasn't a decision I could afford to make alone. Choosing an engagement ring for Violet wasn't something I was willing to mess up.

Under other circumstances, I might've asked Nikki and Tatum and Jules. But it didn't feel right after Violet had revealed Tatum's feelings for me. I knew better than anyone what it felt like to have an unrequited crush. I felt pretty stupid for never having picked up on the signs. Tatum was just so friendly.

Hey, man. Where you at?

I finally texted him at 12:05. Kimballs was a fine establishment—the kind where you made an appointment instead of walking in, an appointment to which I was now officially late. Thankfully, Forrest's responding text was immediate.

I'm thirty seconds out. Don't kill me.

Sure enough, Forrest's truck turned into the parking lot seconds later, followed by another truck on its heels. After that was another truck. Then a minivan, then a sedan. The way they parked together—pretty maids all in a row— explained Forrest's plea. He hadn't come alone.

The next thing I knew, I was being greeted by every single member of the Secret Poker Society. Some guys were two-to-a-car. Dan had come with Buck. Forrest had come with Grizz. Jed and Sebastian had brought their own cars, and—incredibly—the chief had come. This was turning into quite a family affair.

"They wanted to come."

Forrest threw up his hands in the universal sign of peace as he approached me.

"How'd they even know where you were going?" I asked, suspicious.

"It's Taco Tuesday. I dropped by the firehouse for lunch."

I rolled my eyes. Forrest knew every free meal in town.

"And you just happened to mention that I was getting ready to propose to Violet?"

By then, Grizz was walking up to us. "We've got expertise."

I pinned him with a look that told him I called bullshit. "Man, you ain't never proposed to anybody."

"Maybe not. But I've got six and a half brothers, gay and straight. Three of them are happily married. But the other three and a half really fucked up their proposals."

I shook my head quickly, as if to free it of the Grizz effect. I had no clue what the hell he had just said. Buck and Dan were the next ones to come up.

"I was only recently in the same boat myself." Buck announced the rationale for his own inclusion and greeted me with a hug.

"I didn't want to have FOMO," Dan admitted, offering the same.

"I've been married the longest," said the chief. "And, let's face it—you and Violet are the talk of the town."

It was true. Firefighters were big gossips and formidable storytellers. Nothing stayed a secret for long. The courtroom drama that had ensued during Violet's trial against the insurance company was the stuff of legends. A full year had passed and people still asked me to tell the story. I'd even overheard recountings from strangers several times myself, as a bystander.

"Alright," I said, conscious of time as I waved them all inside. At this rate, I wouldn't make my appointment until 12:10. And I wanted—no, needed—to be ready on the correct day for the proposal.

Violet and I had made an agreement. Three months to make sure the two of us were viable. Six months before we told the kids. Another six months to make sure the family unit worked together. We'd mapped everything out—said we wouldn't even consider moving in together sooner than a year. A year would come at our staff meeting on Tuesday.

Tuesday was why I absolutely could not miss this appointment—why I couldn't take time to question why all my friends were there—why I had to roll up into the most elegant jewelry store in Knoxville with a posse.

"Hello. I have an appointment," I said to the receptionist as nonchalantly as possible when I walked in. "Chase Greenleaf? I'm here for bridal."

From the look on the receptionist's face, she wasn't accustomed to this many guys in her lobby.

"Are these your groomsmen?"

In my mind, I hadn't gotten that far. But, the truth was, these guys had been there. They had seen me through thick and thin this past year. These were guys I could trust.

"Yeah, I guess they are."

"We're firefighters," Grizz said, sidling up against the counter and making eyes at the attendant. "We're here to help our buddy propose to his woman."

I threw Forrest a look that said, "Really?" He threw back a look that said, "You don't choose family—family chooses you."

The attendant took us to a back area. What happened from there was closer to what I had expected. A salesperson had been assigned to meet with us. Said salesperson asked about Violet and showed me an array of rings. I had it on good authority that Violet adored Sierra's. That was why I had invited Forrest.

The man gave good advice. I took his word about the pluses and minuses of various ring styles and how many carats. But the other guys turned out to be more helpful than I thought.

"I think you should go for three carats," Grizz chimed in at some point. He'd insisted upon looking at every diamond with a loupe, as though he himself were some sort of master appraiser. "Two carats might not be enough. She's a wealthy woman now."

Violet was, indeed, a wealthy woman. Not only had she accepted the $2.5 million settlement for the wrongful death suit, she had proceeded with a civil suit against the senator. Not only had she won a landmark settlement against the senator—she'd organized a separate class action suit with more than thirty plaintiffs who had been in battles with DCH over jurisdictional issues. With Katrina at the helm, they'd been able to make obstruction and corruption charges stick. Not only had Violet won a financial settlement—Morone himself had gone to jail, marking the end of a multi-year scheme of internal insurance fraud.

Violet had kept enough of the money to properly set up herself, and Bri, and Trey. She'd donated the rest to families of survivors who—like her—had been caught up in red tape and been denied their benefits.

"I'm not buying Violet a three-carat diamond," I made absolutely clear.

"Her hand is far too small," Buck said wisely.

"Less is more," Dan said.

"Three carats is a lot of ring," Forrest agreed.

The ring I finally settled on was a 2.25-carat lab-grown diamond, cushion-cut with pavé diamonds all around.

"Should I even get a diamond?" I had asked, having second thoughts after Forrest and Buck had explained to me the blood diamond thing. "Maybe I should just get her, like, a plain band made out of really nice platinum."

"No!" every last member of the Secret Poker Society cautioned in unison. Grizz looked up from the pinky ring he was trying on.

The saleswoman looked at me accusatorily. "Women like shiny things, too."

* * *

BEFORE I COULD TAKE the ring home with me, I had one more stop to make, to a place I hadn't been in a long time. Todd was buried thirty miles away at a cemetery called the Great Smoky Memorial Gardens. It sat atop a beautiful vista halfway between Green Valley and where Todd's parents lived. As its name announced, it boasted a gorgeous view of Great Smoky Mountains National Park.

When the time had come to bury him, we had spared no expense. His headstone was large and bore the insignia of the Green Valley Fire Department. Apart from his name and the dates of his life, his headstone bore an epitaph.

Firefighters never die.
Their memories burn forever
in the hearts of their families, friends,
and those whose lives they have saved.

"Hey, brother." I sat on the memorial bench we had placed upon his gravestone. "I know it's been a long time. Too long. If you were still here, you'd give me shit. You'd have asked me what the hell was so important I hadn't been to visit my best friend."

I paused. I hadn't even been on the bench for more than a few seconds when I felt the sting of tears—tears of sadness and guilt.

"They say grief gets easier," I began again. "Honestly, it doesn't. The longer you live, the more people you lose. It's been five years since we lost you and it still seems fresh."

I fingered the ring box in my pocket but paused on pulling it out, hesitating to say what I had to, stalling a little as I meandered through. I'd been thinking on this for a while, how to tell Todd about marrying Violet—how to tell him that I wanted to adopt his kids. How to move forward without a blessing he could never give.

"I know I came here a while ago, to tell you me and Violet are a thing. I know I promised to protect her, and told you if I ever hurt her, you could come back and haunt me and shit. I'm here to tell you, I kept my promise. When it comes to her, I've kept every promise I've ever made. And I don't plan to stop that now."

Finally, I did what I'd come to—I took out the small box and opened up its lid to look at the ring. A thought struck me then that had me laughing through my tears—the joke that Todd would crack if he were here.

"No, asshole. I'm not proposing to you. I want to propose to her. I want everything between us to be official. And it's not just for me or for her or for the sake of what we mean to each other. I want us to be a family for those kids."

Now, I was really crying.

"I wish you could see them, man. Bri's turning out just like you said. Sweet, just like her momma. Both of them are smart like her. But I see so much of you in them. Trey's got your sense of humor, and your same sense of adventure. I like to hope that maybe you and Trey had a chance to meet on the other side."

From there I quieted, and I let my gaze fall upon the ring. For minutes, I sat and thought of how life could feel so short, but also so long. I thought of the time I had left with Violet, and how much we'd already been through, and how much more I wanted to go through with her.

I wanted to be there every single day to see those beautiful kids grow up. I wanted us to share a home. I wanted us to become whoever we were supposed to be in this stage of our lives. I wanted us to go on adventures together. I wanted us to be even better partners to one another in business, and life. I wanted us to achieve every single thing we ever set out to. And then I wanted to grow old with her.

"Wherever you are, brother," I finally said. "I hope I have your blessing. And if you can find a way to swing it, I sure wouldn't mind a sign."

Violet

"Hey there, baby…"

I peered down from my perch in my office loft to see Chase walking inside. He was right on time for our Tuesday morning meeting. The one we'd always called our staff meeting had turned into a leadership meeting, mainly because the events department now had an actual staff.

I'd bought the building on Main Street and opened up my shop. For six months, I'd been seeing private clients. But I still directed the events business for Noble Farms. This only became possible after hiring two more people—events coordinators who reported to me.

"I brought you something sweet," Chase said slyly, crossing the showroom quickly and beginning to climb the stairs.

"You always bring me something sweet." I was talking about his lips.

"Even sweeter than that." The smell emanating from his direction foretold what was in the bag.

"Chase. Did you bake cinnamon rolls?"

He reached me quickly enough that he skipped giving me an answer in favor of giving me a kiss. There was no such thing as a peck on the lips or the cheek with him. When Chase kissed me, he really kissed me—like he meant it and wanted me to know.

"Cinnamon rolls are your favorite." He murmured it against my lips for a few short seconds when we came up for air. Then, he went back in, kissing me like we hadn't seen each other in years, even though we'd awakened in each other's arms that very morning.

It was an open secret among the staff that our "leadership meetings" were half-code for alone time. They all knew not to disturb. Just in case, we'd taken to locking the events barn from the inside. The loft bed Chase had built me years ago had started to come in handy, not for naps but for sexy times, back when we'd lived apart.

For the time being, Chase had more or less come to live with me in the name of normalizing things for Bri and Trey. We didn't want to change too much for them too soon. But we all spent our weekends at the farm together. The endgame was for all of us to live at the farm, in the farmhouse. All of that would come in time.

"Shall we get down to business?" I asked after we had kissed a good, long while.

He raised an eyebrow and shifted his gaze to the bed.

"Real business." I shook my head and rolled my eyes. "You know we're going into busy season. Besides, today is the day of our monthly."

Among the things that had not changed were me running the numbers and showing them to Chase. Splitting my time between the farm and my interior design clients had made me even more committed. And I was more than a little proud to see on paper the kinds of results that were coming in. I was even getting better at taking credit for my work.

Not that I could take credit for all the good ideas. Bri had suggested in the spring that Noble Farms host a pumpkin patch—that we do our own hayride and corn maze and bring in our own rides. So we'd grown pumpkins and tested the idea for a few weeks. It had brought in so much money, I wanted to talk to Chase about how to scale it.

After we pulled our lips off of each other, we spent the next half hour running numbers on revenue potential versus the potential liability of bringing in more rides. We also went over the plan of events for the week coming up and when to plan a blackout period to do repairs in the farm's commercial kitchen. We ended with reviewing the report.

"I have one more order of business." Chase closed his copy of the printouts I'd given him. "There's been a cancellation. "The Ogawa wedding, in June."

"I didn't hear anything about that." I frowned. "Did they call the main number or something?"

It wasn't like Chase to not forward anything having to do with the events business to me.

"No, it was me who called them."

Now I was really confused. "Called them to say what?"

Chase looked at me calmly as he set the report down. "Called them to say the venue was no longer available. That an unavoidable conflict arose."

I stared at him in sheer disbelief.

"Chase," I admonished. "You've got to leave the wedding bookings to me. The third Saturday in June is highly sought after. They'll never find another venue for that date."

"All that's taken care of, darlin'." Chase had the nerve to smile. "I called in a favor from a friend. They're very happy with the alternative venue."

I blinked. What friend? And what did that even mean?

"Why did we even need to cancel and why didn't you just let me take care of it? Events are literally my job."

Chase stood up like we were done talking. "I needed to open it up for a VIP."

"VIP" was the shorthand we used to describe events we ran for our friends. Chances were, one of the guys down at the firehouse had told Chase he needed a venue and Chase had asked him for a date.

"Oh. Who's getting married now?" I swiveled a bit in my chair, eager to get into the calendar. It was a part of the system that Chase rarely touched. All I had to do was go in and delete the Ogawa wedding and open a new file for the VIP.

I navigated to June 23, but something was wrong with the booking. The Ogawa file had been deleted but something different was in its place. It looked like another event, but instead of a name, it said, *Blank slate. Blank check.*

"Babe, you added it to the calendar, but you forgot to put in the name. Who's getting married?" I asked again.

When he didn't answer, I swiveled my chair back around. Chase was down on one knee.

"Hopefully, me and you."

My jaw dropped wide open as I comprehended the moment. Chase was proposing to me. He'd just flipped open the box of an enormous ring. Now, it all clicked—why his hair was trimmed and his beard was groomed and why he looked so nice on an average Tuesday. Because this Tuesday wasn't average at all.

"Yes!" I blurted enthusiastically.

"I haven't asked you a question."

"I'll marry you!" I underscored.

"But I had a whole speech."

"Cha-ase…" Now I bounced in my seat, somewhat exasperatedly.

"At least let me promise to love you, and Bri and Trey forever and do everything in my power to make you the happiest woman in the world." Now, he was holding the ring away from me, out of my reach.

Him being on one knee and me being on my feet meant he couldn't take it far.

"Come on, now. Don't play with me." Even as I scolded him, I was grinning widely. "You can give me your speech right after you put on that ring."

Chase

"May I have this dance, little lady?"

I held out my arm to Bri, who wore a white dress just like her momma. Whereas Violet's was yards and yards of fine, flowing lace that flattered her womanly beauty, Bri's was embroidered with vines. They were leaves and stems that started at her hem and ended at her waist in colorful flowers. She floated on a cloud of sweetness and tulle.

"Yes, sir, I will." She curtsied, having gotten it in her head that dressing formally meant putting on airs. I was glad to indulge her. She had barely been able to contain her excitement about the wedding and looked almost as joyful as me. To be clear, no person in the history of forever had ever been as happy as Violet had just made me. I was living the dream.

We made our way to the dance floor for the evening's second dance. My first, of course, had been with my bride. As we swayed, not a single word had passed between us. It hadn't needed to. All the spaces within us and around us, flowing between us and to us from our family and friends, were filling us with love.

"You were great up there, shortcake," I praised Bri as soon as we were dancing. She'd gone through a growth spurt and was taller to me than she once had been. It made talking a lot simpler.

"I wasn't nervous at all."

She hadn't seemed it. She'd scattered petals with aplomb, smiling at the guests as she did. Bri was, as ever, a chatterbox, and spent at least half of the dance recapping her favorite moments from the ceremony—the banjo rendition of "Here Comes the Bride," me promising to love and cherish not just Violet but also Bri and Trey, my and Violet's long kiss. I listened with delight, content to hear her go on about the wedding.

Whereas she had been the flower girl, Trey had been the ring bearer. His dog, Butterscotch, had been the official ring dog. He'd negotiated having his canine companion come with him down the aisle when we'd all planned the wedding. It had been important to us that Bri and Trey be a part of things.

"My friend Tyler has two daddies," Bri suddenly announced.

"Are Tyler's daddies nice?"

"They're okay."

I hummed to demonstrate my interest.

"He calls his one dad 'daddy' and the other 'dad,'" she reported.

"Makes sense," I affirmed. "If both were 'daddy' or both were 'dad,' folks could get confused."

Bri quieted for a moment. When she spoke again, her voice was small.

"I thought maybe it would be okay if I had two daddies. I have lots of uncles, like Uncle Forrest and Uncle Grizz. And I know Daddy's *Daddy*…but maybe you could be Dad."

I didn't think I could take it—the emotion that swelled in my chest from having the love of this little girl, gratitude for the family I found, the fierceness with which I would always protect them. I lifted Bri easily, until we were eye to eye and she rested on the seat of my forearm. I could see it cost her something to ask, so I didn't make her wait.

"'Course I'll be your dad, sugar. I was waiting and hoping you'd ask me, and trying to gather the courage to ask you myself."

Afterword

I cooked up Chase's story back in 2020 when I was writing Forrest for the Trees. I knew that he was in love with Violet even then. I also knew that Todd, despite never coming on to the page, would serve as a central character in most of these books. The tragic manner of his death is my way of talking about wildfires.

We've been fighting them for years in California, where I live. School children in my town have never had a snow day, but they've had air quality days. Friends of mine have lost homes, pets and belongings they cannot replace. As I write this note, the Park Fire has burned more than 400,000 acres, including parts of Lassen National Forest, my family's happy place where we've spent every Memorial Day weekend for more than ten years. It is only 34% contained. I cannot stop crying.

An increasing number of firefighters are losing their lives due to the sharp increase in major blazes. An unprecedented number of firefighters are crossing state lines to help other agencies save what they can. I think a lot about how much suffering this creates. Even the corruption themes exposed in Wild Goose Chase, which were sensationalized in this book, are rooted in real complexities. There are some who stand to gain from outcomes driven by climate change.

All of this is to say, keep reading romance but don't be afraid to read stories that deal with serious themes. Stories are meant to expand our worlds and make us more aware. Especially in romance, they are doing their jobs if they make us more compassionate and empathetic, if they make us want to spread more love.

This is also a long way of telling you to thank your local firefighters. Find one and give them a hug (only if they're a hugger because, boundaries). Write a letter. Visit the website for your local fire service and learn more. These are people who run into burning buildings and forests to protect life, limb, and property. They are first responders to a litany of other scenes. The absolute least that we owe them is our thanks.

Acknowledgments

I want to thank all my friends who provide me with daily inspiration, reminding me constantly how blessed I am to be in this world. My Struggle Bus Crew is at the top of that list. We talk about all the things, but we also do all the things. I'm grateful for their support and am unspeakably proud of them in all they continue to achieve.

Folks who follow me on Facebook know that I am otterly enamored with otters and that Alexa Santi is my otter-loving twin. The joy I receive on a daily basis from the otter love she sends keeps me going in a big way. My Facebook family in Kilby's Corner and beyond also sustains me. I'm probably late on my deadline because I'm having too much fun hanging out with you.

A few specific people helped Wild Goose Chase come together. Eva Moore is my plotting guru. Her fingerprints are all over pretty much everything I write. I am deeply appreciative of her energy, her encouragement and her consistent ability to get me unstuck. Renita Pavia was my beta reader and offered not only fantastic insights but also some of the most supportive and encouraging feedback I've ever received. I will never forget it.

Big thanks also to Stephanie and Andi, who sat with me in Anaheim and came up with the cutest detail of my book: Jamieson's name and his breed and his greater role in helping Chase get out of a bottle of whiskey and take back his life.

Everlasting thanks to my editor, Reina Robinson, who makes me a better writer with every single book and who is consistently flexible, which really helps when I'm off track with my deadlines. Thanks to the team at Valentine PR for all your work in helping get the word out and for being a top-notch partner.

And the biggest thanks goes to Penny for letting me write in the very best fictional world.

About the Author

Kilby Blades is a *USA Today* Bestselling author of Romance and Women's Fiction. Her debut novel, *Snapdragon*, was a HOLT Medallion finalist, a *Publisher's Weekly* BookLife Prize Semi-Finalist, and an IPPY Award medalist. Kilby was honored with an RSJ Emma Award for Best Debut Author in 2018, and has been lauded by critics for "easing feminism and equality into her novels" (*IndieReader*) and "writing characters who complement each other like a fine wine does a good meal" (*Publisher's Weekly*).

During her career as a digital marketing executive, she moonlighted as a journalist, freelanced as a food, wine and travel writer and lived it up as an entertainment columnist. She has lived in five countries, visited more than twenty-five, and spends part of her year in her happy place in the Andes Mountains. Kilby is a feminist, an oenophile, a cinephile, a social-justice fighter, and above all else, a glutton for a good story. Follow her everywhere @kilbyblades.

http://www.instagram.com/kilbyblades
http://www.facebook.com/kilbybladesauthor
http://www.twitter.com/kilbyblades
https://www.bookbub.com/authors/kilby-blades
https://www.goodreads.com/kilbyblades
https://www.amazon.com/Kilby-Blades/e/B01N4770M0

Find Smartypants Romance online:
Website: www.smartypantsromance.com
Facebook: www.facebook.com/smartypantsromance/
Goodreads: www.goodreads.com/smartypantsromance
Twitter: @smartypantsrom
Instagram: @smartypantsromance

The Story Doesn't End Here

I always like to share bonus content related to my books. Sometimes they're lost scenes, sometimes they're FAQs. You can find bonus materials for Wild Goose Chase right here: http://www.kilbyblades.com/wild-goose-chase-bonus-materials.

And if you missed bonus materials for Forrest for the Trees and Young Buck, check them out right here http://www.kilbyblades.com/forrest-for-the-trees-bonus-materials and here http://www.kilbyblades.com/young-buck-bonus-materials.

Also by Kilby Blades

Gilded Love Series

Snapdragon

Chrysalis

Vertical

Loaded: A Holiday Romance

Hot in the Kitchen Series

The Secret Ingredient

Spooning Leads to Forking

Modern Love Series

Friended

Ended?

Also by Smartypants Romance

<u>The Green Valley Library Series</u>

<u>Prose Before Bros by Cathy Yardley (#1)</u>

<u>Shelf Awareness by Katie Ashley (#2)</u>

<u>Dewey Belong Together by Ann Whynot (#3)</u>

<u>Checking You Out by Ann Whynot (#4)</u>

<u>Scorned Women's Society Series</u>

<u>My Bare Lady by Piper Sheldon (#1)</u>

<u>The Treble with Men by Piper Sheldon (#2)</u>

<u>The One That I Want by Piper Sheldon (#3)</u>

<u>Hopelessly Devoted by Piper Sheldon (#3.5)</u>

<u>It Takes a Woman by Piper Sheldon (#4)</u>

<u>Park Ranger Series</u>

<u>Happy Trail by Daisy Prescott (#1)</u>

<u>Stranger Ranger by Daisy Prescott (#2)</u>

<u>The Leffersbee Series</u>

<u>Been There Done That by Hope Ellis (#1)</u>

<u>Before and After You by Hope Ellis (#2)</u>

<u>The Higher Learning Series</u>

<u>Upsy Daisy by Chelsie Edwards (#1)</u>

<u>Green Valley Heroes Series</u>

<u>Forrest for the Trees by Kilby Blades (#1)</u>

<u>Parks and Provocation by Juliette Cross (#2)</u>

<u>Letter Late Than Never by Lauren Connolly (#3)</u>

<u>Peaches and Dreams by Juliette Cross (#4)</u>

<u>Young Buck by Kilby Blades (#5)</u>

<u>Package Makes Perfect by Lauren Connolly (#6)</u>

<u>All Fired Up by Allie Winters (#7)</u>

<u>Wild Goose Chase by Kilby Blades (#8)</u>

<u>The Teachers' Lounge Series</u>

Passing Notes by Nora Everly (#1)
Band Together by Piper Sheldon (#2)
Ex Marks the Spot by Hazel James (#3)
Past Tents by Stacy Travis (#4)

Story of Us Collection
My Story of Us: Zach by Chris Brinkley (#1)
My Story of Us: Thomas by Chris Brinkley (#2)
My Story of Us: Grayson by Chris Brinkley (#3)

Seduction in the City
Cipher Security Series
Code of Conduct by April White (#1)
Code of Honor by April White (#2)
Code of Matrimony by April White (#2.5)
Code of Ethics by April White (#3)

Cipher Office Series
Weight Expectations by M.E. Carter (#1)
Sticking to the Script by Stella Weaver (#2)
Cutie and the Beast by M.E. Carter (#3)
Weights of Wrath by M.E. Carter (#4)

Common Threads Series
Mad About Ewe by Susannah Nix (#1)
Give Love a Chai by Nanxi Wen (#2)
Key Change by Heidi Hutchinson (#3)
Not Since Ewe by Susannah Nix (#4)
Lost Track by Heidi Hutchinson (#5)
Ewe Complete Me by Susannah Nix (#6)
Meet Your Matcha by Nanxi Wen (#7)
All Mixed Up by Heidi Hutchinson (#8)
Write or Wrong by Heidi Hutchinson (#9)

Bad Habit Book Club Series

Nun Too Soon by Lissa Sharpe (#1)

Educated Romance

Work For It Series

Street Smart by Aly Stiles (#1)

Heart Smart by Emma Lee Jayne (#2)

Book Smart by Amanda Pennington (#3)

Smart Mouth by Emma Lee Jayne (#4)

Play Smart by Aly Stiles (#5)

Look Smart by Aly Stiles (#6)

Smart Move by Amanda Pennington (#7)

Stage Smart by Aly Stiles (#8)

Lessons Learned Series

Under Pressure by Allie Winters (#1)

Not Fooling Anyone by Allie Winters (#2)

Can't Fight It by Allie Winters (#3)

The Vinyl Frontier by Lola West (#4)

Out of this World

London Ladies Embroidery Series

Neanderthal Seeks Duchess by Laney Hatcher (#1)

Well Acquainted by Laney Hatcher (#2)

Love Matched by Laney Hatcher (#3)

Wolf Brothers Series

Truth or Wolf by Anne Marsh (#1)

Wolf and Bare It by Anne Marsh (#2)